THE MAGIC CHAIR MURDER

Recent Titles by Diane Janes

Fiction

THE PULL OF THE MOON
WHY DON'T YOU COME FOR ME?
SWIMMING IN THE SHADOWS *
STICK OR TWIST *

Non-fiction

EDWARDIAN MURDER: IGHTHAM & THE
MORPETH TRAIN ROBBERY
POISONOUS LIES: THE CROYDON ARSENIC
MYSTERY
THE CASE OF THE POISONED PARTRIDGE
DEATH AT WOLF'S NICK

* *available from Severn House*

THE MAGIC CHAIR MURDER

Diane Janes

Severn House Large Print
London & New York

This first large print edition published 2018
in Great Britain and the USA by
SEVERN HOUSE PUBLISHERS LTD of
Eardley House, 4 Uxbridge Street, London W8 7SY.
First world regular print edition published 2017 by
Severn House Publishers Ltd.

British Library Cataloguing in Publication Data
A CIP catalogue record for this title is available from the British Library.

ISBN-13: 9780727829023

Severn House Publishers support the Forest Stewardship Council™
[FSC™], the leading international forest certification organisation. All
our titles that are printed on FSC certified paper carry the FSC logo.

MIX
Paper from
responsible sources
FSC
www.fsc.org   FSC® C013056

Typeset by Palimpsest Book Production Ltd.,
Falkirk, Stirlingshire, Scotland.
Printed and bound in Great Britain by
T J International, Padstow, Cornwall.

In memory of Ann and Alastair

One

The car was still blazing by the time Sergeant Graydon arrived. He allowed his bicycle to free-wheel the final few yards along the lane, swinging his left leg over the crossbar so that he was standing upright with one foot balanced on the right-hand pedal for the dismount; a rather flashy method of arrival which he had favoured ever since joining the Lancashire Constabulary back in 'twenty-one. He steered the bicycle into the side of the lane, applying his brakes just enough to bring the machine to a halt alongside the young constable awaiting him.

'Now then,' Graydon said.

Police Constable Hamilton had only been in the job a matter of months, but he already knew that this gruff introduction was a question, to which a response was required.

'The fire was spotted by Mr Birkett, sir. He'd been to a bit of a do at one of the farms over the top, and was walking back. He reckons he saw the fire start when he was only about five minutes from home. Says he knocked on my door as soon as he got to the village. I logged the time as two twenty-three a.m., so if Mr Birkett is right, then it didn't catch alight much before a quarter past two. Then I telephoned you, got into my uniform and came straight to the scene, sir.'

Graydon made a humphing sound. The lad was

1

overeager, the polish not yet knocked off him by a few years of rural beat work.

'I didn't pass anyone on the road,' Hamilton went on. 'There's no sign of the driver, nor yet another vehicle. It doesn't look like there's been an accident, or a collision or some such.'

Graydon continued to contemplate the vehicle in silence. He had occasionally known motorcars to overturn and catch alight after an accident, but this one looked for all the world as if it had been neatly parked at the side of the lane. Funny place to leave a motorcar, a good mile or more away from the nearest dwelling, just where the lane dipped between high banks before disappearing beneath the stone arch of a railway bridge. A back of beyond kind of a spot, where the initial glow would have been well concealed by the overgrown banking at either side of the road, though not of course from anyone walking the hilltop track. It might have gone unnoticed until morning if that bloke had not been cutting across the hill on his way home from a party.

'So . . . no sign of the driver, then,' he said at last.

As if in response to an instruction, Hamilton leant his bike against the bank and approached the car, raising a hand to shield his face in defiance of the heat.

'Hey,' Graydon shouted. 'Back off, you soft bugger. You're not Douglas Fairbanks.'

'Douglas Fairbanks?' Hamilton retreated a couple of yards, as instructed.

'Douglas Fairbanks – in *His Majesty, the American.*'

'Would that be a film, sir?'

'Oh, never mind.'

'Do you reckon it was a fault with the engine? Or something else?'

'Could be something, might be nothing. Get your torch and let's have a look round. Don't get too close.' Hamilton was too young, the older man thought. Too raw and inclined to get over-excited. Most likely it was no more than a fault of some kind in the engine, and the driver gone off in the other direction to find his way home. Motorcars were unreliable buggers and always breaking down. They burned easily, what with wooden floorboards and leather seats and a tank full of petrol, and indeed, as the men approached the flames suddenly leapt higher so that some overhanging branches glowed red for a moment or two, but it was still early in the year and too damp for there to be any real risk of the fire spreading to the surrounding trees and bushes.

Keeping the blazing car at a discreet distance, the two men checked the ground for anything from a spent match upwards, but they found nothing more remarkable than some of last year's damp leaves, and after a couple of minutes they returned to stand beside their bicycles. The air was filled with the stink of burning fuel and rubber. Palls of smoke surged upwards, temporarily obscuring the stars. The brightness of the blaze made everything else seem darker and, beyond the burning wreck, the lane ahead appeared to end in a solid wall of black, where the railway bridge cut across it.

'What now?' asked Hamilton.

'You've telephoned for the fire brigade, I suppose?'

'Yes, sir, but they've a good way to come.'

'Right, then. We wait until they get here to damp it down and then we're away.'

'Suppose there's something in the boot?'

'What did you have in mind? Posh folks' picnic hamper? If there is, the sandwiches will be well and truly kippered by now. If there's anything to see, we'll find it right enough in the morning. We can't stand around here all night, waiting for this lot to cool down.'

Two

At the exact same moment as PC Hamilton was preparing to lever open the boot of Linda Dexter's burnt-out Talbot 105, Hugh Allonby, chairman of the Robert Barnaby Society, was flagging up her absence to a select group of members who were gathered on the terrace of the Furnival Towers Hotel. It was the mid-morning break on the first full day of the society's annual conference and the terrace was crowded with delegates taking full advantage of the unseasonably warm weather to enjoy their tea and coffee. An onlooker might have wondered what sort of occasion would bring together this disparate mix of people and perhaps been further perplexed by the sprinkling of unusual costumes on show, which suggested that a relatively staid gathering had somehow been infiltrated by a group leftover from a fancy dress ball.

A man in a Viking helmet, a strangely fashioned canvas jacket and trousers which resembled nothing more than the bottom half of a bear, was conversing in animated fashion with an elderly woman whose greying hair had been coaxed into a pair of unlikely pigtails beneath a milkmaid's cap, while a few yards away a tweedy academic was sharing his opinions with a woman sporting a coolie hat as wide as a banqueting platter, who was nodding enthusiastically while attempting to

5

balance not only the hat but also three biscuits on the saucer of her coffee cup.

Chairman Allonby, who was reckoned to be one of the greatest living authorities on the late Robert Barnaby, and already had two books on the subject to his name, was not among those who had dressed as a character from one of Robert Barnaby's poems. Indeed, had it been within his power to do so, Allonby would have prohibited this frivolity on the grounds that Barnaby's poetry – though originally written for children – had now attained a status which ought to have ensured that it was approached with an appropriate level of seriousness at all times. He made a point of never speaking to any member clad in a costume, if he could possibly avoid it, a snub which was lost upon most of the perceived offenders, since Allonby generally emphasized his importance in the scheme of things by maintaining a discreet distance between himself and the ordinary rank-and-file members, their mode of dress notwithstanding.

It therefore attracted no undue attention when Mr Allonby gathered half-a-dozen members of his executive committee on the terrace, lowered his voice to maintain discretion and said, 'I daresay that some of you must have noticed the absence of Mrs Dexter. Under normal circumstances, of course, I wouldn't notice one way or the other whether Mrs Dexter was in the hall, but I don't need to remind you that she has been scheduled – against my better judgement – to give the first presentation this afternoon, so I find it a trifle disquieting that she did not appear at breakfast this morning, or attend the first of the morning lectures. I sincerely hope that she is not going to let us down after such a fuss was made about including her in the programme.' He punctuated this last statement with a glare in the direction of one of the newest committee members, Frances Black – or Fran – a handsome woman in her late twenties, who was notably younger than most of the others.

Fran Black reddened slightly but her voice emerged confidently. 'I'm sure Mrs Dexter will appear. She was really keen to speak.'

'But suppose she doesn't? What if I'm up there on the platform and I announce her and . . .' The voice of Mrs Sarah Ingoldsby was rising to a squeak of indignation.

'Don't worry, Mrs Ingoldsby. We will have things sorted out long before it comes to that.' Hugh Allonby patted the woman's shoulder.

Sarah Ingoldsby might be an irritating and generally useless fusspot, thought Fran, but the fact that she was employed at the Vester House Museum, which held a large collection of Robert Barnaby's private papers, to which Hugh Allonby required frequent access, would always guarantee her a place in his inner circle of Barnaby-ites – an elite little clique of members to which Fran neither aspired nor belonged, her recent election to the national committee of the society notwithstanding.

Allonby turned back to the others and asked, 'Does anyone have any idea why Mrs Dexter has not appeared? Presumably none of you have seen her this morning?'

The enquiry met only with a general shaking of heads and murmurs of denial. It seemed that Linda Dexter had not been seen since she left the hotel lounge late the previous evening.

The sensible voice of Miss Jean Robertson, small, brisk and chairman of the Scottish Chapter of the Barnaby Society, cut across the others. 'Has it occurred to anyone that she might be unwell?'

'Possibly someone should check her room,' suggested John James. As the new membership secretary, he had also taken on the task of liaising with the hotel over the room allocations and, as he spoke, he extracted a folded delegate list from his jacket pocket and began to consult it.

Somewhat to everyone's surprise, Allonby himself, though normally a delegator par excellence, immediately announced that he would go in search of the missing speaker's room. Jean Robertson demurred that perhaps it would be better if someone else (meaning a female) went, but Hugh Allonby was already heading purposefully back into the building.

As he left them, Fran Black glanced around the terrace, still vainly hoping to see Linda Dexter somewhere among the groups of people, standing chatting in the glow of spring sunshine. There was the inevitable group of blue stockings, loudly attempting academic one-upmanship in that tiresome way of university women fixated on English literature; the fancy-dress brigade, of course, overgrown children every one, and a couple of gatherings made up of ex-servicemen, easily marked by their vaguely military bearing, as if the years in khaki hung invisibly upon them still

– one or two of them, of course, more obviously marked by the war: an eyepatch here, a walking stick there. Strange how they tended to gravitate towards one another in any gathering, she thought. Like belonging to a secret society. If her own brothers had survived they would have belonged too. The words of Brooke's poem came to her unbidden, and she had to turn away and swallow hard.

'Don't worry.' It was the kindly voice of Tom Dod (with one 'd', as he invariably had to specify). Like herself, he was a few years younger than the rest, another newcomer to the committee, and had presumably mistaken the source of her emotion. 'I'm sure Mrs Dexter will turn up.'

Meanwhile, Hugh Allonby was locating the room which had been reserved for Linda Dexter: a room inconveniently situated at the furthest end of a ground-floor corridor, next to some recently installed fire doors. When he reached it, he found the door to the room wide open and the sound of a woman humming was issuing from within. Advancing to the threshold, he realized at once that the sounds were emanating from a hotel chambermaid who was in the act of remaking the bed. He attracted her attention by briskly rapping his knuckles on the door.

The humming ceased abruptly. 'You want come in?' The girl was a foreigner. 'You want I go? Come back later?'

'No – no,' Hugh said impatiently. 'I'm looking for Mrs Dexter.'

The girl looked at him blankly. 'You want more towel?'

9

'No.' His voice began to betray his notoriously short fuse. 'I am looking for Mrs Linda Dexter – the woman who is staying in this room. Is she here?' He took a step into the room, enough to confirm that there were no occupants other than himself and the foreign girl, who was watching him nervously, poised with a half-plumped pillow in her hand. As he stood looking around, several things struck him, the first of which was that it was a noticeably larger room than the one which had been allocated to him – he would have to have a word in someone's ear about that – but there was something else too. Hugh Allonby was not an especially tidy man. His own bedroom had been left in a state of minor disarray: a couple of ties draped over the back of a chair, yesterday's newspaper tossed on top of the dressing table, among his brushes and a bottle of hair oil, his suitcase left half unpacked and open on its stand. This room was pristine. Once the maid had finished making the bed, there would be nothing to indicate that it was being occupied by a guest at all.

'Open the wardrobe,' he instructed. The girl stared at him. He couldn't decide if she had understood him or not.

'I should call manager,' she said. It was not exactly a question or a statement.

'Never mind, I'll do it myself.' Why on earth they had to employ a foreign girl, with half the country out of work, he couldn't imagine.

She backed away, still clutching the pillow as he advanced into the room and threw open the wardrobe doors. There was nothing inside except vacant coat hangers and a spare blanket neatly folded on the top shelf. From where he stood he could now see that the dressing table was completely devoid of brushes, cosmetics and the like. He turned on his heel and marched back towards Reception, his first instinct being that James had given him the wrong room number. Time was running out. The morning coffee break was almost over. It would not do for the chairman of the Robert Barnaby Society to hold up proceedings. He liked to time his entrance at the point when the lecture theatre was almost full, making a steady progress up the central aisle, pausing to acknowledge a favoured few members who were already in their seats, and being noticed by the newer members, who sometimes recognized him and nudged their companions, whispering, 'It's Hugh Allonby,' while he modestly pretended not to have heard.

Back in Reception, the desk was unattended, so he had to ping the brass bell. When the pimply youth who generally presided over the desk arrived, it took him an age to check the big ledger on the desk and confirm that the room number Mr James had given him was the correct one and that no, Mrs Dexter had not checked out.

Hugh Allonby received this news with an exasperated clicking of his tongue, then glanced around the big entrance hall of the hotel, temporarily at a loss. Through the French doors he could see a tail-end group of delegates drifting back to the Wordsmith Room in readiness for the next lecture. The group to whom he had confided his concerns a few minutes before had just come in from the terrace too, but were clearly hanging back for news. He strode across to them, confiding in a low voice: 'It's most peculiar. There's no sign of her anywhere. Her room appears to have been cleared, but the boy at the desk claims that she hasn't checked out.'

'What are we going to do?'

'There's nothing to be done now. Come along. We can't hold up the next lecture.' Allowing no opportunity for further discussion, Allonby strode into the hall, leaving the others to file in after him, exchanging doubtful glances as they found their seats.

As the next lecturer, a Cambridge professor, was introduced, Fran puzzled over what Hugh Allonby had just said. Surely Linda Dexter hadn't got cold feet and done a runner? It was only the Robert Barnaby Society, after all, not the Royal Institution Christmas Lecture. Of course, some people did freeze at the thought of speaking in public, but surely not Linda Dexter, who had been so enthusiastic when first invited, and had appeared to be her usual confident self over dinner the night before. Fran recalled the conversation clearly. They had been talking about the forth-coming general election and the annoying way in which the press were describing all the newly enfranchised women as 'flappers', leading Miss Robertson to comment that it would be good to see more women being offered a chance to take to the platform at the Barnaby Society meetings, a sentiment with which Linda Dexter had agreed wholeheartedly. Couldn't she see, Fran thought angrily, that if she chickened out at the last minute, it would look bad for the whole of the women membership?

It was not as if she had been pressured into speaking. On the contrary, the original impetus had come from Mrs Dexter herself, who had talked in somewhat enigmatic terms about some research that she had been doing into the provenance of Robert Barnaby's famous 'magic chair'. 'You should put a paper together, for the conference,' Fran had suggested, to which Linda had replied, 'Yes, I've found out some things which the members would find *very interesting*.' Far from being a reluctant speaker, Linda Dexter had appeared keen. She had placed considerable emphasis on those words 'very interesting', and when formally approached to speak she had accepted without any apparent hesitation.

She wouldn't just clear out without saying anything, Fran thought. There's something . . . *wrong* about this. She realized that she had already lost track of the presentation in progress (*Robert Barnaby and Walter de la Mare: Parallel Paths or Divergent Expeditions?*) and spent most of the next forty-five minutes wondering what the hell was going on with Linda Dexter. Maybe Mr Allonby was mistaken? Could he have got the wrong room? Then again, it was an unexpectedly lovely morning – perhaps Linda had merely gone for a walk? But Linda never normally missed the lectures. So . . . maybe she had been unexpectedly called away but still intended to get back in time to deliver her own lecture in the afternoon? If someone had telephoned for her in the middle of the night, she naturally wouldn't

13

have wanted to disturb anyone else . . . but of course the call could only have come through the hotel reception, so they would have known that she had been called away, and the same thing applied to the arrival of a telegram. It was ridiculous, of course, but Fran could not help entertaining the awful foreboding that something bad had happened to her.

While the learned professor quoted from 'The Listeners' to a rapt audience in the Wordsmith Room at the Furnival Towers Hotel, Sergeant Graydon, who had been recalled to the scene by PC Hamilton, was probing the charred remnants of what had once been a suitcase full of women's clothing. It could have been worse, he thought. Car fires occasionally left them with far nastier things than cremated underwear to deal with. As he lowered the lid of the Talbot's boot, a puff of ash escaped, like a visible sigh.

'Pretty fancy car,' Hamilton said. 'Funny that no one's got in touch about it.'

'I suppose the owner must have walked back to the main road and managed to flag a lift from someone after the car caught fire.' Graydon was phlegmatic. 'No doubt someone will come back to claim it soon enough.'

Three

Linda Dexter had been a regular attender since the society's inaugural conference in 1926, so it was inevitable that her absence would be noticed by others beyond the executive committee, and speculation about her possible non-appearance had begun to thread its way through the lunchtime conversation. While the other delegates were lingering over their coffee, Hugh Allonby called the committee together again in the hotel lobby.

'The difficulty which faces us is that Mrs Dexter's presentation, *The Magic Chair: Fact or Fiction*' (he winced as he spoke the title, as if confronted by an unpleasant odour), 'is no more than twenty minutes away, but there is still no sign of Mrs Dexter.'

Fran, who had originally recommended Linda as a possible speaker and could feel a mantle of blame descending upon her, felt obliged to speak up for the absent member. 'I can't believe that she won't be here in time to give her talk. I don't know her all that well, but she just doesn't seem the type to go off without a word. If she'd been called away, or taken ill, or something, she would surely have left word for us. She wouldn't just buzz off.'

'As the hotel has no record of any such message,' said Hugh Allonby, pure acid lacing his tone, 'I am unclear as to how you can advance such a statement.'

Fran, however, was only half listening, because as she finished speaking she had caught sight of Jean Robertson's anxious expression. Whereas Hugh Allonby cared only for the conference, it was evident that some people were becoming concerned for other reasons.

'Look here, Allonby old chap, she may have just gone off somewhere for the morning.' Tom Dod spoke up. 'There's nothing to say that anyone has to sit through everything on the programme.'

Fran flashed him a look of gratitude for his support.

'And taken all her luggage?' Hugh Allonby was contemptuous. 'I'm afraid we have to face up to the fact that dear Mrs Dexter has got cold feet and made a run for it. That's the last we'll hear of *The Magic Chair: Fact or Fiction*. In fact, after this debacle, it wouldn't surprise me if it isn't the last we hear of Mrs Dexter.'

For some reason, Fran noticed, he seemed to find this conclusion oddly satisfying, in spite of the immediate problem that this presented them with.

'Well, I really think that it is perfectly awful of her to let us down like this.' Sarah Ingoldsby simpered up at Allonby. 'Thank goodness Mr Allonby has offered to step in.'

'Maybe she sat in the magic chair and got spirited away?' Gareth Lowe was a hale and hearty member, who appeared to think it incumbent upon him to introduce an element of humour into every proceeding. He adopted a costume

16

from a different poem each year and was currently wearing a white cotton bedsheet, which had been fashioned into a floor-length robe, and which might have been an attempt to conjure up anything from a citizen of Ancient Rome to a druid.

Partly as a welcome respite from looking at a middle-aged man making a complete fool of himself, the whole group turned away from Gareth and looked towards the large carved chair which took pride of place in the hotel lobby – the famous magic chair itself. More of a throne than a chair, carved in oak and painted in scarlet and gold, it was generally acknowledged to be the inspiration for Robert Barnaby's famous magic chair, in which the child characters who peopled his poems were transported into the past for a series of adventures. The chair and indeed the hotel itself were a magnet for fans of Barnaby's work. Though archetypally English, Barnaby's work had been acclaimed all over the English-speaking world, and tourists from as far afield as America and Australia had been known to drive out to Furnival Towers in order to gaze at and even to sit in the famous chair. The discovery of the chair had indirectly led to the foundation of the society itself and the hotel had, of course, been the automatic venue for the society's annual conferences, each of which bore witness to the power of the chair upon the imagination of the author's fans. Of course, with Barnaby himself lost in the Great War – one of the many casualties of the conflict whose last resting place remained unknown – the chair provided a place where one might pay homage. Some people approached it deferentially, as one might a holy relic, reaching out tentatively to stroke its arms, and of course everyone wanted to take a turn at sitting in it. Just at that moment, however, the chair stood in splendid isolation at the centre of the lobby.

'I must go and check the platform.' Sarah Ingoldsby invariably managed to make the provision of a couple of glasses and a jug of water sound like a major feat of organization. She turned away, followed by Hugh Allonby.

'Just time for another cup of coffee, I think,' said Gareth Lowe.

As the group dispersed, Fran found herself standing alone with Tom Dod. Like Linda Dexter, he was someone she knew no more than slightly, but they had begun to gravitate together at society meetings and soon discovered that they shared a similar outlook, for though Fran loved Barnaby's books, enjoyed the society's quarterly journal, the lectures and visits which were arranged, she found it difficult to take it all quite so seriously as some of the leading lights and had instantly warmed to Tom when, at one meeting where the discussion became somewhat heated, he had dared to comment that, 'We are only a small literary society – it's hardly something to fall out about,' a sentiment completely out of step with Hugh Allonby and his immediate circle, who took themselves and the society very seriously indeed. The more intense among them vied to outdo one another's knowledge of Robert Barnaby's life and work. It was said that one member, if supplied with any line from a Barnaby poem, could

18

immediately quote the following line straight off the top of his head. The 'literary' members spoke pompously of 'the canon' when referring to Barnaby's work en masse, and the pseudo religious analogies did not end there. Every issue of the society's quarterly journal seemed to include at least one piece penned by a Barnaby devotee explaining how they had first encountered Barnaby's work – often in tones which conjured up the road to Damascus rather than a childhood visit to a bookshop or a public library. One woman had gushed about the 'life-changing' nature of Barnaby's work, while several had written pieces for the journal which spoke of their embarkation on 'literary pilgrimages' to sites associated with the poet's life and work.

As soon as Tom Dod sensed that he and Fran were on the same wavelength, he had given her the full benefit of his irreverent asides. It was Tom who had privately coined the orders of Barnaby-ites, starting with the High Priests – led by Hugh Allonby – people who for one reason or another were perceived as having a special insight into Barnaby lore, followed by the Acolytes, led by silly little Sarah Ingoldsby, who fluttered around the High Priest, hanging on his every word. The joke had reached the point where Tom had only to nod in the direction of a member and whisper the words 'a true pilgrim' for Fran to be convulsed. Just lately, she had begun to wonder whether she didn't get more fun out of Tom Dod's wicked observations on the society than the actual business of belonging to it.

'Trust old Allonby to step up,' said Tom in a

voice low enough that only she could hear him. 'Another chance to hog the spotlight and be the Saviour of the Society.'

'Oh dear – I bet it'll be The Time I Met Robert Barnaby again.'

'I'm afraid so. But you know how the pilgrims love it – and at the end he gets to do that thing where he walks down the central aisle, shaking hands with people so that they can touch the hand that once touched the hand of the Great Man himself. Seriously, though . . .' Tom's expression changed. 'It does look jolly strange, Mrs Dexter going off like this. What do you think's happened? Could it just be cold feet?'

'She *might* have gone for a walk or something. I know Hugh Allonby said she'd taken all her things, but you know that men never look properly for anything – and he does tend to exaggerate if there's a chance of creating a drama; besides which, he's absolutely dying to take centre stage himself. Maybe she had advance notice that listening to the professor would be about as exciting as wading through treacle?' Even as she spoke, Fran knew that she was clutching at straws.

'Maybe . . . What sort of car does she drive?'

'It's a big saloon. Two shades of blue, quite flashy. Why?'

'Do you mean that rather jolly Talbot? Why don't we have a look and see if it's still in the car park?' he suggested.

Furnival Towers had originally been a private country house, built with a generous carriage drive which swept up to the front door, but the majority of its clientele now arrived by motorcar and charabanc, and to accommodate this change a car park had been cut into the hill, on a lower level to the building and masked from the terrace by a great bank of rhododendrons. As they descended the stone steps together, Tom said, 'I'll take the far end and you try along the side nearest the hotel. If I find a two-tone blue saloon I'll give you a shout and you can see if you recognize it.'

It took them no more than a couple of minutes to establish that the vehicle they sought was not there. As they came together again at the foot of the steps, Fran decided that the time for speculating about country walks was past. 'I know it sounds silly,' she said, 'but I have the creepiest feeling about this. Why on earth would someone go off without saying anything to anyone? And I can't believe she just got nervous. She's never struck me as the nervous type.'

'Not nervous.' He hesitated. 'But I've always thought there was something a little bit odd about her. Something I could never quite put my finger on.'

Both of them glanced back to the top of the steps, where Gareth Lowe and a companion could be seen crossing the terrace, the former having hitched up his robes to reveal a pair of hairy knees, which were no match for the hairy trousers worn by his friend in the home-made Viking helmet.

'Hmm . . . a member of the Robert Barnaby Society accused of being a bit odd – now there's a first,' Fran mused, and they both laughed. 'What do we do now?' she asked when they had fallen silent again.

'There's not much we can do. Go inside and listen to old Allonby pontificating, I suppose.'

When they got back to the entrance hall, they found that another hasty conclave had been assembled, including Marcus Dryden, the owner of Furnival Towers, an avowed Barnaby fan and enthusiastic society member. Sarah Ingoldsby was in the middle of telling Jean Robertson that even if Linda Dexter did appear, she had forfeited her right to speak after causing everyone so much upset. 'Some people think only of themselves.'

'Not much chance of her showing up, I'm afraid,' Tom cut in. 'We've just checked around the grounds and her motor is definitely not there.'

'Perhaps there's been an accident,' Jean Robertson said doubtfully. 'Perhaps she slipped out for a wee while this morning and something happened on the road.' Fran noticed again that, apart from herself and Tom, only Jean seemed to be genuinely concerned that something unfortunate might have befallen their missing speaker.

'Surely someone would have let us know—' Marcus Dryden began.

'Not necessarily,' Fran cut in. 'If there's been an accident the police wouldn't think to contact us here. They would try to contact her family first.'

'Does anyone know anything about her family?' This from Tom. 'Is there someone we could contact to ask if they've heard from her – just to make sure that she's all right?'

Doubtful glances were exchanged. When members of the society got together, they talked about Robert Barnaby and various other literary matters, seldom mentioning their private lives.

After a brief silence, Sarah Ingoldsby said dismissively, 'It's just a case of nerves. She's run off and left us in the lurch. I always thought she was a rather unreliable person.'

'I'm sure we would all much rather hear Hugh speak anyway,' said Marcus – and something in the way he said it pulled Fran up short again. For some reason, people – or at least some people – didn't seem to be all that sorry about missing Linda Dexter's talk. If anything, Marcus sounded almost pleased.

Four

Saturday evenings at the Barnaby Society Annual Conference were traditionally formal affairs. (It was the one occasion in the society's calendar from which Hugh Allonby had managed to banish character costumes entirely.) The majority of the men wore evening dress, and even the more faded lady academics managed to search out a posh frock. The Lancashire weather was seldom kind, and Furnival Towers was notoriously draughty, but at this, the 1929 annual conference, they had been blessed with unusually fine weather and members sipping cocktails or pre-dinner sherry in the Lacelady Bar were treated to a perfect sunset, with the dark, humped backs of the Pennines standing out against a cloudless sky. At each of the previous conferences, the vista had been obscured by lashing rain, so it was hardly surprising that a good many of the gathering had taken up vantage points near the windows, to admire the very views which Hugh Allonby had assured them that afternoon had inspired Robert Barnaby when he had stayed here himself as a young man.

Fran had joined the group which included Tom Dod, and was thinking how well a dinner jacket and high collar suited him. There's something about a man in evening dress, she thought. She had temporarily forgotten all about Linda Dexter, whose disappearance had proved something of a nine-minute wonder among the rest of the delegates. If anything, the general consensus seemed to be that Mrs Dexter had behaved badly, Hugh Allonby had saved the day and the whole business was better forgotten. Besides which, most members were already looking forward to a good feed, followed by the after-dinner speaker, who was a regular broadcaster on the wireless and could currently be seen standing near the bar, where he was being fawned over by Sarah Ingoldsby.

Not everyone had forgotten Linda Dexter, however. Just as the gong sounded to summon them to dinner, Jean Robertson appeared at Fran's side. 'I was wondering – you're friendly with Mrs Dexter – do you know if she is on the telephone at home? Perhaps there is someone we could get in touch with? It would be good to know that she made it safely home and is all right.'

'I don't know her all that well,' said Fran. 'I believe she lives on her own.'

'Ah,' said Jean. 'She's a widow, then.'

It was the obvious assumption, Fran thought. The war had left so many widows, and Linda Dexter, who was probably in her mid-thirties, fitted the age profile perfectly. But we are not all widows, we married women who live alone, Fran thought, a little crossly. Aloud, she said, 'I'm fairly sure that she is on the telephone. Her number may be in the membership directory, but I don't have mine with me.'

Though she had adopted her helpful face,

in truth Fran was slightly irritated by Miss Robertson's enquiry. She wanted to have another drink and forget all about Linda Dexter. I only know the woman through society meetings, the same as everyone else, she thought. Just because I happened to stumble across the fact that she had been doing some research into Robert Barnaby's life, and suggested that she present a paper at the conference, everyone now seems to infer that we are bosom pals. She pushed her unease at Linda's absence to the back of her mind. If she got separated from the group which included Tom Dod as they were going into dinner, she might end up sitting next to a Barnaby bore, rather than next to Tom Dod as she intended.

'Well, now, who might have the number, do you think?' Jean Robertson mused, either not noticing, or choosing to ignore, Fran's somewhat discouraging tone.

'How about trying Mr James?' Fran suggested.

'I don't think he has ever met her,' Jean demurred. 'This is the first conference he's ever been to.'

'I know, but he's the membership secretary now. If anyone has a membership list with them, it will surely be him.'

'That's a good idea. There he is, by the door – why don't we go and ask him?'

Fran did not see why it had to be 'we', but as she couldn't think of a way to extricate herself from the errand without being rude, she reluctantly accompanied the Scottish branch chairman across the room.

John James was in the process of downing the

last of his sherry. Fran realized that he was standing on his own and, remembering that it was his first conference, she felt a pang of guilt at not making more of an effort to include him and introduce him to people. He hadn't arrived until that morning and evidently wasn't a natural mixer.

'You don't have the membership list here, do you?' she asked. 'Telephone numbers, that kind of thing?'

'We're a wee bit concerned about our missing speaker,' added Jean Robertson.

'Belinda Dexter still not turned up?' he asked.

'Linda,' Fran corrected.

'Of course – Linda. The full list's in my room. Do you want me to go and have a look at it now?'

'Well, if it wouldn't be too much nuisance . . .' wheedled Jean.

'We really don't have time,' Fran objected. 'People are starting to go into dinner. We can't hold everyone up.' Across the room, she could see the tall figure of Tom Dod being borne along by the tide heading for the dining room.

'You ladies go along in,' John James said. 'It won't take me a minute to go back to my room and, if I have a number, I'll jot it down and perhaps one of you can pop out between courses and ask the boy at the desk to try it.'

The membership secretary was as good as his word, but though Fran had them try the number between the spring vegetable soup and the roast lamb, word came back from the telephone operator at the exchange to say that there was no reply.

27

As the soup plates were being cleared at Furnival Towers, PC Hartley was cycling towards an address two counties further north. What with one thing and another, police constable Hartley of the Cumberland force had not been able to cycle across to Ivegill until well into the evening, and it was almost dark by the time he arrived at the gate of Langdale House, where he had been sent to acquaint a Mrs Dexter with the news that her Talbot 105 had been found burned-out near some village that he'd never heard of in the Pennines. Even from the gate, the house looked deserted, with the curtains not drawn and no lights burning, so it came as little surprise to him when his summons on the doorbell elicited no response. Further confirmation that there was no one at home came a moment later when a telephone bell began to ring inside and went unanswered. Evidently he was not the only person looking for this Mrs Dexter.

The unusual sight of a policeman in the centre of a small village invariably attracts attention, and by the time PC Hartley had given the bell another pull and followed that up with two or three good, hard bangs on the front door, an elderly woman had appeared from a cottage across the street and was approaching her front gate.

'Are you looking for Mrs Dexter?' she called across. 'I think she's away. I saw her putting a suitcase into her motorcar on Friday.'

God bless the eyes and ears of the world, thought Hartley. Every village should have its busybody.

'Going away for long, was she?'

'I don't know. It wasn't a very big suitcase. Perhaps just for a weekend.'

'Thank you very much, madam. I'll make sure someone pops back on Monday.'

Inwardly, he shook his head at the downright giddiness of some folk. Perhaps by Monday morning this Dexter woman might have noticed that her car was missing and bothered to report it.

'Of course,' Jean Robertson said when Fran relayed back the information that there had been no answer on the telephone. 'If she was overcome with nerves and fled back home, she must be feeling pretty silly by now, so perhaps she wouldn't answer her phone.'

Fran couldn't help thinking that if this was Miss Robertson's favoured theory, then there had been no point in her breaking away from the table and initiating a telephone call in the first place. She had been lucky inasmuch that she had managed to get a place at the same table as Tom Dod, where she was seated between Richard Finney, the society's journal editor, who could always be counted on for intelligent conversation, and Maggie Lawson, a history teacher, whose encyclopaedic knowledge of children's literature was leavened with a rich sense of humour.

The conversation was lively and their group lingered longer than most at the table, then kept together when they finally moved into the bar. Several cocktails later, with Tom sitting opposite to her across their little circle, Fran found that she was imagining herself swaying against him on a semi-darkened dance floor while the band played 'Stardust'.

'But what about Edith Nesbit?' Maggie was asking. 'Don't you think she has had a huge influence? Not so much with "The Railway Children" but the Bastables . . .'

Fran pulled herself back to reality and tried to concentrate on the discussion, but a few minutes later Richard Finney checked his watch and discovered that it was after midnight. This seemed to be the signal for several people to decide that it was time to retire. As the little group broke up, Fran found Tom Dod standing next to her.

'I can't believe how fast the evening's gone,' she said.

'Yes. It's been a good one.'

'The conferences just seem to get better and better each year.'

'Don't they?'

They had fallen behind the rest of the group as they crossed the big entrance hall, and when she reached the foot of the stairs, Fran realized that Tom had stopped walking. She hesitated, one foot poised on the bottom step. 'Aren't you coming upstairs?'

He grinned. 'Not without an invitation. My room's on the ground floor.'

'Oh.'

'Good night, then.'

'Good night.'

They turned away in unison: he along the downstairs corridor, she to climb the stairs.

A few minutes later, as she unfastened her frock and pulled it over her head, Fran relived the exchange. Perhaps if she had given Tom Dod just a bit of encouragement, he might have been

30

helping her out of her frock right now. Then again, if he had been joking about the invitation, she could have made a terrific fool of herself – and if any of the others had overheard them, or seen him entering her room, it would have caused one hell of a scandal. Besides which, she was not the kind of woman who invited men up to her room.

'You've had too much to drink,' she told her reflection as she cleaned her teeth at the washstand in the corner of the room. For some reason, this reminded her of Linda Dexter. Linda saying that she wouldn't have another drink, thank you. It had been the first night of the conference. A group of them had been sitting together in the bar, and someone was buying a round of drinks, but Linda had declined, saying that she was going to bed. Was that really only just over twenty-four hours ago? Where on earth had Linda Dexter gone? Why had she gone?

Five

After breakfast on Sunday morning, there was a familiar end-of-conference feeling in the air. Fran navigated her way across the lobby, pausing several times in order to exchange farewells, to say nothing of negotiating the obstacle presented by a very large American delegate complete with cabin trunk, who was in earnest conversation with Maggie Lawson about the works of Louisa May Alcott, and then avoiding the dull but earnest member from Derbyshire, who was determined to explain the workings of his camera to a very elderly gentleman who only wanted to be photographed sitting in the magic chair.

Tom Dod had been among the early departures, but Fran was booked on the charabanc for the station. It was not due to depart until 10.30 a.m., and this left her with ample time to order another pot of tea in the hotel lounge. She was awaiting its arrival when Miss Dora Leonard and Miss Amy Coward, wispy spinsters of uncertain age, who always travelled together, came into the room. Miss Leonard and Miss Coward were long-standing devotees of Robert Barnaby's work and to Fran they always seemed to inhabit a sunlit world, not unlike a work of children's fiction, in which everything was wonderful and a source of mutual delight.

'Congratulations on your election to the

executive committee, my dear,' Dora Leonard beamed.

'Thank you. Although I'm not sure they're in order. It was an uncontested election, after all. No one ever really wants to join committees. I'm not sure how I got talked into it.' It was because you'd heard that Tom Dod had agreed to do it, said a treacherous voice in her head.

'Oh, no!' exclaimed Amy Coward. 'You must look on it as an honour.'

Fran could not be sure whether Amy was joking or not. Probably not. She and Dora epitomized the body of members which Tom had dubbed the 'true pilgrims'.

As the two ladies fluttered around the table, they were joined by the more solid presence of Jean Robertson, the Scottish chairman, who, like Fran, was awaiting the departure of the station bus.

'I thought you would already be on your way, Miss Robertson. Such a long way back to Dumfries,' said Dora Leonard.

'It's not so bad. I'll get the ten past eleven and easily be home by three.'

'Did anyone find out what happened to Mrs Dexter?' Amy Coward asked, dropping her voice as if confiding a scandal. 'Such strange behaviour. I heard that she just took herself off without a word to anyone.'

'We asked dear Mr Dryden about it,' said Dora Leonard. 'Thinking that as the owner of the hotel, he would know the facts of the business, but apparently none of the staff saw her go. She left her room key on the chest of drawers, and the

33

girl who does the rooms found it there the next day. Of course, she had paid on arrival, so there was no problem about the bill.'

'I'm afraid we know no more than you do,' said Miss Robertson.

Miss Coward clicked her tongue. 'It's so very inconsiderate. There is too much of that sort of thing nowadays. It's everywhere – even in the Robert Barnaby Society. First Jennifer Rumsey, now this.'

'Miss Rumsey had a sick relative,' Jean Robertson said quickly. 'She had to stand down.'

'Oh.' Amy Coward appeared reluctant to retract the criticism. 'I rather got the impression from dear Mr Allonby that she had left the society in the lurch.'

'Fortunately Mr James was able to step in.' Jean Robertson sounded both brisk and reassuring at the same time.

'That new man?' said Miss Leonard. 'This was his first conference, wasn't it?'

'He's not such a new member,' said Jean Robertson. 'I believe he joined a couple of years ago but he's never managed to get to any meetings before. Rather a high pressure kind of job, I think. That's why he didn't arrive until very late on Friday night and no one set eyes on him until breakfast on Saturday morning.'

'Well, he seems a thoroughly nice man,' said Amy Coward, while Fran thought privately that Miss Coward would probably have declared Kaiser Bill himself a thoroughly nice man if he had turned up and professed enthusiasm for the work of Robert Barnaby. 'And I'm sure we're all grateful to him for taking on Miss Rumsey's role,' Miss Coward continued. 'It can't be easy, being membership secretary.'

'He's a real find,' Jean Robertson agreed. 'He made most of the arrangements for this weekend. No mess-ups over who was in which room this year.'

'Of course, everyone on the committee works hard,' Miss Leonard put in. 'We ordinary members are not nearly as appreciative as we should be, and all the little extra surprises that add to our fun . . . Mr Lowe coming into dinner on Friday night dressed as the Barbary Pirate. I'm not sure who he was supposed to be on Saturday, but he does put heart and soul into it, doesn't he? And I suppose he was the Black Shadow too?' She looked to Jean and Fran for confirmation, but neither had anything to add. Gareth Lowe's escapades were all undertaken entirely on his own initiative without the prior knowledge of anyone else. 'Though I must say it gave me quite a turn for a moment, when I saw him climbing in at that window.' Miss Leonard might have elaborated further, but at that point several others joined the group and, as the chairs were shunted into a wider circle in order to accommodate these extra bodies, Fran forgot to ask Miss Leonard what she meant about Gareth Lowe and the window.

Half an hour later, with her final round of farewells made, Fran carried her suitcase down the stone steps to the waiting motor coach. The driver was talking to someone at the door of the bus, so she hoisted her own small suitcase into the boot and was startled when she straightened up and turned to find someone standing right next to her.

'Sorry, did I make you jump?' It was Stephen Latchford – 'Stephen-with-a-ph' as Tom Dod referred to him, owing to Stephen Latchford's habit of specifying the correct spelling whenever he introduced himself.

Knowing that she had visibly jumped, a denial was pointless. 'I didn't see you,' Fran said.

'Ahh.' He gave a knowing smile. 'That's because I'm like the Black Shadow. I can melt in and out of the scene at will.'

Though references to the Black Shadow, villain of the Barnaby stories, were *de rigeur* at society events, for some reason Fran found this second mention within the space of half an hour unnerving.

'I didn't realize until this weekend that we live within twenty miles of one another,' Stephen-with-a-ph continued. 'I can give you a lift home if you like – save you getting the train. We should definitely travel together in future. Much more economical. Friendlier, too.'

Fran regained some personal space by taking a couple of steps backwards, and forced a smile. 'That's very generous of you, but I have a driver booked to collect me from the station. We'll have to think about it next time.'

'To next time then. Safe journey.' He raised his hat and continued to stand alongside the coach, as if waiting to wave off an old friend. Fran didn't consider Stephen Latchford a particular friend. If anything, she had always thought him a little

36

creepy. An obsessive Barnaby fan, his speciality was finding references to Barnaby in other people's work. He kept a log of all the Robert Barnaby mentions he had discovered in books, newspapers and periodicals, and was always tediously eager to share his latest finds. Funny, she thought, that until now she had never realized that he lived anywhere near her. Well, forewarned was forearmed. She would have to keep an excuse ready prepared in case the suggestion of sharing his motorcar arose again in the future.

The annual conference generally left her in high spirits, but she felt curiously depressed as the motor coach began bumping along the lanes which meandered across the moor away from Furnival Towers. She did not want to think that it was on account of Tom Dod, but she could not help admitting to herself that she had been disappointed when he had left immediately after breakfast, saying no more than a collective 'goodbye' which had encompassed a whole group of people who happened to be around at the time, including herself.

The Barnaby Society – and Tom Dod if he had only known it – had been a lifeline during these past months since Michael had left her. She had a few other friends, of course, but the sheer escapism of the Barnaby Society had plucked her right out of the miserable world which she had been inhabiting elsewhere. Unlike other friends and relatives one ran into, members of the Barnaby Society knew nothing of one another's private lives and troubles. Their conversation focused almost exclusively on books in general and Robert Barnaby's books in particular, which made it easy to forget everything else.

Then there was Tom Dod himself. She found him attractive in all sorts of ways, and she had occasionally considered the possibility that it might be mutual, but he had never made a move. Then again, she thought, neither have I. On reflection, she didn't even know how these things worked. She had been married at twenty-one, after a short but conventional courtship, enacted under the watchful eye of her mother. She supposed now that she and Michael had never been ecstatically happy together, but she had always assumed them to have been happy *enough*, and therefore the news that he intended to leave her for the horrid little woman with whom he had started an affair had blown her world apart.

He and the woman had it all planned. He had obtained a transfer and they had already arranged to rent a house in Nottingham, where no one knew them and they could live as Mr and Mrs Black, pretending to be a married couple, while she, the real Mrs Black, would be left to face the gossip and the stares afforded to those whose marriages had failed. It was not fair.

Michael had tentatively asked her if she would consider a divorce. Not naming the other woman, of course. His idea had involved the usual sordid put-up job – paying some woman to stay overnight in a hotel with him so that Fran could then sue for adultery. She had refused, of course. Why should she make things that easy for them? And anyway, her mother could never have coped with the scandal of a divorce. A separation could be glossed over to a certain extent, but divorces were public property.

'Such a disgrace,' her mother had said. 'But it's not my disgrace, Mummy,' she had protested. Her mother had said nothing in return, and this, she knew, was because privately her mother thought that it *was* her disgrace. It took two people to fail at marriage. Clearly she had not made a success of it, because if she had, Michael would never have left her. And as well as failing Michael, Fran knew that she had failed her mother too, for with Geoff and Cec both dead, the end of her marriage had stifled the sole possible source of grandchildren.

'I suppose you will have to come back and live with me,' her mother had said. But it had not come to that. Her great-aunt Rachel's legacy had provided her with enough to live on and the means to rent a little cottage not too far away from her old school friend, Mo, but well away from the wagging tongues of her own old neighbours or her mother's. And though her mother had initially protested that she ought not to live alone, Fran knew that her mother was secretly relieved. 'No one will know anything about it there,' she had said. 'People will think you're a widow.'

But, of course, she was not a widow and, unlike a widow, she was not free, after a respectable interval, to find another man and marry again. In which case, she asked herself, almost angrily, what was she doing dreaming about Tom Dod? Did she imagine that she was the type of woman who had affairs? Did Tom think she was a widow?

She did not know what he thought, because one did not broadcast one's private situation from the rooftops. She had once indulged in a cosy little fantasy in which Tom had paid court to her, she had divorced Michael and married Tom, but in real life she knew that there was little hope of such an outcome. Even if Tom himself had accepted this state of affairs, his family were unlikely to accept his marrying a woman who was divorced. The whole thing was extremely depressing and, in any case, she reminded herself, there was not the slightest suggestion that he even regarded her as anything more than a casual acquaintance.

She had already begun to regret her election to the society's executive committee. She knew that she would find Hugh Allonby hard work, to say nothing of his chief acolyte, the tedious Mrs Ingoldsby. Perhaps her glum mood wasn't just about Tom Dod, she thought, because there was also this strange, unfathomable business about Linda Dexter too.

She was still thinking about it when the motor coach trundled to a halt in the cobbled forecourt of the railway station, and she suddenly remembered that she did have a note of Linda Dexter's telephone number after all – it was in the back of her pocket diary, where she had jotted it down when Mrs Dexter had first mentioned the possibility of giving a lecture. Glancing at her wristwatch to confirm that she still had time before her train, Fran carried her case across to the public call box, pulled the coppers out from her purse, lifted the handset and asked the operator for the number. After the usual plinks and clicks, the line went silent while the request was relayed from one exchange to the next. While she waited, Fran began to have second thoughts. She did not know what she was going to say when the call was answered. Wouldn't Linda Dexter think it strange, presumptuous even, of Fran to call? It was not as if they were really friends – only people who knew each other slightly through mutual membership of a club. But when a woman's voice came on the line at last, it was not Linda Dexter but the original operator, informing her that there was no reply from the number she had requested.

As she replaced the receiver, a knock on the window of the booth startled her into a stifled scream. She turned to find Stephen-with-a-ph-Latchford smiling at her from the other side of the glass. Shaken and astonished, Fran pushed the door open and stared out at him.

'Problem with your train?'

She supposed that he thought he was being helpful, but it was still hard to keep the annoyance out of her voice. 'No, everything is fine. I was just making a telephone call.'

'Right-ho. You know, I was passing the station and I saw the chara and suddenly had a thought – if I took you home by way of the station, we could let your driver know that he wasn't needed and I could drop you at your door. It's scarcely out of my way.' He was filling the space she needed to step into, inadvertently penning her into the phone booth.

'On the contrary,' she said, 'I think that is

41

asking you to go much too far out of your way. Thank you for stopping, but if you'll excuse me, I really must get across to the other platform for my train.' She all but pushed past him, forcing him to step backwards in a hurry, so that he almost fell over a couple of wicker hampers which were standing on the platform. It was barely polite, but it was the second time he had frightened the life out of her in the past hour and she was not amused, however generous his intentions. Normally she would be only too glad of a lift, for she liked driving, and of course it was much more direct than taking the omnibus or the train, but something about the way Mr Latchford was pressing her to accept made her all the more determined to refuse.

It was a dispiriting homecoming. The train seemed to trundle at half its normal pace under ever greyer skies and spots of rain began to hit the windshield of the taxi when she was still about a mile from home. By the time Freddie Dyson, the local driver who could easily have doubled as the village idiot, drew up at the cottage gate, rain was beating feverishly against the car, and even in the few seconds that it took her to run up the path and get the front door open, the hair which protruded from under her hat had become a tangle of rats' tails.

Mrs Snegglington, her cat, who had been named for a character in a Robert Barnaby story, did not come to greet her when she let herself in. Sulking, probably, Fran thought, having been left with no one but Ada, the daily maid, to minister to her needs. Ada had not put a match to the fire before she left to catch her afternoon bus back to Ulverston and the place felt chilly, almost damp. Fran had a love-hate relationship with Bee Hive Cottage. When she had first seen it, on a summer afternoon, with shadows dancing on the walls and birdsong pouring in through the open windows, she had thought there could be no better place to be. But it was very different on these darker days, with the stone floor echoing her footsteps as she made another solitary homecoming.

At least the fire was laid. She only had to apply a match and within moments the kindling had caught, the silence dispelled by a series of snaps and hisses as the smaller stuff surrendered to the flames. Good old Ada – she certainly knew how to lay a fire. The logs would catch in no time.

Ada was a bit of a luxury on her relatively small income and something of a sop to her mother, whose ideas of Armageddon included the thought of being without help in the house. Fran knew that she was perfectly capable of managing the little place herself, and what was more, having Ada in to help with the chores just left her with more time on her hands. After Michael left her, she had initially attempted to find some work. She was an able typist and bookkeeper, but with so many people unemployed, firms were able to pick and choose, and most employers flatly refused to take on married women. One hope had been snuffed out when she arrived at the interview to discover that they had mistaken Frances for Francis. Another had told her, in a pseudo kindly voice, that it would be different if she had been a war widow. In what way would it be different?

43

she had wanted to scream. Is a woman any less in need of supplementing her income just because her husband has fallen victim to a frizzy-haired little tramp with skinny ankles rather than the bloody Hun? She had not screamed, of course. It wasn't something a well-brought-up young woman did.

After taking off her outdoor things and warming her hands in front of the glowing fire, she went into the kitchen and attempted to make her peace with Mrs Snegglington, who only agreed to thaw at the prospect of some tinned sardines. Fran made a pot of tea and, having set the tray with cup, saucer, milk jug, tea pot and strainer, she carried it into the sitting room and placed it on the small table alongside the armchair closest to the fire, where she sat with her legs curled under her, glancing idly through the minutes of the last meeting of the Barnaby Society executive committee. Homework from Hugh Allonby in preparation for her new role.

Liaison with the Vester House Museum over next year's proposed exhibition . . .

Proposal for lapel pins for purchase by members . . .

Motion to raise subscriptions . . .

The telephone startled her. She reached across to grab it, almost upsetting her part-drunk cup of tea, which rattled precariously in its saucer.

'Hello?'

'Fran, darling, it's Mo.'

'Hello, Mo. How are you?'

'I'm fine. So how about you? How did it go?' Mo's voice was full of expectation.

44

'How did what go?'

Mo made an impatient noise down the line. 'Your weekend . . . with that chap.'

'What do you mean, with that chap?'

'You know, this Tom chap. The chap you keep on talking about.'

'I told you before, there's absolutely nothing in it. We see each other at Barnaby meetings and that's it. We're just friends.'

'You need to make a move. Get back in the game. It's the only way you'll ever get over . . . Anyway,' Mo changed the subject abruptly. 'What's his other name – this Tom?'

'It's Dod,' she said reluctantly.

'Dud!'

'No. Dod.'

'As in D-O-D-D?'

'No. As in D-O-D.'

'Gosh, how unusual. Like Lottie Dod, the tennis player.'

'Before my time, darling.'

'But everyone knows about her – first woman to win the Ladies' Championships three years in a row. I say, do you think Helen Wills will make it three in a row this year? Of course, now that *Mademoiselle* Lenglen has gone and won it five times in a row, the gloss has rather gone off a mere three victories, don't you think? Anyway, talking of pairing up for mixed doubles and all that, let's get back to this Tom character . . .'

Mo was her oldest friend and Fran loved her dearly, but Mo's fixation with getting Fran 'back in the game', as she put it, had already led to a dull dinner with a bachelor accountant, to say nothing of an excruciating evening with an old letch from Mo's tennis club, and just now she didn't feel in the mood to talk about Tom Dod, over whom she was beginning to feel rather a fool, so she changed the subject by telling Mo about the strange disappearance of Linda Dexter instead.

When she had finished, Mo said, 'She might have been kidnapped. Why, the whole thing sounds straight out of an Agatha Christie. Didn't anyone think to ring the police?'

'That's a bit overdramatic. She's a grown woman and I'm afraid that the obvious answer is that she just panicked and cleared off.' Yet even as she said it, Fran could hear that alarm bell of worry clanging faintly in the back of her mind again.

'Nope.' There was undisguised mirth in Mo's voice as she continued, 'She's been done away with. Probably about to reveal something terrible in the sainted Robert Barnaby's past and had to be silenced. This woman disappears into thin air and there's a chap called Dod at the same conference. I mean, you don't have to look far for a suspect, do you?'

'What on earth are you talking about now?'

'Didn't you know that dod means death in some of the Scandinavian languages?'

'Of course I didn't. Only someone like you, whose husband is permanently globe-trotting, would know a thing like that.'

'Heavens, it's just as well the two of you don't appear to be getting together. I mean, imagine if the names were hyphenated . . . black-death . . .'

'Oh, yes, very droll,' said Fran sarcastically.

'Anyway, if nothing's come of the Tom thing . . .'

'There is no Tom thing.'

'Then there's another really nice unattached chap, just joined the tennis club . . .'

'Please, Mo. No more chaps from the tennis club.'

A call from Mo normally cheered her up, but when their conversation was over and Fran recalled her friend's question about 'the Tom thing', it depressed her. She hadn't realized that she had gone on about him to Mo. It made her feel immature and desperate. It wasn't as if she even knew anything about Tom Dod, except that he shared her interest in Robert Barnaby and made her laugh. Was she really so desperate that any man who made the slightest friendly overture became some sort of target? Of course not. She had not gone on about him. It was just Mo's interpretation of things.

It seemed particularly quiet in the cottage after the constant background chatter of the conference. She could have put on the wireless, but it smacked too much of an admission that she didn't like the silence of the place at night. Perhaps it had been a mistake to come and live here. Pig-headedness winning out over common sense. Sometimes the cottage felt very empty with just her and the cat. She had begun to drink too many pink gins to see her through the evenings, and caught herself talking a little too frequently to Mrs Snegglington. That's how I'll end up, she thought. A batty old woman who lives on her own, with a regiment of cats. I'll drink too much and go senile, thinking I'm a child again, with my pets named after characters in bloody Robert Barnaby books . . . and Mo will still be ringing up to tell me about a really nice chap who's just joined her Retired Gentlefolk's Dining Club. She grinned in spite of herself. Pull yourself together. You're only twenty-eight. That's a year younger than that dull little woman was when she snared Michael. Winifred – the wouldn't-say-boo-to-a-goose scorer at the cricket club. Well, she'd scored with Michael all right. She actually called herself Winny, which rhymed very nicely with ninny. It made the whole thing sound rather ridiculous. My husband's run off with Winny the Ninny.

Six

The branch line between Clitheroe and Shieldsby had been constructed solely for the purpose of carrying aggregate from Shieldsby Quarry. In its heyday, the line had sometimes seen the passage of several trains per day, but for many years now the number of train movements had been reduced to fewer than a dozen each week. From Monday to Friday, one heavily laden beast would carry away a full load of crushed stone in the hour before midnight, and from Monday to Friday another sturdy workhorse would come steaming in the opposite direction a few hours later, its trucks clattering and empty in readiness to stand in the sidings and be loaded afresh. These were slow-moving trains, which were only allowed to join the main line in the wee small hours of the morning when the more glamorous expresses were scarcer and the solid bulk of goods traffic held sway. The routine varied at the weekends, for the quarrymen had a half day on Saturdays and did not work at all on Sundays, so once the sound of the fully laden wagons had faded into the distance on Friday nights, the line fell silent until around six on Monday mornings, when the rails rang again to the rattle of the empty wagons.

Throughout the winter months, Driver Tyler made the inward run to Shieldsby Quarry under cover of darkness, but as April advanced towards

May, he completed the last few miles of his journey in the grey half-light which precedes dawn, the visibility increasing week by week as the hour of sunrise crept inexorably forward. He knew the line intimately and was immediately alert to any changes, so although the brief glimpse of something on the track just after Bridge 485 did not look like anything in particular – just a bag of rubbish or some discarded clothes – Driver Tyler knew at once that it had not been there before the weekend. They were past the place before he even had time to point the object out to his fireman and it was neither practical nor possible to stop the train. He sensed rather than felt the impact as the wheels brushed whatever it was contemptuously aside. He knew instinctively that there was something not right about the bundle on the line. Someone would have to be told about it.

Fran's telephone rang at just after half past six that evening. Although he had never called her before, she immediately recognized Tom Dod's voice on the line.

'Fran.' He always called her Fran these days, never Mrs Black. It had come about at a society meeting a couple of months ago, when he had said, 'I say, do call me Tom,' and she had naturally reciprocated by inviting him to call her Fran. It was part of his air of easy informality which she found so attractive. There was nothing stuffy about Tom Dod. 'Have you heard the news?' he asked.

'What news?'

'I think you had better prepare yourself for a shock. I believe they've found Linda Dexter's body on a railway line.'

For a moment, she was too stunned to say anything. 'You're joking! No, obviously you're not joking. No one would joke about a thing like that.'

'It was in the evening paper. Of course, it doesn't actually say that it's Linda Dexter, but apparently the police found a burnt-out motor car in the early hours of Saturday morning, standing in a lane not far from the spot where the body was. It's a Talbot 105.'

'But they haven't said that it's her? Are you sure, Tom? What makes you think it's her?'

'It's less than a dozen miles from Furnival Towers, and the police are saying that the body could have been on the track for most of the weekend. Apparently there are no trains running along that line between just before midnight on Friday and quite early on Monday morning, which fits with the timing of her vanishing act. Maybe I'm jumping to conclusions. Do you take an evening paper?'

'I have the *Post* delivered but I haven't read it yet. I'll check it now and call you back.'

She found the story on an inside page. A blazing Talbot 105 found in a country lane in the early hours of Saturday morning was thought to be linked with a body which had been discovered that morning alongside the railway line, only fifty yards or so away. The remains had not been formally identified and the police were refusing to confirm the identity of the car owner, or whether the two incidents were linked. They had not ruled out foul play.

Tom answered the telephone so quickly that he must have been standing over it.

'It could be Linda Dexter,' she said. 'It does fit. The car was found in the early hours of Saturday morning and Linda was last seen in the bar late on Friday night.'

'If it is her, then someone ought to telephone the police and let them know that she was at the conference. Shall I do it?'

'I don't know. If someone else has seen the news, they may have called already. Hugh Allonby or someone might have done.'

'Actually,' it sounded as though Tom was thinking aloud, 'we ought to mention it to the old boy first, as a courtesy if nothing else. He is the national chairman, after all.'

Fran agreed immediately. 'He will probably want to tell the whole committee. Better people hear it sooner rather than later. It's going to come as a bit of a shock and the police may want to take statements from people. You'd better telephone the High Priest.'

'Right-ho. I'll ring Allonby first, then the Old Bill.'

Fran spent a few more minutes searching through the paper, but there was nothing else about the story. Then another thought struck her. Suppose they were wrong and it wasn't Linda? She pulled her diary out of her handbag, dialled up the operator and asked for Linda Dexter's number again but, just as before, the operator was unable to connect her. The thought of a telephone bell echoing through an empty house sent a goosey chill from her shoulders to her wrists.

A moment later, her own telephone rang again and she picked it up full of hope, but it wasn't Linda Dexter saying that she hadn't got to the phone in time, it was Tom again, sounding more than slightly angry. 'I've just spoken to the High Priest and Grand Panjandrum himself, Mr Hugh Allonby. Apparently he believes that it is up to him to ring the police on behalf of the society, as and when he has satisfied himself that it's necessary to do so.'

'But that's ridiculous!' exclaimed Fran.

'Not according to Allonby. He says that we must not start rumours leading to the society's involvement in a police enquiry based on nothing more than guesswork and supposition. Apparently he intends to alert the rest of the committee to the situation as soon as possible and sound everyone out before he does anything which might associate Robert Barnaby's name with an unknown body on a railway line.'

Fran hesitated. 'I can see what he means but I think he's wrong. If it is Linda Dexter, then the police need to know as soon as possible what she was doing in the area that weekend.'

'I agree, but he's the chairman, so it's his call up to a point.' Tom sounded doubtful. 'And we don't know for certain that it is Linda Dexter. If it is, I suppose a few hours' delay in calling the police won't make any difference. The police might already be in touch with her family and know that she was attending the conference. We

53

could be worrying about telling them something that they already know.'

'That's true, I suppose.'

'Anyway, I'll get off the line, in case Allonby is trying to get through to you.'

'All right. When he speaks with me, I'll vote for contacting the police straight away, just in case it is Linda.'

After replacing the telephone she went into the kitchen, but the idea of supper had little appeal. It was impossible to settle to anything while she waited for Hugh Allonby to call, and one scenario after another presented itself. She thought of the body lying undiscovered for two nights at the side of the track. Supposing Linda hadn't been dead? Suppose she had fallen down and injured herself and cried out for help and no one came? It was too horrible to contemplate.

Every so often she glanced up at the clock on the mantelshelf. It was taking Hugh Allonby an awfully long time to call everyone. She thought of ringing Tom again, but of course that would block any incoming call. Eventually, when the clock had struck ten, she checked her member-ship list for his number, then called the operator and asked for the number herself. She half expected his line to be engaged, but there was no problem in getting connected.

'Good evening, Mr Allonby,' she began, feeling absurdly nervous. 'I have been expecting you to call me about Linda Dexter, but I began to think that perhaps you had experienced some difficulty in getting through.'

'Mrs Black? I would not have dreamed of

disturbing you at such a late hour.' The tone was reproving. 'I have written a note to go in tomorrow's post, but you have pre-empted me.'

As he seemed disinclined to elaborate further, Fran said, trying to keep it light, 'Perhaps you could save the stamp by telling me what the note says.'

'Certainly. It is a general note and reads as follows: *Dear Fellow Committee Member, a suggestion has been made that a body found near Clitheroe today is that of Mrs Linda Dexter. It has been decided that members of the committee should under no circumstances contact the police in connection with this matter until confirmation of identity has been established and the committee has had the opportunity to discuss the matter further. Hugh Allonby, Chairman.*'

A flush of anger spread through her chest as she listened. Who exactly had decided this and why hadn't she been consulted? She was on the committee, after all. 'I'm sorry,' she said, 'but I'm afraid I don't understand.'

'Really? Isn't it self-explanatory?'

'What I mean is that I want to ask how you can say that a decision has been made? I am on the committee and I haven't even been consulted.'

Hugh Allonby's voice was smooth as syrup. 'The general view was that until such time as there was a definite link between this tragic affair and Mrs Dexter, any suggestion of involving the society was utterly mistaken – little more than wasting police time. As the executive committee, we have to consider any possible adverse impact on both the society itself

55

and the reputation of Robert Barnaby in everything we do. Starting a wild goose chase which associates the society with a sordid police enquiry would be thoroughly irresponsible. There is absolutely nothing to connect a member of the society to this incident, apart from some very wild speculation.'

'I tried to telephone Mrs Dexter's number again tonight,' Fran said. 'There's still no answer.'

'That is neither here nor there.'

'I don't see how you can say that a decision has been reached when we haven't had the chance to discuss it. You didn't telephone me, and I have been at home all evening.'

'One doesn't have to consult every member in order to reach a consensus. Once more than half the members of our committee have assented to something, that's a majority.'

'I feel that we should all have been given the opportunity to discuss it,' Fran persisted. 'I happen to believe that someone should inform the police that Linda Dexter disappeared from the conference—'

'I think disappeared is an overdramatic way of expressing it.'

'—and so does Tom Dod.'

'You've discussed it with Mr Dod, then?'

Fran felt a sudden need to defend herself. 'He rang me to ask what I thought he should do.'

'And why did he ring you in particular?' The tone was unmistakably nasty.

Up to that moment, it hadn't occurred to Fran to question why. The obvious answer was that perhaps as Jean Robertson had done at the

56

weekend, Tom had inferred a stronger link between herself and Linda Dexter than actually existed, probably thanks to her suggesting Linda for the conference programme, but since she didn't want to remind Hugh Allonby of that particular connection just then, she said lamely, 'I don't know.'

'There are proper channels of communication when something as important as the society's reputation is at stake. Serious matters like this need to go through the elected chairman, and that is me.'

'Yes, of course. I suggested to Mr Dod that he ring you,' Fran said, and instantly despised herself for a suck-up.

'Well, he did ring me and I have dealt with the matter. Now, it is really very late. I was on my way to bed when you rang.'

'Which other committee members did you talk to? Did Miss Robertson think we ought to go to the police?'

'It is very late,' he repeated. 'And I do not propose to discuss the matter any further. Goodnight, Mrs Black.' A loud click in her ear indicated that the chairman had hung up.

Seven

Dear Fellow Committee Member,

Now that the body of Mrs Dexter has been formally identified, I have notified the authorities of her involvement in our annual conference. It is possible that some of you may be contacted by the police in furtherance of their enquiries. Should this occur, I would appreciate your keeping me informed. In the meantime, may I remind you that any enquiries from the press should be directed to me. It is most important that the society speaks with one voice at a time like this and avoids any negative publicity.

Hugh Allonby,
Chairman

The letter was waiting for Fran on Wednesday, when she arrived home after spending the day at Kendal market. Absolutely no expression of regret, she noted. Nothing about sympathy for Linda Dexter's family. She did not care for the tone of the letter at all and wondered whether or not to phone Tom Dod. She decided against and called Mo instead.

'So, my dear, what's up with you?'

'To tell you the truth, I've had a bit of a shock. Are you busy?'

'You know I'm never too busy for you. Actually, I'm lying with my feet up on the sofa, drinking whiskey and lemonade.'

58

'Why? Have you caught a chill?'

'Of course not, I've just run out of gin. What's happened to you?'

'Nothing's happened to me; it's someone else. Have you heard about the woman who's been found dead on a railway line in Lancashire, close to a burned-out motorcar?'

'Can't say that I have. You're not going to tell me . . . don't say it's that woman who disappeared at your conference?'

'It is. It's Linda Dexter.'

'Good heavens! How on earth did she get there?'

'I don't know.'

'Come on, Fran. You must have a theory. It's got to be murder or suicide. You don't end up on a railway line by accident.'

'I don't know. It's very peculiar.'

'Was she depressed? The type to kill herself?'

'Is there a type? I don't know what to think. Maybe she did kill herself . . .'

'But you don't really think so.'

'I don't know. I mean, I don't even know her all that well. It's a funny time to choose, don't you think? We all spent the evening chatting together in the hotel bar and she seemed happy enough. I got the impression that she was really looking forward to giving her talk the next day. And if you're about to top yourself, why on earth set your car on fire first?'

'What sort of place is it?'

'What do you mean, Mo?'

'Where she was found. Is it busy? Easy to get to?'

'Neither. After I read about it in the paper, I checked on the map, and basically it's at the back of beyond. She would have had to set fire to her car, then climb up the railway embankment by the bridge, and then walk a few yards along the line. It's not even a proper railway line – just this funny old single track railway which serves a quarry.'

'People don't go to railway lines to commit suicide, unless they want to throw themselves under a train,' observed Mo. 'Did she actually throw herself under a train?'

'I suppose so. The paper doesn't really say how she died, but that's the obvious assumption.'

'Well, I agree that it all sounds jolly off-key. Why climb up an embankment in the dark? Had she got a torch with her – and what sort of shoes was she wearing? If you wanted to chuck yourself in front of a train, wouldn't you do better to drive to a mainline station, leave your car in the station yard and wait on the platform? I told you so, didn't I? I said she'd been kidnapped and murdered, right from the start. What does your Tom chap think?'

'He's not my Tom chap. I don't know – I haven't asked him.'

'Well, call him. Perfect excuse.'

'Honestly, Mo!'

'Seems reasonable enough to me. The whole Robert Barnaby Society is going to be agog with it. Only natural to get in touch, I'd say.'

Fran was still contemplating this advice when the question was resolved by Tom ringing her. 'You've seen Allonby's note?' he asked. Having received her affirmation, he went on, 'I know this probably seems like a strange question, but do you happen to know what Linda Dexter was planning to say at the conference?'

'Not really. The lecture title was *The Magic Chair: Fact or Fiction*, and she was going to speak about some research that she had just finished.'

'Did she tell you anything about this research?'

'Just that it was something completely new – information which had never been published before. She said the members would find it very interesting – as if, well, I don't know – she thought it might create a bit of a stir.' Fran hesitated, because she knew it sounded crazy, but then she said it anyway. 'Do you think that perhaps someone wanted to stop her from making that speech?'

Tom gave a half-hearted laugh. 'Sounds pretty melodramatic, doesn't it?'

'I don't know what to think,' Fran said slowly. 'I do find it hard to believe that Linda Dexter killed herself. Surely you don't go from being jolly in the bar to chucking yourself under a train in the space of a couple of hours?'

'Funny time to choose to kill yourself.'

'Funny way to go about it as well. I was talking to a friend earlier and she said she couldn't imagine why anyone would set fire to their car, then struggle up a railway embankment, when you could far more easily drive to a mainline station and simply walk out on to the platform. My friend thinks that she must have been abducted from the hotel and murdered.'

'I would say that there's a lot of sense in that,' Tom said.

'But you can't just walk into the Furnival Towers Hotel and attack someone. The doors are locked at night and surely Marcus Dryden would have said something if there had been any sign of a break-in.'

'So the chances are that no one broke in.'

'Do you really think that someone killed her? A member of the society?'

'Do you think I'm absolutely barking to suggest it?'

'No,' she said, 'I don't. Do you think it might be something to do with Linda's research?'

'It doesn't seem very likely, does it? I mean, what could possibly be that important about the Robert Barnaby Society?'

'Would the police take it seriously?'

'I'm not planning to suggest it to them,' said Tom. 'In a sense, I'm with old Allonby inasmuch that we do have a responsibility to protect the society from wild rumours, and I do appreciate that it won't do the public image of Robert Barnaby any good to be at the centre of a police investigation. Besides which, the idea sounds so farfetched that the person who put it forward would look like a prize idiot, particularly when it turned out to be a load of tosh. I mean, it can't be much better than a million-to-one shot.'

'But what if your million-to-one shot is right?'

'If we could somehow get hold of a copy of Linda Dexter's lecture, or better still, see her research notes, the two of us know enough about Robert Barnaby to see whether or not the idea is a runner. If it turns out that there is something in it, well, that would be the time to involve the police. Though quite honestly I can't imagine what anyone could possibly discover about a dead author which would be worth committing a murder to keep it quiet.'

Fran thought for a moment before she said, 'Linda's family might be willing to give a copy of her research papers to the Robert Barnaby Society.'

'They might, but an official approach from the committee wouldn't be the best way to go about this.'

'Why not?'

'Think about it,' said Tom.

'Because if your million-to-one shot comes in, the person who killed Linda is probably someone who is at the heart of the society.'

'Precisely.'

Eight

It was around eleven o'clock the following morning when Ada answered a knock at the front door and then hesitantly announced, 'It's a policeman to see you, Mum.'

Police Sergeant Godfrey seemed anxious to put her at her ease. Just routine enquiries, he said, on behalf of the coroner. He supposed that she was aware of the recent demise of Mrs Linda Dexter?

'I read about it in the paper,' Fran said. 'Please, do come in and take a seat.' She extended a hand in the direction of the sofa while simultaneously nodding in the direction of the kitchen, by way of dismissing Ada, who was lurking in the doorway with her mouth open.

'The police in Cumberland have received information from one of their local telephone exchanges that a call had recently been placed from a telephone listed at this address, asking for the number belonging to Mrs Linda Dexter of Ivegill, and it was thought possible that, as a friend or relative of the deceased, you might be able to throw some light on her state of mind.'

'You're treating it as a suspected suicide, then?' asked Fran.

'I'm afraid I couldn't possibly comment, Mrs Black. I'm not directly involved with the case myself. I'm just the local officer who is to take down any statement you may care to make, which I will then pass to the officers who are conducting the enquiry.'

She knew from the newspapers that an inquest had been opened and adjourned. Linda's identity had been established with reference to her dental records (Fran shuddered at the implications of this), and though there was nothing official, it was hinted that the cause of death was probably the result of being struck by a train. The papers had so far exhibited little interest in the Robert Barnaby Society, with some merely mentioning that Mrs Dexter had been staying at a nearby hotel, or else naming the hotel and adding that she had been at a conference or a 'private event'. Only one newspaper had bothered to contact Hugh Allonby, who was quoted as saying how deeply saddened the society had been to learn of the death of a well-loved member. Hugh himself was described as president of the Robert Barnaby Society and the author of several books, including *The Sheer Magic of Barnaby*. 'I don't believe it,' Tom had said when they'd spoken on the telephone later that evening. 'He's turned the whole exercise into a bit of self-publicity.'

In spite of being assured that it was 'just routine', Fran felt uncomfortable about the visit from the local constabulary. She had scarcely known Mrs Dexter, she told Sergeant Godfrey, while realizing how thin that sounded, when she had to explain that she had telephoned the dead woman's house not once but three times during the weekend of her death. She wondered if he would ask her what Linda had been going to speak about at the conference, but he didn't, though he did want to know whether Linda had appeared in any way upset, or had been behaving differently to her normal self during that Friday evening at the Furnival Towers Hotel, and finally whether Fran had been aware of anything which might have been worrying Linda.

'There was nothing out of the ordinary at all. Of course, I don't know anything about her private life. She never really talked about herself. We usually talk about books, you see. She was very knowledgeable: very well read.'

'She never mentioned anything about men friends? You see, she was divorced, Mrs Black, so there was no husband on the scene, if you see what I mean.'

'No, I don't,' Fran said coldly. 'And as I've told you already, I knew nothing of her private life.' And yet, she thought, little by little, I am becoming involved. I have started to think of her as Linda rather than Mrs Dexter. Perhaps it's because no one else – except Tom and Mo – seems to care. All Hugh Allonby thinks about is his precious society.

As she shut the door behind the policeman, Fran said aloud, 'Well, I don't believe she killed herself.'

Mrs Snegglington was lying on the window seat, a vantage point from which she had been able to observe the visitor through narrowed eyes, refusing to acknowledge all Sergeant Godfrey's friendly overtures. As if in response to Fran's comment, she raised her head and looked Fran straight in the eye, as if to say: *So what are you going to do about it?*

'Did you call, Mum?' Ada, clearly agog, emerged from the kitchen, where she had no doubt been listening to every word.

'No, thank you, Ada. I was just talking to the cat.'

Nine

'So,' said Mo. 'How's your sleuthing going?'

It was Friday evening, two weeks to the day since Linda Dexter had last been seen at the Furnival Towers Hotel. Mo had driven over to Bee Hive Cottage by prior arrangement, bringing the constituents of cocktails and canapes, to be consumed before a light supper provided by Fran.

'You know that Tom Dod has this idea that perhaps there was something in Linda's research that someone didn't want to be made public?'

'Sounds a bit farfetched, doesn't it, darling? I mean, we're talking of a children's author here, not the memoirs of a double agent.'

'Yes and no. Some people do have a monetary interest in Robert Barnaby.'

'You mean the people who inherited his estate, his publishers, that kind of thing?'

'Well, yes, of course, but not so much them. I think Robert Barnaby books would probably carry on selling, whatever anyone dug up about his private life.'

'Who else has a stake in it?' asked Mo. 'Oh, do look out, Mrs Sneggers – there now, at least three drops of gin splashed into my lap!'

'Here, have my napkin. No, Tom's theory is that there are one or two other people who have a vested interest. Hugh Allonby is the main one. If Linda had discovered something which discredited his books . . . although I can't imagine what it could possibly be . . .'

'Maybe your Tom is wrong.'

Fran ignored the 'your'. 'I think he probably is, but at the same time why would anyone agree to give a lecture, drive all the way across the country, appear perfectly normal all evening, then pack up all their things, sneak off and top themselves on the railway line?'

'I wouldn't do it like that,' agreed Mo, helping herself to another square of toast topped with anchovy paste. 'I read somewhere that hypothermia is a painless way to die. Walk up into the hills with a bottle of whiskey, sit in the snow and let nature take its course. Apparently you just fall asleep.'

'Slight problem with the shortage of snow in late April.'

'Well, I wouldn't use the railway line method,' Mo reiterated. 'Anyway, with my luck, there wouldn't be a train coming.'

'Mo, I can never decide if you're an idiot or a genius!'

'Gosh, thanks. Now what have I said?'

'The line where they found Linda is a little branch line, serving a quarry. The reason it took two days to spot her was because hardly any trains use it. So how would she have known when there was a train due?'

'Maybe she didn't.'

'No, no, think it through. It's an absolute maze of little lanes round there. If you're planning to kill yourself, you don't drive around rural Lancashire on the off chance of finding a railway

69

line. Even if you do spot a railway bridge, any fool knows that you can't just set fire to your car, then climb up the embankment on the assumption that there will be a train coming. Some rural lines carry hardly any traffic, and Linda wasn't stupid. If she chose to kill herself there, that presupposes that she knew the line was still used and exactly when she could expect a train.'

'Do you think she was the sort of person who would know about railway trains?'

'Not really. I imagine her knowledge of trains began and ended with Edith Nesbit.'

Mo looked blank.

'*The Railway Children*,' Fran prompted. 'Linda knew lots and lots about children's literature but I don't suppose she'd have known anything much about railways. The sort of trains which ran along that line wouldn't even appear on an ordinary passenger timetable.'

'But whoever took her up there did know about that train,' said Mo. 'So we're looking for a train-spotter with a vested interest in Robert Barnaby. That ought to narrow the field considerably. Are you going to ring Tom and tell him?'

'Not now,' said Fran. She didn't want to ring Tom with Mo listening in. 'I'll have plenty of time to tell him about it on Tuesday.'

'Why? What's happening on Tuesday?'

'We're going to Linda Dexter's funeral.'

'We?'

'Yes, we. Tom Dod and I are attending Linda's funeral on behalf of the Robert Barnaby Society.'

'Good move,' murmured Mo.

Fran leant across to refill their glasses, neatly discouraging Mrs Snegglington's interest in the anchovy toasts with her free hand. 'Hugh Allonby got a letter from Linda's sister, telling him about the arrangements and asking whether anyone from the society would like to be there.'

'So you and Tom . . .'

'I seemed to be the person on the committee who had had the most to do with Linda – not that that amounted to much – and Tom happened to have a business appointment in Lancashire the day before, so he said he would stay overnight and we could go to the funeral together on Tuesday morning.'

'So you've offered him a bed for the night.'

'Of course not. He's going to stay in a hotel and then pick me up on his way.'

'You mean you didn't even offer? Good grief, Fran, there's just no hope for you. A chap gives you the broadest of hints—'

'He didn't give me any hints.'

'It all depends if he's keen enough. It's still not too late, you know. You could telephone him and say you've just thought—'

'It isn't like that. The only reason we're both going to the funeral is that we both happen to be available: I've always got time on my hands these days and he is working somewhere convenient the day before. The point is that we may be able to find out more about Linda – specifically, who is going to inherit her estate and thereby her research. Besides which, someone from the society really ought to go and no one else volunteered.'

'I suppose a trip in his motorcar is a good way

71

of getting to know more about him. If I'd had the benefit of a few long journeys *a deux* with a certain person, I might have avoided the matrimonial shackles myself.'

'Really, Mo, you are terribly naughty about poor Terence.'

'My dear, "poor Terence" as you call him is perfectly happy living on the other side of the world, mashing up rubber, or whatever it is that he is doing at the moment. I can tell from his letters that he doesn't exactly miss me.'

'That's hardly fair,' Fran protested, 'when he invariably suggests in his letters that you ought to go out there and join him.'

'That's just a matter of form. He knows perfectly well that I hate the climate. Believe me, he has far more fun when I'm not there. He wouldn't keep on asking if he thought there was the slightest chance that I'd say "yes".'

'And in the meantime, you have your fun here.'

'There is hardly a shortage of men who like to chaperone a grass widow around the town. As you would find out, if you would only dip your toe into the social pool a little more often.'

'But I am not any sort of widow,' Fran said, suddenly weary. 'I am separated from my husband, which makes me dangerously uncommitted and unspoken for.'

Ten

It was a slow drive up and down the steep inclines which led over the shoulder of Shap Fell, but being with Tom Dod made it shorter. They had talked almost non-stop on the way, only falling silent when they had parked the car in the lane and approached the little church in Ivegill, where a black-clad woman was handing out service books at the door. It was not a large building, but fortunately there did not appear to be many mourners requiring accommodation. The usual neighbours and church ladies had gathered respectfully in the back pews, and Fran and Tom shuffled into a vacant bench just in front of them. Along with the service book had come a neatly engraved, black-edged card bearing the words,

Funeral of Linda Ann Dexter
1893–1929
The Lord giveth and the Lord taketh away

'I didn't think she was as old as that,' Tom whispered.

'Well preserved,' Fran whispered back.

They sat in silence for another couple of minutes, before Tom whispered, 'There aren't many people here.'

'Perhaps they're all following the hearse.'

By the time the funeral party arrived, there were no more than two-dozen people waiting in the church, but nor was the procession which followed the pale oak coffin a large one. There was a dark-haired woman on a man's arm – possibly a sibling and their spouse, Fran decided – followed by two little boys, looking uncomfortable in school uniforms augmented by hastily obtained black ties and armbands. After them came a small miscellany of much older men and women, probably uncles and aunts in their dark suits and coats, funeral veterans every one.

An air of awkwardness hung over the service. There was a particularly ragged rendition of 'The Lord's My Shepherd', with only the church ladies at the rear putting heart and soul into it, and a reading from St John, presumably recommended by the vicar, who did his best, in spite of apparently having known little of Linda or her family. The eulogy confirmed Fran's theory about the mourners, with its mention that Linda's only sister, Christina, should be comforted in her loss. No one displayed any obvious emotion.

After the interment, the church ladies hastened ahead to get the kettles on at the village hall, while the remainder of the small congregation followed them up the hill at a more desultory pace. As they strolled along at the rear of the group, Tom said, 'If we split up when we get inside, we can probably manage to speak to everyone here.'

'Good idea.'

'What did you think of Linda's house?'

They had spotted the property in question – easily

identifiable by the name on the gatepost – just before reaching the church, so there had been no time for discussion until now.

'I'd say that it was a big place for one person on her own,' murmured Tom.

'Perhaps she wasn't always on her own.'

'True.'

Inside the village hall, tables of sandwiches and home-made cake had been laid out, far in excess of anything likely to be consumed. Fran found it easy to mingle and get people to talk to her. A good opener was 'Have you come far?' which eased them gently towards, 'How did you come to know Linda?'

Fifteen minutes into the proceedings, Tom joined her beside the plates of ham sandwiches. 'We're in good company,' he said quietly. 'Half the people here seem to be representing other literary societies. That lot,' he indicated a plump quartet of middle-aged women, with a sideways movement of his eyes, 'are from the Guild of Girls' School Stories.'

Fran nodded. 'I've just been talking to a couple who could bore for England on some children's writer I haven't even heard of.'

'There's also a small contingent from the local bridge club.'

They separated again to complete their task, but as Tom made for a tall, thin man who was currently standing alone in one corner, she found the tables momentarily turned when the woman she had marked down for Linda's sister approached to thank her for coming and asked, 'Have you come far?'

'The next county,' Fran said. 'I live not far from Ulverston, if you know it.'

'Know it? I should think I do. I live in Kendal.'

'Kendal?' echoed Fran. 'I thought you would be local – I mean, that you would live up here, near Linda.'

'None of the family have ever lived up this way, except for Linda.'

'I was so sorry to hear what happened,' Fran said. 'It must have been an awful shock.'

'Oh, it has been. A terrible thing to happen to anyone.'

And yet, she didn't sound exactly devastated, Fran thought. Sad, yes, but not distraught. Not the way she had been when those telegrams had come about Geoffrey and Cecil. It was the same story with everyone, she thought. No one really seemed close to Linda – not even her sister.

'Well,' said Tom as they walked back to his car, 'I must say that was a pretty rum affair. So far as I can make out from my chief informant, Linda's Aunt Lilian, unless Linda has unexpectedly left everything to the cat's home, the sister, Christina, stands to get everything, so she's the one we're going to have to approach about Linda's papers. And by the way, you were right with what you said on the way up here – it's pretty obvious that Linda didn't have a living husband, or a job, but there's some substantial money somewhere in the background.'

Fran didn't reply until they were both inside the car again and Tom had fired up the engine. Then she said, 'Do you think we're terrible people?'

'What do you mean?'

'Going round, systematically quizzing everyone at a funeral. Poking our noses into other people's business.'

'Not at all. People don't mind talking about themselves. In fact, most people quite like it. Linda's Aunt Lilian had a lovely time explaining her entire family tree to me. I know all about Jack, who served with the navy, and young Alec, who's done so well for himself down in London. Anyway, we're acting in the interests of the Robert Barnaby Society.'

Fran wanted to say sod the society. We both just fancy ourselves as Sherlock Holmes, but she didn't. The wind had turned chilly and made her nose run, so she opened her bag for a handkerchief and, as she extracted it, she caught a glimpse of the funeral card, which she had stuffed inside. Maybe we're doing it for her as well, she thought. Because no one else seems to care what really happened. Aloud, she said, 'Very well then. What have we come up with so far?'

'Well, I've been to some funny funerals in my time,' Tom began, 'but that was about the funniest.'

Fran, in whose experience funerals had been events singularly lacking in comedic possibilities, was tempted to ask him for details of these other funny funerals, but decided that it was best to stay on track. 'It reminded me a bit of a great-aunt's funeral I went to once,' she said. 'No one was particularly upset because she was really old. She'd outlived pretty much everyone who was close to her, so the people who came were relatives like me who scarcely knew her, or people who'd come out of a sense of duty – neighbours and people from the church she used to go to. The only person who cried was the house parlour maid.'

'Exactly,' said Tom. 'Linda was only thirty-six, but none of her relatives appeared to be close to her and she didn't seem to have any real friends.'

'The nearest thing to a friend that I came across was a lady who knew her from the bridge club. She said that they occasionally used to meet up in a tea shop in Carlisle, if they were both going in for shopping, but she appeared to know next to nothing about Linda and said that they always talked about general things.'

Tom nodded. 'Very few relatives at all. Just the sister and her family, a handful of aunts and uncles and a few random cousins. The people from the various literary societies were just the same as us – they knew Linda from meetings, nothing more.'

'My guess is that she and her sister didn't get on,' said Fran. 'Her sister made the arrangements for the funeral, but only because there isn't anyone else. I'd say there's no love lost between them. She wasn't even upset.'

'So the picture we're getting is of a woman who lived alone and had very few friends. Maybe she did throw herself under a train.'

'Excuse me, I live alone. That isn't a motive for suicide.'

'But you've got at least *one* friend,' Tom said, mischievously emphasizing the 'one'. 'You told me about her on the telephone.'

Fran gave him a sidelong look, but he was concentrating on the road, so she continued, 'I'm not convinced that Linda was lonely. You know how some lonely people are obviously needy. They latch on – especially to other people in clubs and societies. Linda wasn't like that. She was comfortable with herself. Sort of . . . self-sufficient.'

Tom digested this for a moment in silence. 'We have to remember that to a great many people, suicide is still a sin. If they all believe that Linda took her own life, there might be a degree of embarrassment there. Guilt, too, thinking that she had been so unhappy and nobody even knew.'

'I'm more and more convinced that someone killed her,' Fran said. 'Either they pushed her in front of a train, or else she was already dead when she was dumped on the line.'

'Someone who was trying to make it look like suicide,' Tom mused. 'A train must make an awful mess of somebody. It mightn't be possible to tell if they'd been hit on the head first or exactly how long they'd been dead.'

'If someone did kill Linda, it might not be your million-to-one Barnaby revelation theory. There could be other motives.'

'Fair enough,' said Tom. 'What else have we got?'

'Money, for starters. That house must be worth quite a bit if it belonged to her. Linda always dressed well and she ran a nice motorcar. I've heard her talking about taking holidays on the Continent. And another thing: where did her money come from? Her sister looked . . .' she hesitated, not wishing to appear snobbish, '. . . she looked quite . . . ordinary. No holidays on the Continent for her, I'll bet. Her shoes looked quite worn.'

'Gosh, you are observant,' said Tom, and Fran tried not to feel childishly pleased. 'Maybe Linda married into money?' he continued. 'Or . . . oh, I don't know – maybe she was a blackmailer. You know, keeping quiet about the affair between the High Priest and the Head Acolyte.'

'Hugh Allonby and Sarah Ingoldsby?'

'Yes. Didn't you know?'

'No. But I should have realized. He's forever pawing her. And she's always looking doe-eyed at him. Yeuch.' Fran shuddered before asking, 'How did you find out? Or am I the only person in the society who hadn't guessed?'

'Oh, I think they manage to keep it pretty much a secret, but I'd overheard a couple of things which made me wonder, and then I happened to see him going into her room at last year's conference, which pretty much confirmed it. In fact . . .' he hesitated, then decided to plough on, '. . . I had a bit of a laugh with John James over it this year. You know, it's his first year sorting out the accommodation at the Furnival Towers and he told me that old Allonby called him up especially to tell him that he and Mrs Ingoldsby always had adjacent rooms at the conference for "organizational purposes". I've heard it called a few things, but never that before.'

Fran laughed before she could stop herself. It was hard to imagine either of that creepy pair having an affair with anyone, but maybe that was what made them so well suited to one another. 'Well, well,' she said. 'Who would have imagined such goings-on at the Robert Barnaby Society? I believe there is both a Mrs Allonby and a Mr Ingoldsby. I suppose needing to be at society meetings is an ideal cover for their affair. No wonder Little Miss Fuss Face got so upset when she thought that she would have to stand down from the committee this year and managed to wangle a co-option on account of her connection with the Vester House Museum. I wonder how many extra-curricular committee meetings take place at various secluded little venues which the rest of us know nothing about. I don't suppose either of them would be best pleased to have their spouses let in on the secret, but then again, I don't think Hugh Allonby's book sales would run to paying off a blackmailer either.'

'It certainly wouldn't run to the price of a Talbot 105,' said Tom. 'But Linda's money came from somewhere and the origin of it might be relevant, because if someone is being fleeced in some way, they'd want to put a stop to it.'

'So.' Fran counted the theories off on her fingers. 'There's possible blackmail, there's someone hoping to inherit, there's the dark secret she may have been on the point of revealing about Robert Barnaby, there's the sinister man in the background . . .'

'What sinister man?'

'She was an attractive woman. You can't ever rule out the possibility of there being a sinister man. Don't you read detective stories?'

'Very well then. We won't rule out the sinister

81

man – whoever he might be. And finally, there's suicide.'

'She didn't kill herself,' said Fran. 'I just know she didn't.'

'Nothing at all was said about her husband,' Tom mused.

'People don't always want to talk about their husbands.'

'Of course not,' he said quickly. 'Please don't think . . .' He trailed into awkward silence, adding, when she gave him no help, 'I know that it can be incredibly difficult. People lost in the war and so on.'

Fran took a deep breath. 'I have to go to the unveiling of a war memorial on Sunday. My mother wants me to go along because both my brothers' names will be on it. My husband did serve in the war but he was a non-combatant. There was something wrong with his hearing, so he got a desk job, I believe. I didn't know him then. We were married in 1922, but a few years later he met someone else that he liked better than me and took himself off to live with her instead.'

'You still wear his ring.'

'I am still, technically, his wife.'

'Beastly business, these war memorials,' he said quietly. 'The war has been over for ten years and some districts are still squabbling about how to remember, as if any of us is ever going to forget. I'm sorry about your brothers. I lost an older brother too. His name was William but we always called him Will.'

They travelled the next mile or two in silence.

It was a comfortable silence, Fran thought, into which the difficult topics of lost lives and a failed marriage could fade without any need of further explanation. At least now he knew how things stood.

In spite of the darkening skies, her heart felt light. The front seat of his Hudson brought them into such close physical proximity that when he changed gear the sleeve of his overcoat brushed lightly against the dark fabric of her jacket. She did not want the journey to end, but they had almost reached the turning for her cottage.

'It's the next left,' she said. 'Thank you so much for driving me. I hope you will come in and have some tea.'

'I wish I could, but I'm running late as it is after getting stuck behind that slow lorry, and I promised to be home by six without fail. My parents have organized some blasted dinner at their place this evening and I really have to be there.' He sounded genuinely disappointed. 'In the meantime, what's our plan of action?'

'This is it.' She managed to keep the disappointment out of her voice as she indicated the cottage and he obediently slowed the car to a standstill at her gate. 'One of us obviously has to contact the sister and tactfully ask about Linda's research papers and who is going to get them. I should probably do it as I live nearest.'

'Better if you do it,' Tom agreed. 'As you don't live very far, you might be able to wangle an invitation to call on her and explain about the material on Robert Barnaby. Then you could get her talking, see if you can find out a bit more about Linda herself.'

'And in the meantime, what angle will you be following, Special Agent Dod?'

'I thought I might book myself a night at the Furnival Towers. I could let on that I was working in the area. I want to test out how easy it would be to kidnap someone from the hotel.'

'Do you think that's wise? I mean, aren't there laws about that sort of thing?'

Tom laughed. 'You know perfectly well what I mean. Checking how you would get in and out of the building at night without being spotted and all that kind of thing.'

The wild idea ran through Fran's mind that he might be waiting for her to suggest that she should spend the night there too. There was an expectant pause while they watched the wind tearing at the bushes outside. The weather had worsened considerably in the past half hour and it buffeted the car in unsteadying gusts. An old cigarette packet catapulted unexpectedly from beneath the hedge and skidded across the road at high speed.

'I'll need both hands on the wheel at this rate,' he said. 'It's a pig of a road in weather like this.'

'Thank you so much for driving me up there,' she said again. The moment had passed. It was somehow too late now to say anything about staying the night at the Furnival Towers.

As he got out and came around to open the car door for her, she wondered whether a friendly parting peck on the cheek would be appropriate. She was still considering the point as he opened the door, at which point the wind tried to snatch his folded map from the dashboard, leading to an undignified scramble as they both tried to grab it. 'Hurry up.' He laughed. 'Everything's blowing away.'

There was nothing for it but to exit the car as fast as she could and shut the door. She knew that she must look like a scarecrow with one hand restraining her hat and her hair blowing all over her face. She staggered across to the gate and then had to wrestle her hat and handbag under control while she attempted to unlatch it. Once that had been accomplished, she turned back just in time to see him raise his arm in a lazy salute of departure. She waved in return, standing in the gateway and watching as his car rounded the bend.

To her considerable surprise, no sooner had Tom's car gone out of sight than a dark blue Austin 7 appeared from the other direction and glided to a halt. She was even more astonished when the driver's door opened and Stephen-with-a-ph-Latchford got out and walked towards her.

'What jolly good luck,' he said. 'I thought I'd missed you. I was passing by, so I decided to call in and show you this fascinating piece I've just come across about dear old Barnaby.'

Fran gathered her wits, dragging down her windblown skirt with as much dignity as she could muster and forcing her mouth into a thin smile. 'I've just got back from a funeral.' It was of course a socially acceptable time to make a call, but she hoped that he would take the hint and realize that it wasn't a convenient moment. Instead, he stood his ground and adopted a solicitous smile, saying, 'Oh dear. Is it anyone I'm liable to know?'

'It was Linda Dexter's. I attended on behalf of the society.'

'Oh dear. I hope it wasn't too sad for you. I'm very curious about Mrs Dexter; you must tell me all about it.'

To Fran's irritation, he had by now sidestepped her at the gate and was standing on the path, holding it open, on the clear expectation of being admitted to the house. It would be impossible to get rid of him without being downright rude. She had some difficulty locating the front door key within her handbag, the wind was shrieking through the nearby trees, making them moan like old men in torment, and here was Stephen Latchford, following her up to the front door, with the memory of his strange persistence about the lift on the last day of the conference surfacing to add to her general sense of discomfiture.

Once she had the front door open, he followed her into the cramped little hall, exclaiming at the sight of the living room. 'What a super room.' He walked in uninvited and held up one of the tapestry sofa cushions. 'Did you sew this yourself? No? It's very well chosen. Shall I light the fire for you?'

She wanted to tell him not to touch anything, but that seemed ridiculous. The fire was ready-laid and putting a match to it the obvious thing to do, while at the same time his offer represented an inappropriate degree of familiarity in the house of someone he hardly knew. To her astonishment, after lighting the sitting-room fire, he then followed her into the kitchen while she made a pot of tea. She didn't want to offer him a cup but she was gasping for one herself, and anyway, it would appear churlish not to offer him something.

When they were back in the sitting room, he asked her again about Linda's funeral and she told him that it had been a simple service. 'She didn't have a big family, so there weren't exactly regiments of people there.'

'Very sad for her family,' he said. 'Inconsiderate of her, though. Topping herself at the conference like that.'

'Is that what you think? That she killed herself?'

'Well, it's pretty obvious, isn't it? That's what everyone thinks. The police are certainly taking that line. They as good as said so when they came to see me last week.'

'Why did the police want to see you?'

'I was in the room directly across the corridor from her the night she decided to pop out and throw herself under a train, so naturally they wanted to know if I'd seen or heard anything that night, but of course I hadn't. I went to sleep at about midnight and didn't stir again until half past seven. I understand they called on the person who'd been in the room next door to her too, but apparently no one saw or heard anything. Well, it's not as if members of the society spend their nights creeping around the hotel corridors, is it? Not unless they're Mr Allonby and Mrs Ingoldsby.' He gave her a knowing smirk, which made her squirm inwardly.

Was she the only person who hadn't known?

Aloud, she prompted, 'You said you had something to show me.'

'Of course, of course.' He produced a folded sheet of paper from his inside pocket, opening it out before he handed it across. It was an article neatly cut from what appeared to be a local history magazine, which mentioned that Robert Barnaby's signature had been found in a guest-book which belonged to a well-known local family who had a house a few miles away, near Millom.

'Fascinating, isn't it?' he said. 'A Barnaby connection, right on your doorstep. I shall have to do a bit more digging into this one.'

Fran attempted to be interested, but what on earth was there to say? Robert Barnaby had once spent a weekend in the Lake District. Well, who hadn't?

When he eventually said that he would have to be going, she made no attempt to discourage him. Even so, he made a prolonged farewell, thanking her for the tea again and saying what a nice place she had. 'Off the beaten track, but not too difficult for me to find.'

She shut the door behind him with a sigh of relief, not bothering to wait on the step until his car had pulled away.

Eleven

Fran caught the early bus on Sunday morning, in order to be in plenty of time for the grand unveiling of the Cleppington War Memorial, which was scheduled to take place at eleven. The original idea had been to coincide the ceremony with the tenth anniversary of Armistice Day, but then the thing had not been ready on time, and having waited almost a decade for their memorial, the villagers had not been minded to hold a service of commemoration before the cross was finished and the names of the lost inscribed upon it. Not that Cleppington was by any means the last place to get its war memorial organized. Nearby, the community of Harlingdale were still getting their fund together, while in Kinthwaite Bridge there was an ongoing dispute between those who wanted a statue of a soldier with bowed head and those who favoured a cenotaph-like structure.

The memorial at Cleppington had become something of an obsession for her mother. In the years immediately after the war, she had been among the first to agitate for it, and then one of the first to write a cheque when subscriptions were initially sought. During the intervening years, she had seemed to Fran to be constantly preoccupied with the efforts of the War Memorial Committee and forever regaling her daughter with tales of disputes regarding the inclusion of various names – 'the point is that their boy never actually lived here in the parish at all' – to say nothing of arguments over the form that the memorial should take. 'A public hall may well be an asset to the village, but as Mr Laker said, "I don't like the notion of my boy's name being an excuse for folk to get rowdy playing darts and dominoes, or worse still, cards."'

Fran, though sorely tempted, had never told her mother that she thought fun and laughter and people playing cards and games were far more evocative of her brothers than a cold stone cross towering above a corner of the churchyard.

Dora, the house parlour maid, answered the door to her – she had never used her latch key since leaving home to be married.

'Ah.' Her mother held out both hands and sighed as her daughter entered the drawing room. 'I did so hope that you might have changed your mind and prevailed upon Michael to come and stand alongside you at the ceremony.'

'Mummy, I told you that was not going to happen.' Fran attempted to keep the irritation out of her voice.

'People will notice.'

Privately, Fran thought that people had probably noticed already that her husband had not accompanied her on any of her visits to her mother for almost a year now, but remembering the sensitivities of the day, she resolved to err on the side of kindness and said, 'I'm sure no one will think it in the least strange. After all, Michael never knew Geoffrey or Cecil.'

'That's true.' Her mother sighed again. 'Oh dear, oh dear. So many lives ruined.'

Fran had the strongest suspicion that her mother was not just referring to those lost in the war, and this was confirmed a moment later when her mother added, as if to herself, 'Perhaps if you had given him children.'

Fran reddened and was about to reply when her Aunt Violet and Uncle Henry were shown in and they all became caught up in greetings and polite remarks about the sadness of the day. They were followed by Uncle George and Aunt Lizzie with news of Cousin Edwina's new baby. Fran found herself blushing for no reason. It isn't that I mind at all, she told herself, it's just that I mind that they think I mind. She could not meet her mother's eye and, as she fiddled with her gloves, it occurred to her that she was dressed in the same slate-grey two-piece and black hat that she had worn for Linda Dexter's funeral. At least it had been a proper funeral, with Linda laid to rest in home soil. The men and boys who had not come home had been interred elsewhere or even completely lost in the Flanders mud.

The little party walked the short distance to church and took their places at the front of the small crowd which had gathered in the church-yard. Though referred to as an unveiling, the memorial cross already stood bare to the grey sky, the names of almost thirty souls inscribed upon it. There was a hint of drizzle and a strange, bitter taste in the air. The taste of collective loss, Fran thought. As the preliminaries began, she tried to picture her brothers' faces, but instead

91

found herself noticing the piece of cotton which had come adrift from Reverend Lewis's surplice and was dangling limply against his dark clerical gown. The breeze stirred against the thread and then unexpectedly blew it against the nose of Harry Postlethwaite, the plump, red-faced village newsagent who had never seen military service but was standing stiffly, as if to attention. Evidently not wishing to spoil the dignity of his pose, Mr Postlethwaite, unaware that he was being observed, attempted to remove the offending strand of cotton by twitching his nose. Fran experienced an abrupt and irreverent desire to laugh.

It's no good, she thought. You can't stay sad forever. And yet, you sort of have to. The sacrifice made by her brothers had placed obligations upon her. She had been transformed from the youngest of three into an only child, with a particular duty to keep her widowed mother happy. That meant keeping up the pretence that she was still married – even when no one was fooled – and trying to protect her mother from the perceived scandal of a divorce. The scandal of an affair would be even worse, of course. If Geoffrey and Cec had been alive, marrying nice girls and producing grand-children, she might have somehow managed to vanish behind the distractions they provided, but as it was, she would always be under the spot-light, centre stage.

When the time came to enter the church, she slipped her arm through her mother's and they walked at a measured pace immediately behind Colonel and Mrs Dillington-Smyth, whose heir had been lost at Passchendaele. The relatives of the lost were afforded precedence as the crowd processed into the church, their order of entry dictated by an unspoken acknowledgement of social position, so that the Dillington-Smyths took the lead, with the other middle-class families following on and Mr and Mrs Needham, who lived in one of the tied cottages at Ranelagh Farm and had lost all three of their boys, bringing up the rear. This too, Fran thought, did not reflect the reality of her brothers' loss. She recalled a letter from Cec, in which he had spoken of his fellow Tommies. *We are all like brothers here . . . A lot of things will change when the war is over.* But they had not changed, she thought sadly. Or at least, not in the right way.

Twelve

Mo could hardly wait to get in the door before announcing, 'You'll never guess! I've been given a pair of Wimbledon tickets. Let's go down and stay with my friends the Radleys for a couple of days. We can shop or visit galleries on the second day.'

'I'd love to,' Fran said. 'It's simply ages since I've been down to London.'

Mo flopped onto the sofa, still looking pleased with herself. 'I've had such a splendid week. First our Ladies A team won their match, and now I've got a pair of Wimbledon tickets. It should be second-round matches, if play is running to schedule.'

'It sounds wonderful. What would you like to drink?'

'Better make it a coffee. Oh, on second thoughts, I'll have a small G and T. Any progress on your enquiries, Sherlock?'

'Nothing much since I brought you up to date after the funeral. I gave it a couple of days, then wrote a little note to the sister. I found their address in the postal directory; they don't appear to be on the telephone.'

'So what did you say to her?'

'I offered my condolences, obviously, then said that I was from the Robert Barnaby Society and that I would appreciate her contacting me because Linda and I had shared some particular interests.'

'And how about that Stephen-with-a-ph fellow? Heard anything else from him?'

'No, thank goodness. Don't you think it was a bit suspicious, the way he was all but waiting on the doorstep after the funeral? Maybe he knew where I'd been and came on purpose. Anyway, I certainly think he should be on the list of suspects.'

'But where's the motive? He may have chosen his time because he was just being plain nosy.'

'I suppose so.'

'And how's Watson doing?'

'Watson?'

'Well, if you're Sherlock – though it's more like Shylock – look at the size of this measure.' Mo held up her glass in feigned disgust.

'You said a small one. Anyway, I thought you were driving.'

'I did. I am. Go on – has he found anything out yet?'

'Not yet, but he's going to stay at the Furnival Towers on Friday night. There's a Barnaby Society executive committee meeting in Stafford this Saturday, and I've arranged to take an earlier train so that we can meet up beforehand and compare notes. I'm hoping that Linda's sister will have got back to me by then.'

There had been some difficulty with her mother regarding the Barnaby Society meeting. After the War Memorial had been officially consecrated and they had returned to her mother's house to consume roast beef and

Yorkshire pudding, her mother had raised the question of the church bazaar on the following Saturday, which she had assumed that Fran would attend with her, as she always did.

'Oh, I'm sorry, Mummy, but I can't. I have to go to a committee meeting.'

'A committee meeting? What sort of organization holds its committee meetings on a Saturday afternoon?'

'A society which has committee members drawn from all over the country, some of whom have to work on weekdays.'

'You can send your apologies.'

'Oh, no, Mummy I really can't.' Fran forked in a mouthful of spring cabbage to play for time. Why couldn't she? Inspiration. 'It's the first full meeting since I was elected. It would be terribly bad form to cry off at less than a week's notice.' She swallowed the cabbage, barely chewed and hurried on. 'I know the bazaar is in a terribly good cause, but I really do have to go to the Barnaby Society meeting.' And not just because Tom Dod will be there – the thing about being newly elected is true.

The meeting was at a small hotel near the railway station. It was not difficult to find and she recognized Tom's Hudson parked on the forecourt. He was waiting for her in the hotel's lounge-cum-reception and stood up when he saw her approach, his features blossoming into a broad smile of welcome.

'Let me get you a cup of coffee. Or would you rather have a pot of tea?'

'Tea would be lovely, thank you.'

After he had summoned the waiter and placed their order, she launched on to the business in hand right away, still basking in the warmth of that smile. 'I've had no joy with Linda's sister, I'm afraid. I've tried writing to her and, when I was in Kendal, I even called at the house but there was no one at home. I popped my card through the letterbox, with another little note scribbled on the back, but there's been no response. I don't want to call again in case I put her off by being too pushy.'

'Oh, well, maybe we need to give it time. I've done quite well, I think. I got a lot from Furnival Towers. First of all, there's very little to prevent anyone from being kidnapped.'

'Good heavens! Don't they lock the front door at night?'

'They do. But as security goes, that's about it.'

'And I suppose you can open the front door from the inside? And there isn't anyone on the Reception desk at night?'

'No, there isn't. But I don't think that's how Linda left the building . . .'

'Go on,' Fran prompted as he left the phrase hanging in the air.

'First of all, I had quite a long chat with Marcus Dryden. All friendly, conciliatory stuff. I think he pretty much guessed that I was on a fishing expedition but he didn't seem to mind. He isn't too pleased about any of this, as you can imagine. He's very much down the suicide track, and let's face it, he would be, because it wouldn't do his business much good if women are afraid to stay there because someone was abducted from one of his hotel rooms.'

'Quite,' said Fran. 'Though I suppose we can't rule out the possibility that Linda left under her own steam to meet someone and was murdered at the rendezvous.'

'Yes, I wondered about that. But why would she take all her clothes if she was just slipping out to meet someone? Also, you would expect her to leave by the front door and that was still locked next morning, according to Dryden.'

'Looking at it another way,' said Fran, 'why would the kidnapper bother to take all her clothes either?'

'I think I can see why. Supposing someone wanted to prevent Linda from giving her speech? If they left the speech behind in her room, it would fall into someone else's hands. If they only took Linda and the speech, someone might realize that it had gone and that would actually draw attention to it. But if they took everything . . .'

'That's very clever of you. And would explain why the car and everything in it was burnt!'

Tom nodded. 'But there won't just be one copy of her speech – there's sure to be another draft at the very least, to say nothing of whatever notes she was working from.'

'It looks as if your million-to-one shot just narrowed down to ten thousand to one.' She noticed that he couldn't help but look pleased with himself.

'Of course, there may be other reasons for removing all her luggage.'

'You said there was another way of getting out instead of the front door,' Fran prompted.

'I found out from Dryden that Linda was in

room seven. Later on that evening, I had a mooch around and found number seven. It was very easy to find because it's along that ground-floor corridor where I was staying myself. Room seven is right at the end, next to the fire door, which is one of those push-bar types that you get in cinemas. I tried it, on the off-chance that it set off an alarm somewhere. If it did, I was going to say that I was just nipping out for a cigarette.'

'You don't smoke, do you?'

'No, but I didn't think anyone would actually check my pockets for gaspers and a lighter in order to dispute the point.'

'And did an alarm go off?'

'No. I left the door open for ages but no one came to investigate. In fact, I wedged it open a crack with a bit of brick that I found just outside the door and left it like that while I went outside to have a scout around. The fire door comes out on the side of the building where there are no windows directly overlooking it, and from the fire door it's barely a couple of yards to a little path which runs straight down to the car park. There is a slight risk that someone might see you as you go down the path, but only if they happened to be looking out of their bedroom window at the right moment; and once down on the car park, you can't be seen from the hotel windows at all. When I got back to the fire door it was still wedged open, just the way I'd left it.'

'So you think someone forced Linda to pack up all her stuff and exit via the fire escape?' said Fran.

'You sound doubtful.'

99

'Why didn't she shout for help?'

'I don't know. Maybe she couldn't. Maybe she was gagged. Maybe she was tied up and it was the kidnapper who cleared all her stuff into the case. It wouldn't have taken long. It was only a weekend trip and I don't suppose he was worried about creasing anything. She was quite small and slight. I reckon I could easily have carried her down to the car, providing she wasn't putting up much resistance.'

'Maybe she agreed to do it because she didn't realize how much danger she was in.'

Now it was Tom's turn to look doubtful. 'Why on earth would she agree?'

'Perhaps she thought it was a sort of joke,' Fran said doubtfully. 'Some sort of Gareth Lowe-type escapade.'

'In the middle of the night?'

'I admit that it's far-fetched, but you never know with Gareth Lowe. He's completely barking.'

'Anyway, there's something else about taking all the luggage,' Tom said.

'Go on.'

'According to Dryden, the police told him that it's pretty much scuppered their chances of proving one way or the other whether there was anyone else in the room with Linda. You see, by the time Linda was missed, the girl who cleans the room had already changed the bedding and wiped everything clean. A hotel room is a nightmare from the point of view of fingerprints at the best of times, because dozens of different people are coming in and out, but if Linda's things had still been there, the chambermaid

100

wouldn't have assumed that the guest had checked out and probably wouldn't have cleaned the room so thoroughly.'

'All of which makes a hotel room a far better place to abduct Linda from than simply murdering her in her own house, where you might leave traces that were harder to explain,' mused Fran. 'And I suppose setting fire to her car would destroy any fingerprints you'd left inside it.'

'One other thing Marcus Dryden said—'

But Fran was not destined to hear what else Mr Dryden had said just then.

'Hello, you two. You're early.' Gareth Lowe – mercifully clad in an ordinary tweed jacket over flannels – had entered the room without either of them noticing him. 'Awful weather again, isn't it? You wouldn't think it was May. Doesn't bode well for the summer, what?'

Having just described him as barking, Fran was only too glad to let Tom make the conversational running with Mr Lowe. Thank goodness he hadn't arrived a moment earlier! She would really have to be much more careful what she said about people in public. It was partly Tom's fault, she thought. He made her feel so at ease that she forgot her manners and said things which were really not nice at all.

Soon after Gareth came Jean Robertson, and after her John James. Hugh Allonby and Sarah Ingoldsby arrived together, closely followed by Ruth Winterton, the formidable retired headmistress of a girls' school, and finally came Vivian Blakemore, a fussy, middle-aged bachelor who always wore a flower in his buttonhole and was half a minute the right side of arriving late.

Hugh Allonby led them into a small, private room which had been reserved for the occasion. It had faded wallpaper and even more faded hunting prints on the walls. The windows were rendered opaque by dusty net curtains and most of the floor space was occupied by a square table surrounded by about a dozen chairs. They seated themselves around three sides of the table: Hugh Allonby took the central seat, furthest away from the door, flanked by Jean Robertson, who acted as secretary, and Vivian Blakemore, who was the society's treasurer. Ruth Winterton, Sarah Ingoldsby and Gareth Lowe chose seats with their backs to the windows, while the three newcomers to the committee, Tom, John James and Fran sat facing them. Apologies had been received from Richard Finney, the journal secretary.

Fran wondered if Hugh Allonby would begin with a word about Linda Dexter's death, but once everyone had finished shuffling papers and filling water glasses, he went straight into the formal agenda: minutes of the previous meeting, matters arising, correspondence received and so on. There were no contentious issues, but even so, Fran could gauge the extent of Hugh's influence on proceedings by the way Ruth Winterton and Gareth Lowe deferred to him on every question, while Vivian Blakemore was obviously content to bumble along in whichever direction Hugh led, even if he was not entirely certain of the ultimate destination. With Sarah Ingoldsby's loyalty factored in, she thought, Hugh could always be confident of the committee's support. Even if she and Tom were to form an alliance with those lesser-known quantities, Jean Robertson and John James, they could only achieve a tie, at which point Hugh had his chairman's casting vote. It was not that she had joined the committee to wreak change or cause dissention – far from it – but she found it vaguely dispiriting to think that the committee's sole purpose was to rubber stamp Hugh Allonby's decisions.

The business was conducted at a stately pace, so it took almost two hours to reach Item 6: The Annual Conference 1929. Hugh portentously cleared his throat. 'Now, Miss Robertson, I suggest that there is no need to minute what I'm about to say next. I think we are all aware – even Miss Winterton, who unfortunately could not be with us this year – of the unfortunate event which some-what marred this year's conference. Fortunately Mrs Dexter's body was not discovered until after everyone had gone home, so the conference was not spoiled for most of those who attended.'

It had become very close in the stuffy little room. Noticing Fran reach for her almost empty glass, John James pulled the jug towards him, lifted it and poured her some water. 'Thank you,' she whispered.

'The police have of course been making enquiries and I think I can safely say that they will conclude that Mrs Dexter committed suicide. She was, as I think some of you are possibly aware, a rather unbalanced woman, given to some very peculiar ideas. This is clearly not the sort of person, still less the sort of episode, with which the society would want to be associated. I think

103

I have done quite well in keeping the press at bay.' He paused long enough for Vivian Blakemore to murmur something approving and Gareth Lowe to add a gruff: 'Hear, Hear.'

'I have had a word with Mr Finney regarding our journal, and let him know that no mention of this unpleasantness should appear—'

'Excuse me, Mr Chairman, but when a member dies, there is normally a brief obituary—' Jean Robertson began.

'Not in this case, I think.' Hugh cut straight across her. 'I've also had a word with Marcus Dryden. It has all been most upsetting for the Dryden family, and of course it is not at all good for their business. I am sure none of us would wish anything that happened at a Barnaby Society event to have a detrimental effect on the Dryden family and Furnival Towers. Now Mr Dryden mentioned some time ago that the displays in the Barnaby Room are getting a little tired and the magic chair itself needs re-gilding. Under the circumstances, I think it would be appropriate for the society to make a grant out of its funds.'

'Oh, what a good idea, Mr Allonby,' gushed Sarah Ingoldsby, as if this was the very first she had heard about it, which Fran knew instinctively it was not.

'Hold on,' said Tom. 'I think we need to tread very carefully on this. Surely we shouldn't be offering money from the society's reserves to a private commercial undertaking?'

'You seem to forget Mr Dod,' boomed Ruth Winterton, who addressed any meeting as if it were a two-hundred-strong school assembly, 'that there is a unique connection between Robert Barnaby and Furnival Towers.'

'Which doesn't alter the fact that Furnival Towers is a commercially run hotel.' Tom spoke calmly and politely, but Ruth Winterton looked as outraged as if he had blasphemed in church.

'The Dryden family have been very good to the Robert Barnaby Society over the years,' Hugh said. 'We have derived considerable benefit from being able to hold many of our meetings there.'

'We also pay normal commercial rates to do so,' Tom said. 'The Barnaby connection is their big selling point; lots of people go and stay there because of it. I'm not sure that society money should be—'

Tom got no further. 'I suggest we put the matter to the vote,' said Hugh. 'Do I have a proposer that we financially support some restorative work to the Barnaby displays and the magic chair? Thank you, Mrs Ingoldsby. Mr Lowe, will you second? All in favour of making a grant to the Furnival Towers? That's everyone except Mr Dod and Mrs Black. Thank you, everyone.' He looked at his watch. 'I think now might be a good time to break for tea and sandwiches.'

At the mention of food, Gareth Lowe immediately bounced out of his chair and began to gather his papers together. Fran glanced sideways at Tom. His face appeared to be slightly flushed, but it might have been the warmth of the room.

Two separate tables had been set aside in an otherwise deserted dining room for them to eat their plates of ham and tomato sandwiches. Tom,

Fran, Jean Robertson and John James took one table while the other five made up the second.

'I heard that you went to represent the society at Mrs Dexter's funeral.' Jean Robertson addressed Fran. 'That was very thoughtful of you.'

'Mr Dod came as well. I'm glad we went, particularly as some people appear to be intent on expunging her from the society's history as swiftly as possible.'

Miss Robertson lowered her voice and glanced sideways at the occupants of the other table. 'I'm not entirely happy about there being no obituary,' she said. 'Whatever the circumstances, Mrs Dexter loved Robert Barnaby's books and she was a loyal member from the very outset, but of course Mr Allonby has the society's interests at heart and I daresay he is looking at it solely from that perspective. At the end of the day, we sometimes have to put our personal feelings aside and decide the best way for the society. That's what the membership have elected us to do.'

'But surely there's no harm in putting some sort of announcement in the journal,' said Fran. 'Just to say that we regret her passing. Linda Dexter was quite well known among the active members and lots of them will get to hear about this, even if they weren't actually at the conference. Complete silence just seems strange and . . . and disrespectful.'

'I reluctantly have to agree with Allonby,' John James interposed. 'Equally, there must be lots of members who have never met Mrs Dexter and aren't aware of what happened. Why upset them? This isn't the sort of thing they joined the society to read about. I probably see it a bit differently to you because I never met her myself, so I don't have to put my personal feelings aside.'

'What I would like to know,' Tom said, 'is what on earth Allonby means about the poor woman being unbalanced and having funny ideas? She always seemed to be perfectly normal to me.'

'I suspect that Mr Allonby is exaggerating a wee bit,' said Jean. 'He's among the greatest living experts on Robert Barnaby and I think that sometimes makes him a bit inclined to ridicule anyone else's interpretation of things if it differs from his own.'

'What ideas did Linda Dexter have that differed from his?' prompted Fran.

'I've really no idea,' said Jean Robertson. 'Though the night before she . . . Well, that last evening, on her way to bed, she remarked that she would be setting some long-held assumptions on their heads. I remember the phrase because it made me think of acrobats, for some reason.'

There was a brief silence.

'How are you finding the membership secretary's job?' Tom asked John James.

'Oh, it's not really onerous. I've been doing it for over six months now and I've managed to fit it in with my work, though I never seem to get to any society meetings – you know how it is – with clashing dates. Unfortunately I may not be able to do the job for much longer. There's a chance that I'm going to be posted abroad and, if that happens, I'm afraid the society will have to find someone else.'

'Oh dear.' Miss Robertson made little noises

107

of consternation. 'Still, I suppose we mustn't begrudge you an opportunity. Where might you be going?'

'It's all very uncertain. No point saying anything at this stage.'

Since Mr James evidently did not want to discuss the matter, Jean Robertson took the hint and, turning to Fran, asked whether she planned to attend the society's summer picnic.

'I expect so,' said Fran. 'Anyway, isn't it part of the committee's job to organize it?'

Hugh Allonby did not allow them to linger too long over lunch. The slight awkwardness over the grant of money to Furnival Towers seemed to have been forgotten and the resumed meeting proceeded smoothly until they came to Item 8: Membership Secretary's Report. After John James had given them the statistics, which demonstrated another small increase in membership numbers, he added, 'I think I ought to mention formally that I may have to step down. It won't be for another couple of months at least, but as I was telling some of you at lunchtime, it's possible that I will be posted abroad in the near future. I thought I'd better give as much notice as possible, so that you have a chance to line someone else up for the job.'

'Oh dear,' said Ruth Winterton. 'That would be a let-down. You're so efficient and it's *so* difficult to get people to do anything these days.'

John James attempted to make light of it. 'It wasn't hard to fill the job last time. I saw the notice in the newsletter and volunteered straight away.'

'But you're the exception that proves the rule,' Gareth Lowe said. 'We usually have to get people in an armlock, or at the very least threaten to set the Black Shadow on them.'

'You don't suppose that Jennifer Rumsey would agree to do it again now that she's had a bit of a break?' asked Fran, and sensed immediately that she had said the wrong thing.

'Definitely not,' said Hugh Allonby. 'Absolutely not a chance.'

'I think Mr James has the right idea,' Ruth Winterton said briskly. 'As soon as we know one way or the other, we should have Mr Finney put an appeal in the journal. Someone is sure to come forward.'

'Let's move on to Any Other Business,' said Hugh.

This final section of proceedings dragged on interminably. Vivian Blakemore had seen a rare Barnaby first edition advertised for sale and wished to draw the matter to the committee's attention, though it was unclear to what purpose. Gareth Lowe had come up with a hare-brained publicity stunt which he had to be talked out of. The suggestion of publicity initiatives sent Ruth Winterton off on a long peroration about whether anything could be done to publicize the society at events such as the Malvern Festival.

By the time they finally filed into the entrance lobby, several people were glancing at their watches and worrying about trains. Tom Dod gave Fran and Jean Robertson a lift to the station so as to avoid the worst of the rain, and as she was getting out of the car, Fran remembered that

Tom had never finished telling her what it was that Marcus Dryden had said to him the night before. I can't say anything in front of Miss Robertson, she thought. I'll have to telephone and ask him later.

The railway journey allowed her plenty of time to contemplate not only the meeting but also whether they had really discovered anything more about what had happened to Linda Dexter. Were the police convinced that the death had been suicide? That's what everyone seemed to be saying, but surely the police would be thinking of all the same things that she and Tom were: in fact, they probably had a lot more to go on. Of course, they wouldn't have told Hugh Allonby, or Marcus Dryden, or Stephen-with-a-ph-Latchford what they were really thinking any more than Sergeant Godfrey, who had given nothing away when she had asked him about Linda's death.

As soon as she opened the cottage door, she saw that there was a letter on the mat which must have come by second post. She turned it over and, not recognizing the handwriting, tore it open before she had even taken off her jacket. It was from Christina Harper, Linda Dexter's sister, apologizing for the delay in responding to her own notes and saying that she was generally at home most afternoons, if Fran would like to confirm a time and date when she would be in Kendal again.

Twenty minutes later, Fran was asking the operator for Tom's number. She was feeling very pleased with herself, having already penned a reply to Mrs Harper, nominating Tuesday for her

110

visit as 'she happened to be going into Kendal that day' – a fib on a par with Tom's needing to pop out of the fire exit for a cigarette. As Fran waited for Tom to pick up, Mrs Snegglington weaved round her ankles, emitting peevish mews, intended to remind her that merely putting down a dish of food was insufficient attention for a cat who has been left alone to amuse herself all day.

'Connecting your call,' came the voice of the operator.

Another, different voice said, 'Hello?'

It was a young woman's voice. Refined. Not like a servant's. Fran waited for one anguished second before cutting off the call. She replaced the receiver and walked into the middle of the room, where she could see her oddly pale reflection in the mirror above the fireplace. The cat trotted after her and jumped on to the back of the sofa, watching Fran expectantly.

A moment or two later, when the telephone rang, she retraced her steps and answered it automatically. This time it was Tom's voice. 'Hello? Is that Fran? Did you just try to ring a minute ago? I checked with the operator and recognized your number. Were you cut off?'

'Yes. Sorry. Not cut off, no. I put the phone down when a woman answered. I was expecting you and thought I'd got a wrong number.'

'It was my wife, Veronica,' he said, perfectly oblivious to the sound of cracking ice at the other end of the line as Fran fell right to the bottom of a very deep pool.

Thirteen

Fran had forgotten, until she plumbed the recesses of the pantry, that they had finished off the gin during Mo's last visit, but she found a bottle of red wine gathering dust at the back of the shelf and decided that would have to do. It was not as if she held dinner parties any more. The cork began to disintegrate before she had the corkscrew more than halfway into it. Michael had always been the one who opened the wine. It was traditionally a job for the man of the house (assuming one wasn't well-heeled enough to have a butler) and although she told herself that there was no reason why a woman should not do it, lack of experience left her making a total pig's breakfast of the whole operation, so that when she finally managed to draw the corkscrew towards her, the upper half of the cork came out in bits while the lower remained firmly in situ. It had turned into such a performance that she had almost lost interest in the idea of a drink but, determined not to be beaten, she made another couple of failed attempts with the corkscrew before resorting to the potato peeler to dig out the rest.

After that, she investigated the cold supper left by Ada, discovering bread and butter, curling at the edges, some slices of cheese and an accompaniment of pickled cabbage (Ada's ideas of catering sometimes left a lot to be desired). Deciding that she was not hungry after all, she replaced the plate under its cover of greaseproof paper and took her glass of hard-won wine back to the sitting room, which seemed emptier now that it was warm enough not to need a fire in the evenings.

Here she sat brooding on her own foolishness. Or maybe it was mere naivety? It had been foolish, yes, to assume that Tom Dod was a bachelor. Had she been wrong in imagining that the attraction on her part was mutually felt? If not, then he must have been anticipating that they would have an affair. Put bluntly like that, it sounded sordid. She did not want to start a cheating game, like the one to which she herself had fallen victim. But then again, perhaps the sense that her feelings had been reciprocated had been mere wishful thinking?

The wine was a source of comfort, in spite of the need to fish out an occasional fleck of cork. Mrs Snegglington insinuated herself on to Fran's lap and began to purr, occasionally kneading with her claws or shifting into a more satisfactory position.

'You're right, Sneggers,' Fran said. 'We must stop being maudlin and focus on the matter in hand.' And I must stop talking to the cat, she added inwardly.

The papers from the meeting were within easy reach where she had tossed them down on the table and with her free hand she began to draw abstract doodles on the back of the agenda, mixed in with occasional questions. *What were*

Linda's 'differing' ideas? Is there some other motive? Why did Jennifer Rumsey stand down as membership sec? Eventually she tipped the cat on to the rug and took her glass through to the kitchen for a refill. On her return, she spotted the card from Linda Dexter's funeral, still propped on the mantelpiece. It was easy to conjure up an image of Linda: a petite woman with bobbed blonde hair, grey eyes and an ordinary-looking face – nothing remarkable. Someone you might pass in the street without a second glance.

'You know, I'm carrying on with this for your sake,' she said aloud. Oh dear, now she was talking to imaginary dead people as well.

She switched on the wireless and tuned it to a programme of dance music, turning it up loud enough for a party; no neighbours here to come knocking on the door. Mrs Snegglington stalked out, flicking her tail a couple of times to indicate her displeasure as she headed upstairs to lie on the bed. One of the great things about living alone is the opportunity it affords for unrestrained dancing around the hearth rug while getting all the lyrics wrong. Fran was midway through muddling the words of 'Has Anybody Seen My Girl' when the doorbell sounded a long, insistent note, just as if the neighbours *had* come round to complain.

Fran stopped dead in her tracks, then stepped across to the open doorway, from whence she could see the front door. It was only just after nine and still daylight, but no one ever came in the evenings except by prior arrangement. Perhaps

114

it was someone whose car had broken down. You could see the cottage rooftop from the main road. If she peered through the front window, whoever was standing at the door would be able to see her. The Palmer Dance Band continued to belt out 'Has Anybody Seen My Girl' but she hardly noticed. The bell shrilled again. Her persistent caller was keeping a finger on the button for what seemed like forever. She reached over and turned down the wireless a couple of degrees, then approached the front door. 'Who is it?' she called.

'It's Stephen Latchford. I've got something here that will interest you.'

Although he couldn't see her, she felt exposed. 'You can't come in. I . . . I'm just about to have a bath.'

'It sounds more like you're having a party.' Although it was delivered as a joke, there was a challenging note in his voice.

'I have it on loud so that I can hear it while I'm upstairs in the bath.' Dammit, dammit. He would not be able to hear any water running, instantly giving lie to her excuse. No, wait, wouldn't the music drown the water out?

'Shall I come back in half an hour?'

'No, it's bath night. You'll have to come another time. It would be much better if you telephoned first to say you are coming, and avoid having a wasted journey.'

There was a moment or two of silence. She was just thinking he had gone when his voice came again. 'Very well. I'll come back when it's more convenient.' He sounded unmistakeably annoyed.

She stepped back from the door and collided with the small table where she had put her glass of wine down a moment or two before. It crashed on to the stone floor, splintering in all directions and sending splashes of red wine up the wall like blood at a crime scene.

'Is everything all right in there?'

'Yes.' She faltered. 'I just dropped a bottle of bath salts. Everything's fine.'

'Are you sure you don't need any help?'

'Of course not, I'm absolutely fine. You'll have to excuse me; I have to clear this up.'

She backed away from the door, doing her best to avoid treading in the mess on the floor, then ran softly up the stairs, sidestepping across her bedroom until she could see out of the window while standing far enough back to be out of sight in the room, which was in shadow now that the sun had sunk below the treeline. She was just in time to see him reach his car. He got inside, but he didn't put on the lights or start the engine. What the hell was he doing? Why didn't he go away?

Surely he couldn't see her watching him? She shrank further back into the room, just in case. The floorboards seemed to be vibrating to the beat of the dance band – or perhaps it was her own heartbeat. 'Just go,' she whispered. 'Just go away.'

Another song ended, the announcer introduced the next tune, and still he sat in the darkened car. What to do? No point telephoning anyone. There was no law against him sitting out there. Then the headlights came on and almost simultaneously the car moved silently away. She realized then that she couldn't hear the engine above the noise of the music. He might have turned it on as soon as he got into the car – maybe he had just paused to consult a road map or something. She ought to stop behaving like a bloody fool. She was starting to make a habit of it.

She took the stairs unsteadily. The cat had preceded her and paused to sniff disapprovingly at the spilled wine.

'Be careful,' Fran cautioned. 'Don't go getting glass in your paws.'

Mrs Snegglington gave her a teach-your-grandmother look and leapt gracefully on to the sofa back. Fran went into the kitchen to fetch a cloth and some old newspaper to wrap the bits of glass inside. Then she knelt on the floor and began to pick out the larger pieces, inching forward with elaborate care until she put her hand down straight on to a curved sliver which bit into the ball of her thumb. As she withdrew her hand, splotches of blood mingled with the spilled wine. She stumbled across to sit on the bottom stair and began to sob.

Fourteen

The Harpers lived in a quiet part of Kendal, their small terraced house pretty much indistinguishable from all the others in the road. Christina Harper opened the door herself and invited Fran in, escorting her to sit in one of the lumpy, horsehair-filled armchairs which stood on either side of the fireplace in the seldom-used front parlour, and offering her a cup of tea with the courteous reluctance of a small businessman greeting a visiting tax inspector. The Harpers evidently did not entertain many callers, and after this uncertain welcome, Fran expected the visit to be uphill going, but to her relief, Mrs Harper thawed quickly once the opportunity arose to have a good moan.

'The whole thing has been a nightmare. We had to get special permission from the coroner to arrange the funeral, because that side of things isn't done with yet. The inquest won't bring in a verdict until the police have finished making their enquiries.'

Fran was dying to ask some questions about this, but she sensed that it was better to let Linda's sister run on.

'Then we found out there's death duties to be paid, if you don't mind – and before I can do that, I have to sort out exactly how much money's involved. I don't know when they expect you to

118

do all this. I have a home and two boys to take care of. Their dad takes them out to the football on Saturday afternoons and that's the only time I get to myself all week. It isn't as if it's a cock stride to Ivegill. Just getting there and back on the bus takes up the best part of a day.' Mrs Harper paused to sip her tea.

'Isn't there anyone else who could help you?' Fran asked. 'Any other family?'

'To mind the boys, you mean? Mam's sister has offered but she's too old; she can't cope with them when they get going. They're not bad lads,' she added quickly. 'But you know what lads are like.'

Fran nodded sympathetically. 'And there's no one who could help sort out your sister's affairs?'

'Not really. Our mam and dad both passed on a couple of years ago and that just leaves me. To tell you the truth, we weren't even close. There's a big gap between me and our Lindy. Six years. I was only eleven when she left home.'

Fran did some mental arithmetic. That only made Christina Harper thirty. Motherhood had evidently taken its toll. Linda had actually looked younger than her sister. Linda had also lost any trace of the local accent which they had once presumably shared.

Mrs Harper was still talking. 'I was surprised when I found out that everything was coming to me. To be honest, I thought she might easily have left her money elsewhere.'

'Did you think she might have left it to a charity or something?' Fran fished.

'Well, it wasn't something that we ever talked

119

about. To be absolutely honest, we didn't talk much about anything. We only saw each other two or three times a year, if that. She had her life and I had mine.'

'But deep down, she must have really cared for you. Otherwise she wouldn't have left you everything.'

'Maybe she didn't have anyone else to leave it to. Mind you,' the woman added quickly, 'I'm not saying that I'm not grateful. It will make a lot of difference to us. No more struggling to make ends meet, that's for sure. We'll be able to move to a bigger place – maybe something up in Ambleside. I've always fancied one of them big houses with a view.' She stopped abruptly. 'Oh dear, I sound dreadful, don't I? Going on about the money. It isn't that I'm glad she's dead—'

'Of course not,' said Fran. 'Anyone would be glad to come into a lot of money. It's only natural. You're just honest enough to admit it.'

'Do you know, that's exactly what the policeman said.' Mrs Harper looked relieved. When she smiled, the crow's feet at her eyes were more sharply defined.

Fran seized her moment. 'Have the police given you any idea of what they think happened?'

'They're keeping me informed, or so they say.' The other woman paused to lower her voice as if sharing a confidence. 'If you ask me, they don't really know what happened. Following up all possible leads, the policeman said. We had to say where we were on the night it happened. Well, we were here, like always. Could anyone confirm it? they wanted to know. Well, of course there isn't anyone who could. I said to them, "I didn't even know she was staying at the whatever-it's-called towers. She didn't keep me informed of her movements".'

'They got in touch with me, too,' Fran said, 'because I had tried to telephone Linda a couple of times after she went missing.'

'There you are.' Christina Harper nodded companionably, as if being a fellow target of police enquiries helped to nurture a growing level of understanding between them. 'They've had a good look through all Lindy's things. They asked me if I wanted to be present while they did it. Well, I didn't, to be honest. The thought of strangers rooting through her things – it's not very nice, is it? And besides which, I didn't want to go all that way just to stand about like a spare part for however long it took, so I told them they could just get the key off Mrs Roseby who lives in the house opposite. We left a set of keys with her so that folk who needed to could get in and out without me needing to be up and down.'

'Did the police find anything useful?'

'Not so far as I know. They came back here after and asked another lot of questions. Had Lindy talked to me about any worries? Was she concerned about her health? Maybe frightened of getting cancer? I said to them, "Well, we're all frightened of getting that," but no, she hadn't mentioned anything about it to me. And nor did I think she was the sort to brood on stuff like that. She never worried about her health, so far as I know. She wasn't daft.'

They're clutching at straws, Fran thought. Aloud, she said, 'So the police do think it could have been suicide?'

'They're not ruling it out. That's what they said to me.'

'And what do you think?'

'Well . . . I don't know. Our Lindy never seemed like the type to do a thing like that. Anyway,' Christina glanced pointedly towards the clock, 'you said in your letter that there was something you wanted to talk about – something about her books and papers?'

Fran went into her carefully rehearsed explanation about Linda's doing some research which had been of great mutual interest, taking care not to suggest that it contained anything particularly exciting or controversial. 'She was going to share her findings with the society and obviously any new insights into Robert Barnaby's life would be valuable – not in a monetary sense, but for future students of his work. It would be terribly sad if the research was lost after all Linda's hard work.'

The other woman shook her head. 'I don't know anything about all that. I wouldn't know where to start looking, or what it was if I fell over it.'

Fran did her best to look sympathetic and appealing at the same time. 'Linda had spent such a lot of time on this and I just feel that she would have wanted the society to have it.'

Christina hesitated. 'Our Lindy did love those Robert Barnaby books. She read them over and over again when she was little. I could never get into them myself. I suppose this research she's done would be a sort of legacy to your society.'

Fran nodded, not daring to say anything.

'Look, I'll tell you what. If you really want this stuff and you're prepared to look for it yourself, I'll drop a note to Mrs Roseby and tell her to let you into the house, to see if you can find it. You would know what you're looking for better than me.'

Fran stared in astonishment: this was much better than anything she had hoped for. 'Don't you want to be there?'

'One lot of folk have already gone through everything, so I don't see what difference another one makes. You know what you're looking for, which is probably more than they did – and I don't want to go trekking up there again. Mr Harper and I have already been twice, getting all the financial stuff and emptying out the pantry, and to be frank with you, I'm not even sure I'll go back again. I might just pay someone else to clear everything once we've got the estate sorted out. There's folk who do that sort of thing. Cart it all off to an auction, like.'

'This is really very kind of you. Would it be all right if I went up later this week?' asked Fran, mentally reckoning the earliest possible date she could manage and all the time fearing that Mrs Harper might have second thoughts.

'I'll drop Mrs Roseby a note, to let her know to expect you.'

'And you're sure there wouldn't be any problem with the police over my taking things away?'

'No – they've finished nosing around. They've been thorough, I'll give them that. Even wanted to know about Lindy's ex-husband, poor old

123

David Dexter. I told them, "He won't be able to help you. He's been dead for about ten years." They always do think it might be the ex-husband, don't they?'

'What do you think happened?' Fran prompted.

The woman hesitated, as if she was trying to decide, saying eventually, 'I think it could have been some maniac who got into her hotel room. Escaped from an asylum, I daresay. Or maybe she did do it herself, after all. She was a funny one, our Lindy. You never really knew what was going on in her mind. We weren't close, because she wasn't the sort of person you *could* get close to – if you know what I mean.'

Fifteen

It took several minutes for Fran and Mo to settle themselves at their favourite table in the tea shop on the promenade, arrange their assorted shopping, order afternoon tea, remove their gloves and straighten their hats, and only when they were completely settled did Mo say, 'Now, have you considered what I said about that chap, Jumbo Fielding, because I can easily introduce you.'

'Really, Mo, I do wish you would stop playing at matchmaker. As it happens, I saw the man in question, or the man I assume to be him, from your description, entering the offices of Fielding and Fielding this morning and I can see at a glance that he's not my type at all.'

'Oh dear,' Mo said. 'I thought he would be exactly your type. He's an absolute scream after a couple of cocktails. You should have seen him imitating Charlie Chaplin at the Willington's last weekend. Honestly, Fran, you could have a much better social life if you were only prepared to make an effort in the right direction.'

'You know very well that the sort of party where people start impersonating Charlie Chaplin after a couple of cocktails is my idea of hell.'

'That's simply not true and you know it. The trouble is that being married to Michael ironed all the fun out of you.'

'Please, let's not talk about Michael.'

'Very well then. Tell me all about your amateur detective friend. I'm up to the point where he was going back to have another look around the hotel.'

Fran took a few seconds to gaze out over the shallow waters of Morecambe Bay, which were glittering silver and gold in the late afternoon sunshine, before she regaled Mo with Tom's discoveries at Furnival Towers. After that she related her own encounter with Christina Harper. 'So the upshot is,' she concluded, 'I'm going up to Linda Dexter's house to have a look for these research papers tomorrow. Do you fancy coming with me?'

'I'd love to, but I've got a prior engagement with my hairdresser. And even if I hadn't, you wouldn't want me along, playing gooseberry.'

'Tom Dod isn't coming. He has to take his wife and son somewhere.'

'His son? His wife?' Mo's voice had risen, but she quickly lowered it again to say, 'I thought you said that he was single. Are you sure?'

'I was mistaken about him being single. If you keep on staring at me like that, instead of watching what you're doing, you're going to pour that tea all over the tablecloth.'

Mo drew in a long intake of breath. 'When did you find this out?'

'When I rang him and his wife answered the telephone.'

'Well, well. So he was up to no good after all. Deceitful devil.'

'There was no deceit involved,' Fran said. 'And

126

he wasn't up to anything. I kept on telling you that there was nothing brewing between us but you wouldn't listen.'

'Oh, come on, Fran. You've known him all this time and he just never happened to mention that he's got a wife and son?'

'Why should he? I don't know him all that well. I don't suppose you know the domestic details of everyone you play tennis with. Your trouble is that you think any man who doesn't have his Happily Married lapel badge on display is up for grabs.'

'That's not a very nice thing to say.'

'You're right. It's not. I'm sorry.'

'This Deathly Dod fellow, though . . . You spent a couple of hours in the car with him, going to and from that funeral. You found out that he's a company director in a family firm of wholesale fruiterers—'

'Because I asked him what he did for a living.'

'—but not that he was married.'

'I didn't ask him that.'

'I still think it's a bit fishy that he never mentioned his wife.'

'It just didn't come up.'

Mo made a disbelieving noise which Fran chose to ignore. There was a short silence while Mo sliced her Madeira cake into tiny, bite-sized squares, then she said, 'Do you think he's still interested in pursuing this theory about what happened to Linda Dexter? Now that you know he's married.'

'What difference does his being married make? He's been married all along.'

'I just think that . . . well, he's suddenly become unavailable . . .'

'You're unavailable too,' Fran said. 'Should I assume that means you're not interested in hearing any more about it?'

'All right, don't get snappy.'

'Actually, he's still really keen. He's given me the telephone number of the relatives they're visiting tomorrow afternoon so that I can get hold of him if I find anything.'

'Or so that you can ring him without any risk of his wife picking up the telephone,' said Mo.

Fran ignored the remark. 'It may be quite a job, going through all her papers.'

'Are you really going to go through all this woman's private notes?'

'Her sister didn't seem to mind. She's virtually given me *carte blanche* to look at whatever I like, though obviously I will only be looking at anything which might relate to her Robert Barnaby research, not private correspondence, diaries, things like that.'

'Things like that might be significant if you're wrong about the Robert Barnaby connection providing a motive.'

'I am not going to snoop about in the poor woman's diaries, if she had such things.'

They continued to eat their tea against the backdrop of the bay and no more was said about Linda Dexter or Tom Dod. The sky had turned overcast again, which made the journey home seem less and less appealing. Mo offered to run her all the way, but Fran knew that her friend had another engagement and insisted on

128

taking the 5.20 p.m. bus, which would drop her at the top of the lane.

In spite of the threatening clouds, she thought that she would manage to get home before it began to rain. According to the newspapers, the weather had been improving steadily throughout the month, but that was in London, of course. Up here the weather often had quite different ideas. Better have an early night, she told herself. She needed to be up early in the morning, because she had to cast her vote at the church hall in Haverthwaite before catching the first of the three buses which would take her on the somewhat convoluted journey to Ivegill.

She had forgotten all about the election when agreeing the day of her visit to Linda's house with Mrs Harper, and casting her vote would be an inconvenience, but she felt that she had to do it for the sake of all those women who had gone to prison and made every kind of sacrifice, just so that she could. Not that she had ever taken much notice of politics before, which made it hard to know who to vote for. Her mother, of course, had been all for Mr Baldwin and his 'safety first', but she had more sympathy with Lloyd George's promise to conquer unemployment. All those men who had fought alongside Geoffrey and Cec, reduced to selling matches in the street or tramping the country looking for work. It was a scandal and something ought to be done. Linda Dexter has been dead for almost five weeks, said a voice in her head: something ought to be done about that too.

She made it to the front door, just as the first

129

spots of rain hit the ground. The day's post was waiting on the mat (why Ada had not noticed it lying there, she could not imagine) and she carried it into the little parlour on the opposite side of the hall to the sitting room, where she liked to use the big, old-fashioned desk which she had picked up cheaply from the auction rooms. She opened the trio of envelopes, all of which turned out to be bills, and as she put them into the designated pigeon hole, she noticed that the papers from the Barnaby Society meeting were still lying on the desk and began to sort through them in a desultory way, deciding whether she needed to keep everything or could consign some of it to the role of fire-lighting material. When she reached the list of membership updates from John James, Stephen Latchford's name jumped out at her. He was listed as a recent change of address, with a new abode at Broughton in Furness. Out of curiosity, she checked the membership list to see where he had moved from and found that it was an address near Carlisle, barely ten miles away from Linda Dexter's home in Ivegill.

She heard herself saying to Tom, 'There's the sinister man. You can't rule out the sinister man.' She had not mentioned Stephen-with-a-ph's visits to Tom or Mo, but this put things in a different light. She picked up the telephone, then hesitated. Perhaps Mo was right and Tom Dod would not want his wife to be forever answering the telephone to her. She would have to leave the news about Stephen Latchford for another time.

Sixteen

Feeling like a pioneer for her generation, Fran was among the earliest to arrive at Haverthwaite church hall and she marched in with her head held high. All that fuss over being allowed to put a cross on a piece of paper, when the stupidest of men had been allowed to do it for years! Now that it actually came to it, the whole business was over in a moment and something of an anti-climax. Anyway, it was a step forward – the time might even come when women were shown how to use corkscrews and put up shelves.

A light drizzle had begun to fall as she waited for the bus on the main road, and by the time she had connected with the route to Carlisle they were driving through fog. Shapes loomed at the roadside like lingering primeval spirits from an earlier age. It was an alien landscape alive with suggestion: sighting a troop of ghostly border reivers seemed a possibility, an encounter with a murderous hitchhiker positively likely, but once the bus had topped the watershed and began to descend again, the mist dispersed entirely, giving way to a pale blue sky.

Fran had spent the past couple of days half fearing that Christina Harper might change her mind and withdraw permission to search her sister's house, so when she got home on Wednesday evening and saw an envelope on the mat, in handwriting that she recognized as Mrs Harper's, Fran had naturally feared the worst. In fact, the woman had written to ask a favour. Would Fran mind bringing a couple of items back with her – a model of a horse's head and an antique clock, both of which would be found in the drawing room? Fran sighed with relief while mentally sending up a prayer that the items in question were small enough to be easily transported on a public omnibus.

Gladness was not her predominant emotion, however, now that the mission was almost upon her. It would be very strange, going into a dead person's house like this. A place, moreover, into which she had never been invited while the owner was alive. She finally alighted from the third bus of the day at half past eleven in the morning and walked briskly down the lane to the cottage, which she easily identified as Mrs Roseby's, feeling that every eye in the village was probably focused upon her. One pair certainly had been, because Mrs Roseby opened the door before she even had a chance to knock.

'You'll be Mrs Black. Mrs Dexter's sister told me to expect you.'

Fran waited while Mrs Roseby handed over the keys, explaining which one related to the front door, which to the back and so on.

'With the police, are you?'

'No. I'm not with the police.'

'Oh, I thought you must be. The sister gave me to understand that you'd be looking for something.' Mrs Roseby was evidently burning with curiosity, but when Fran said nothing to enlighten her, she reluctantly relinquished the keys, saying: 'If you need anything, you just pop across and let me know. I'll be in all day.'

'Thank you.'

Fran crossed the lane, conscious of the thin breeze which found its way into a non-existent gap where her skirt met her jumper. Whatever the national papers might say, it was unseasonably cool for the end of May.

Curiosity killed the cat, said a voice in her head.

Rubbish. No one ever got anywhere without curiosity. She hadn't got up at the crack of dawn only to chicken out at the last minute. She opened one of the front gates and walked up the gravel path which led directly to the front door. A drive led past the side of the building to a half-visible coach house, where Linda had probably garaged her car. Fran noticed that her feet seemed to be making an incredible amount of noise. She wondered if Mrs Roseby was still watching her and whether there was a particular trick to opening the front door – she would feel such a fool if, after all, she couldn't get in, but the key turned easily in the lock and the front door seemed to swing open of its own volition, without her needing to exert any pressure at all. It came up short against two or three election flyers which were lying on the doormat. Christina Harper had probably arranged for the post to be redirected, but that didn't prevent the occasional item being hand-delivered. Fran bent to pick them up before quietly closing the front door behind her.

At first sight, the hall looked reassuringly normal, just as it would have done if Linda had still been alive and someone had been admitting Fran as a visitor to the house in the ordinary way, but a closer look revealed the layer of dust which dulled the surface of the hall table, the five-week-old newspaper which lay forgotten on the seat of a mock-Regency chair, the newsprint already fading where the sun had caught it. It was only a few weeks since Linda had left for the last time, but the house already exuded a sense of being long deserted. Linda's sister evidently saw no benefit in continuing to pay a maid to keep the place up.

Fran stood in the hall, wondering where to begin. When discussing the proposed search with Tom during a telephone call two evenings before, he had suggested that she should look through 'everything' on the basis that should his million-to-one theory turn out to be wrong, there might still be some other useful clues. This comprehensive operation had sounded simple enough when discussed on the phone and she had not demurred, as she had with Mo, over poking her nose into someone else's private life. Now that she was actually standing on the doormat, however, the task seemed altogether more daunting.

'Oh, come on,' she said aloud. 'You're here now. Might as well go through with it.' The house swallowed up her words, converting them into an icy silence as surely as if they had never been uttered.

She cautiously pulled open the drawer in the

hall table, as if she expected something to jump out at her, and sifted through the contents, taking elaborate care not to disarrange anything before remembering that this was not a furtive search where everything must be left exactly in place to avoid the homeowner ever suspecting that it had occurred. The homeowner was never coming back. She could afford a little rearrangement. The drawer contained various odds and ends, including a card advertising a plumbing service, an unused notepad, some loose paperclips and a couple of old receipts. Nothing of significance at all.

To the right of the hall was the drawing room, and to the left a door led into a formal dining room. Fran entered the drawing room hesitantly, still half expecting to be ejected as a trespasser. The room was expensively furnished with modern sofas and ornaments. Large cabinets housed a collection of china figurines, which Fran instinctively knew to be good quality. A gramophone stood on a specially designed cabinet, which included a cupboard for housing the records. It was a collection which ranged from *Swan Lake* to *Lilac Time*, and included some dance music too. There was no sign of anything which might house personal notebooks. Fran tried to stop herself from speculating on which had been Linda's favourite spot. Were those cushions somewhat higgledy-piggledy because the police had searched behind them, or because that was where Linda had last sat to listen to the gramophone the day before she died?

There was a curious kind of anonymity to the

room, she thought. In many ways it reminded her of a large furniture showroom which she and Michael had once visited in order to choose their dining suite. It had occupied the entire upper floor of a big store in Manchester, and had been arranged to display the firm's goods in a series of rooms, which were necessarily somewhat anonymous, devoid of the usual framed family photographs, the sepia brides and grooms, little girls with their hands folded in their laps, their brothers standing at their shoulders, wearing sailor suits and serious expressions, the inevitable beloved son or nephew in uniform, not destined to grow old as we grow old. Just as there had been nothing of that in the showroom, so it was here, in Linda's drawing room. The only exception was a lone framed photograph standing on a side table. It was a picture of a large house: a view from the garden, taken on a sunny day and, on closer examination, the place struck Fran as being oddly familiar. She decided that she must have seen it somewhere before, perhaps in a book or a magazine.

Casting around the room again, she easily identified the clock and the ornamental horse's head which Christina Harper had asked her to bring back. Though they were not particularly large, the items were awkwardly shaped and quite heavy. She lifted them both on to the little table, next to the picture of the house which had caught her eye a moment before. As she examined the picture more closely, it occurred to her that perhaps it could be somewhere which was connected with Robert Barnaby. It was the sort of house in the country to which the author had often found himself invited, particularly as his books began to gain him attention. On a whim, she decided to help herself to the photograph. After all, Mrs Harper had made it clear that she was welcome to take anything connected to Linda's research, and the picture would fetch nothing at auction. She would have to find some newspaper to wrap the things in, she decided, so that they didn't scratch one another as they travelled home together in her wicker shopping basket.

A second door led out of the drawing room directly into a small sitting room, where there was a wireless on the table and a sewing basket beside one of the armchairs. Behind the sitting room lay the large kitchen. Here, too, no expense had been spared. Oak cupboards opened to reveal all the latest kitchen gadgetry and two services, both courtesy of Royal Doulton. There was no paperwork save for a drawer full of handwritten recipes.

From the kitchen, it was possible to re-enter the hall or continue directly into the dining room. Fran went back into the hall and looked doubtfully at the stairs. She swallowed hard and began to ascend slowly, twice pausing to glance over her shoulder as the light played tricks at the periphery of her vision. There were half-a-dozen doors leading off the landing, and the first one she chose was a bathroom. The room next door had obviously been Linda's bedroom. A part-used jar of Pond's Cold Cream and an almost empty bottle of Chanel No.5 still stood on the dressing table, and there were more cosmetic preparations of various kinds visible in a partly open drawer. With fingers which trembled, Fran systematically opened one drawer after another, reluctantly probing to check that there was nothing concealed among the dead woman's sweaters and underwear, all the time resisting the impulse to look over her shoulder, ignoring that ever-present sense of being observed.

You shouldn't be doing this, she said to herself. These are Linda's personal things.

And yet, Christina Harper had given her permission. It came to her that she would never have agreed to a virtual stranger rooting through Geoffrey or Cec's belongings. Nor employed some anonymous company to dispose of them. The woman's actions demonstrated an unusual level of detachment bordering on cold-hearted.

After Linda's bedroom, she tackled the other upstairs rooms. The first two were spare bedrooms – double rooms furnished as if for guests, although there was little sign that they were ever used. All the furnishings were in showroom condition, the drawers and wardrobes either empty or else repositories for pristine towels and bed linen. Fran was reminded again of that large store which she and Michael had visited so many years before. Everything here seemed to have been chosen for looking at rather than living with. Nothing about any of these rooms gave much of a clue to the person who had furnished them.

The last of the upstairs rooms was completely different. Instead of a bed there was a small, comfortable sofa positioned under the window to afford anyone who sat in it the best possible light for reading. Wall-to-ceiling shelves had been built around the other three sides of the room and these were filled to overflowing with books. Robert Barnaby had pride of place but they were all here: Kipling, Stevenson, Alcott, Lucy Maude Montgomery, the early Angela Brazils. It was a shrine to children's literature. For the first time since she had entered the house, Fran felt halfway towards being comfortable. The temptation to browse the nearest volumes was strong. She reached up to remove an illustrated copy of *The Wind in the Willows* from the top shelf, but her sleeve must have caught something because a small pile of books cascaded on to the floor, sending an explosion of noise through the silent house.

'A noise fit to wake the dead,' said a voice in her head before she could stop it. She set about restoring the books to their former positions, pausing every so often to convince herself that the only movements she could hear were her own. The book room felt increasingly like a safe haven from the otherwise hostile house. Here you could shut the door on life in general and immerse yourself in a world where worries dissolved as the pages turned and no bogeyman could come and get you.

She had assumed that the only room left to check downstairs was the dining room but, as soon as she entered it, she realized that there was a door leading into another room beyond it – at last, the room which Linda had used as a study, complete with a shelf of neatly labelled box files and carefully stacked notebooks, with covers got up in a design which imitated marble. The hands of the large wall clock had stopped at twenty-three minutes past two, but its presence provided a reminder that she had to consider the infrequency of the bus service. She did not have an infinite amount of time. Bother, bother – if only she had poked her head into the dining room first.

She scanned the neatly printed labels which had been affixed to both the files and the spines of the notebooks. Immediately after *Household Accounts* came a box labelled *RB*. Robert Barnaby – it had to be. She eased the large rectangular box file down from its place and put it on the desk, dropping into the big leather chair where Linda herself must have sat hundreds of times, and pressed the little release button which allowed the top cover of the box file to be opened.

The trio of bangs on the window made her jump right out of the seat. Mrs Roseby was standing outside, gesturing with her hand and nodding down at a tray which she was balancing on the outside windowsill with her spare hand. Taking in the small teapot and accompanying paraphernalia, Fran had little alternative but to backtrack through the dining room and open the front door.

'Sorry if I startled you. I came to the window because I thought you might not come if I used the knocker, seeing as you're not expecting anyone. I've brought you some tea. Thought you might be glad of it. There's nothing left over here to make yourself a drink, is there? I think that sister's even taken the tea caddy.'

Since Mrs Roseby made no move to actually hand over the tray, Fran made room for her to step inside, which she did, immediately heading straight down the hall to the kitchen. She seemed to know her way around, Fran thought, and the remark about the missing tea caddy suggested that perhaps the police search had not been the only scrutiny to which the premises had already been subjected.

'I thought we might as well use Mrs Dexter's china, to save me carrying anything else over.'

Fran noted the 'we'. Oh, well, perhaps the interlude could be put to some use: and anyway, although she was dying to get back to Linda's study, she genuinely welcomed the tea.

They took their cups and saucers across to the kitchen table, sitting in the pair of hard wooden chairs which had presumably been used by the now-departed staff. Mrs Roseby needed no encouragement to talk. 'To think when I saw Mrs Dexter putting that case into her motorcar, that would be the last time I'd ever set eyes on her. You just can't credit it, can you?'

'You must have been very upset when you heard the news,' Fran prompted.

'Well, yes and no, dear. When you reach my age, you get to more funerals than weddings, if you see what I mean. And it wasn't as if we were really friendly. Oh, she was a pleasant enough lady but she kept herself to herself. In fact, some folk thought she was a bit standoffish. She didn't mix or get involved much in the life of the village.'

'Had she lived in the village for long?'

'Ooh, yes, let's see . . . A good nine or ten years, I'd say. But she didn't join in with anything much. Wasn't a churchgoer. She didn't neighbour. In fact, apart from Mrs Griggs, who used to come in to do the heavy work, I doubt if anyone in the village has ever set foot in this house since she bought it, other than me.'

'Did she have any other help in the house?' asked Fran.

'Oh, bless you, yes. She might not have been one of the county set but she was a lady right enough. There was Mrs Parsons, the cook, who came originally from Penrith, and a house parlour maid called Ethel. They've both been let go, of course, but they got new positions pretty easily, I believe. Well, there's such a shortage of good help these days, isn't there, with so many girls going off to get work in the towns.' Mrs Roseby paused to sip her tea before continuing. 'I don't know that those young women will find such an easy life at another post, mind you. There was never any entertaining and Mrs Dexter was away a lot, of course; always off on trips and holidays, she was. It's all right for some, isn't it?'

'Has she always lived here on her own?'

'Always, just Mrs Dexter and whatever staff she had. Ethel and the cook lived in, and at one time I seem to remember there used to be a scullery maid too, though maybe she went home at nights. And I will say this for her,' Mrs Roseby lowered her voice, as if she was afraid that there might be eavesdroppers lurking in the larder, 'there was never any carrying-on. Not like some I could mention. Strange cars parked outside overnight and men going off the next morning. No, Mrs Dexter wasn't that type of woman. In fact, she had no visitors at all to speak of.'

'That must have been quite lonely for her.'

'I suppose so.' Mrs Roseby paused to look around the kitchen. 'All these lovely things but no friends.' She turned her gaze back on Fran. 'So, what is it you're doing here? A valuation of the estate, is it?'

'I'm looking for some research notes which Mrs Dexter compiled – about the children's author, Robert Barnaby.'

Mrs Roseby looked blank. 'Was that what she did – research? And there's me thinking she didn't have a job.'

'It wasn't exactly a job – more of a hobby.'

It took almost another half an hour to get rid of Mrs Roseby, who apparently knew very little about her long-term neighbour but a very great deal about various other residents of Ivegill, which she was only too eager to share. In the end, Fran became so desperate that she had to say pointedly, 'I'm sorry, but I really do have to get on. Thank you so much for the tea. It was very thoughtful.' She then stood up and headed purposefully back to the study, leaving the other woman to see herself out.

Once back at the desk, she finally opened the box file and began to read.

Seventeen

It was much later than she had intended when Fran finally left Langdale House, and by the time she had extricated herself from the errand of returning the keys to the garrulous Mrs Roseby, she only just made the last possible bus and then had to wait over an hour for one of the connections. The journey home seemed endless: each of the buses crawled and coughed up the inclines as if they would never make the top, and on the final leg, the thought of what had happened to Linda grew in her mind. It was horribly easy to imagine all sorts of things, travelling along darkened roads with passing images half glimpsed in the gathering darkness beyond the bus windows. There were only a handful of other travellers on the bus, and once she got down on to the road she was completely alone. She paused a moment or two as the bus trundled off in the direction of Ulverston, in order to let her eyes grow accustomed to the dark. After that, it was not difficult to negotiate the familiar unlit lane, though the combination of the clock and the horse's head requested by Christina Harper, together with the notebooks and picture removed on her own initiative, weighed heavily in her basket.

When the bulk of Bee Hive Cottage appeared at last, she saw that it was completely in darkness. Ada had of course departed at the usual hour, not thinking to leave a light burning in the sitting-room window, since she would probably have expected her employer to arrive home during the hours of daylight. Fran was therefore forced to negotiate the short distance up the path, which led from the lane to the front door, through a garden full of shadows. Then she fumbled the operation of unlocking the door, at one point almost dropping her key. Just the thought of that made her heart beat faster. She would never be able to see a key in the pool of blackness at her feet.

You're going to have to sell, said a voice in her head. *You can't go on like this, getting the wind up every time you have to come home after dark.*

As she had expected, Mrs Snegglington was in a haughty mood over the lateness of her supper and, once she had wolfed down her food, adopted a policy of non-fraternization. Fran left her sulking in the kitchen. Now that she had lit the oil lamps and done her duty by the cat, she could scarcely wait to telephone Tom, all the worries and the frustrations of the journey forgotten in her eagerness to pass on what she had found out. Then there seemed to be an interminable delay while the operator was connecting them, but at last she heard his voice on the line: 'Hello? Is that you, Fran?'

'Yes. Yes, it's me. I found Linda's notes and a copy of her speech and I've read it all the way through. Believe me, *The Magic Chair: Fact or Fiction* is pure dynamite.'

'Wait, hang on. Let me shut the door so I can hear you properly . . . Go on, what does it say?'

'If Linda is right – and I suspect that she is

145

– the magic chair in Furnival Towers is a complete fraud. In fact, the whole Furnival Towers connection is a sham. According to Linda's presentation, she was rereading Hugh Allonby's original Barnaby biography about six months ago when she realized that something didn't quite fit, so she went to the Vester House Museum and checked Robert Barnaby's diaries and there's no record in them of him ever staying at Furnival Towers at all. In 1891 he stayed with an old friend who had a house on Longridge Fell, so he would certainly have seen Furnival Towers from the outside, but Linda couldn't find any evidence at all that he'd ever actually set foot in the place. Then she went to the county archives and did some digging about Furnival Towers itself. Back when Barnaby began writing the Magic Chair books, it was still owned by the Furnival family, but they sold it to the Drydens back in 1910.'

'And that's when it was converted into a hotel.'

'Exactly. But the thing is, the Drydens only bought the house – not the contents. Apparently the original sale bills and advertising still survive and the sale particulars are absolutely clear on that point. The original contents had been sold about eighteen months before the house was auctioned off, and there's more. According to Linda, there are some old photographs in *Country Life* showing the interior of Furnival Towers before the big sell-off, and there's absolutely no sign of the magic chair.'

'So when the hotel brochure says that it stands in the entrance hall, as it has done for generations . . .'

'It's basically a lot of drivel. Linda couldn't find any reference to the chair being there until Hugh Allonby mentioned it in an article he wrote for a magazine not long after Robert Barnaby died.'

'But that wasn't until 1915?'

'Quite. It sounds as if the magic chair wasn't based on a real chair at all. It just came out of Robert Barnaby's imagination, and the house in the stories probably isn't Furnival Towers either. Barnaby himself never said it was. It just happens to be similar in one or two respects, and I suppose an awful lot of other large country houses would fit the bill just as well. The Drydens must have acquired a suitable chair at some point and painted it up.'

'The Barnaby connection is a huge selling point for the hotel,' Tom said. 'In fact, it's their main selling point. It won't do Marcus Dryden's business any good if news gets out that essentially there is no Barnaby connection.'

'It won't do Hugh Allonby any good either. He's built a reputation as *the* Robert Barnaby expert, but his research can't have been up to much if he just accepted a story the Drydens told him and has helped to peddle the myth ever since.'

'Do you suppose Linda's right?'

'I don't know. I suppose she could have made it up – maybe it's a spoof?'

'We can always check it ourselves,' Tom said. 'Has she given details of all her sources?'

'Yes. Unlike Hugh's books, which always have gushy acknowledgements about the generous help and advice he's received from the Dryden

147

family and Mrs Ingoldsby at the Vester House Museum, but no actual document references, Linda actually numbers her sources and gives chapter and verse on absolutely everything. I've still a couple of notebooks to look at yet. I'm going to finish going through them this evening.'

'Then I'll let you get on,' said Tom. 'You're doing brilliantly.'

Fran spent the next four hours poring over Linda's copious notes. In her determination to ferret out the truth, she had forgotten how hungry she ought to be and made do with occasional pots of tea. Linda's methodical approach made things easy for her. Inside the notebook labelled 'RB/Magic Chair', Linda had not only transcribed the relevant information but had also included the reference numbers by which she had called up the original documents. As she read page after page of Linda's neat, upright handwriting, Fran became ever more convinced that Linda had not made anything up.

Robert Barnaby wasn't the only author Linda had interested herself in, but so far as Fran could see there was nothing else contentious in the files. Linda's interests had lain in biographical detail, sources and inspiration. She had not been routinely digging dirt, Fran thought – she had merely opened up a book one day and been hit in the eye with something inconsistent.

It was only when she finally looked up from her labours that her eye fell on the trio of irregular bundles, wrapped in old newspaper, which had travelled in her shopping bag alongside the notebooks and papers. The first two were the items which Christina Harper had asked her to collect. She suspected that their value was to be reckoned more in monetary worth than sentiment. Whereas Mrs Harper had coveted a clock and a drawing-room ornament, Fran guessed that the thing Linda had prized above all else in the house was her collection of books, which was now destined to be hauled off to a sale room and dispersed to the four winds. She hoped their new owners would cherish them as much as Linda clearly had.

Belatedly realizing that she was ravenous, she went into the kitchen and cut some doorsteps of bread, which she used to make navvy-like cheese and pickle sandwiches that would have horrified her mother, who always had all the crusts cut off. As she chomped her way through her impro-vised supper, Fran reflected that it looked as if Tom's million-to-one shot had come in after all. Linda Dexter had been silenced for the sake of a research paper which challenged the prove-nance of a piece of old furniture. The police obviously hadn't envisaged anything like that, otherwise they would surely have taken away all the relevant papers themselves.

It was only then that she thought about explaining their theory to the police and realized how thin it would sound. Did one paper at an obscure conference really matter that much? Even if Linda had delivered her lecture, wouldn't Hugh Allonby have simply pooh-poohed the whole thing? If he had politely dismissed Linda's discoveries – saying that she was confused or mistaken – he would probably have received unquestioning support from the vast majority of the society's membership, most of whom believed him to be an infallible source on all things Barnaby. The more she thought about it, the greater became her certainty that when the chips were down, many of the members would not have *wanted* to believe Linda. The chair was almost sacred to them, representing one of the few tangible links to their favourite author. Would it really have mattered all that much to Hugh Allonby and Marcus Dryden if Linda's paper had been delivered? Wasn't this whole thing the very thinnest of motives for murder? But if that was so, then there must be something else . . .

From nowhere in particular, a vision of Stephen-with-a-ph-Latchford drifted into her mind. She had seen and heard nothing of him since her refusal to admit him to the house a few days before and, with a bit of luck, he would take the hint and not come back. Even so, there was this odd coincidence that Stephen-with-a-ph had until recently lived not far from Linda Dexter. Well, so what? That didn't prove anything.

Eighteen

Fran had arranged to convey the clock and the horse's head to Christina Harper's house the following morning. The man who sat in front of her on the bus had a newspaper and Fran could see the headline over his shoulder: *No Clear Victory In Election – Count Continues.* She thought of the pitiful queue outside the Labour Exchange and sighed. Mr Lloyd George's message had evidently fallen on deaf ears. She had rewrapped the items requested by Mrs Harper in brown paper and string and, taking a leaf out of Mrs Roseby's book, made no attempt to extract them from the confines of her bag when she presented herself on the doorstep, an act of cheek which was rewarded with admission to the house and the offer of another cup of tea.

'Did you find what you wanted?' Mrs Harper asked when they were seated again in the front parlour, a teapot under a cosy standing on the table and the two objects of the errand safely handed over.

'Yes, thank you. I've got the notebooks and things with me, just in case you wanted to see what I've taken.'

Christina Harper waved the idea away like someone discouraging a gnat. 'It's all the same to me. I don't suppose it would interest anyone outside your society.'

'Probably not,' Fran said, while attempting to banish the image of a large policeman from her mind.

'I can't remember if you take sugar,' her hostess said as she proffered a bowl which did not match the teacups.

Declining the sugar and putting the imaginary policeman firmly to one side, Fran embarked upon the other topic towards which she intended to steer her hostess, saying casually, 'Mrs Roseby mentioned that Linda had lived in that house for quite a long time.'

'That's right. Let's see now, it would have been about 1919 . . . That's right. It was the year me and Mr Harper got married. Ironic, really. I was getting into one marriage while she was getting out of another.'

'She couldn't have been married very long.' Fran adopted a sympathetic look, which she hoped would encourage confidences.

'Hardly any time at all. It was a funny business altogether, if you ask me.' When Fran smiled encouragingly, Christina Harper continued, 'I never understood why they got married in the first place. I'll be honest with you – they got married in such a rush, our mam thought at first that David Dexter must have got our Lindy into the family way. She was old fashioned, see, our mam; she wouldn't have asked how things stood outright. Well, they didn't in those days, did they?'

And nor do they now, so far as I'm aware, thought Fran, who was surprised and somewhat embarrassed at being the recipient of such indelicate information from a relative stranger.

'Well, anyway, there wasn't a baby on the way. They moved up to Carlisle – that's where he came from originally – and we didn't see much of them after that. Seemed like no time at all they were going their separate ways again. I used to say to Mr Harper, if you had to explain a marriage the way you had to explain a murder, our Lindy would have said that she married David Dexter while temporarily of unsound mind.' She chuckled to herself and Fran joined in politely.

'Why do you say that?'

'Well, it was in that year or two just after her father died, and to be honest, she was never the same person after that.'

'*Her* father?' Fran prompted politely.

'That's right. We were only half-sisters – didn't I tell you that? Same mother, different fathers. Lindy's father left my mother for another woman. Just walked out on her, he did. Mam only found out after he was gone that she was carrying our Lindy. She wanted him to stand by her but he wouldn't, and in the end she agreed to divorce him. He had the money, you see, and could make it worth her while. Mind you, he didn't give her much by comparison with what he should have, not by a long way. But he was a clever one, you see. Self-made man, he was, and I daresay he could afford clever solicitors and all, whereas our mam was just ordinary and didn't have anything behind her. Anyway, after a short time Mam got married again. He was a grand fellow, my dad. He always treated our Lindy like she was his own, made no difference between the two of us at all. Although Lindy knew our dad wasn't

153

her real father, she called him Dad and every-thing. She never saw her real father back then, not when we was little; he was still busy making his fortune down south and he was never talked of. It didn't seem to matter to Lindy – not then. She was always a happy little kiddie, Mam said – though she generally had her nose in a book, but some little 'uns are like that, aren't they?'

Fran nodded in confirmation and Christina continued. 'Of course, when she started growing up a bit, well – you know what girls can be like. Whenever our dad told her off about some-thing she'd start going on about how he wasn't her real Dad and how she had a right to know who her father was, all that sort of thing. A lot of chaps would have given her a good hiding and told her to pipe down, but as I've said, my father was a gentle sort of man and eventually he and Mam said that if Lindy really wanted to meet her other Dad, maybe it could be arranged, and perhaps that would put her mind at rest and she'd stop going on about it. So then Mam wrote to Lindy's father and it was all fixed up for them to meet.'

'Gosh,' said Fran. 'What a peculiar situation. How old was Linda by this time?'

'She was about fifteen or sixteen, I think. I don't really remember much about it, but of course it was talked about later on, when I was older. Anyway, they met and he made a great big fuss of her. What Mam and Dad hadn't realized was that by that time he'd had this great big place built on the edge of Windermere, where he came every summer, and all the while

154

we'd been living in a two-up two-down in Kendal.

'Of course, Lindy went off to see him, all got up in her Sunday frock, and came back full of it. Talking about his fancy house and his boat on the lake. Our house wasn't good enough for her after that. Instead of making things better, it made things worse. "The Little Princess", my mam used to call her. Talk about big ideas. Why couldn't we have nice new clothes and why didn't we have any maids? Then her own father started taking her about in his ruddy motorcar and buying her presents: expensive stuff. All those years that he'd never bothered with her, never so much as sent her a birthday card, and suddenly all this.' Mrs Harper spread her arms wide, as if to encompass the whole world.

'Did she ever say that she wanted to go and live with him?'

Linda's stepsister gave a hollow laugh. 'There was a fly in that pot of ointment. His second wife was still alive then and for all that she pretended to be nice to Lindy and make her welcome, she didn't want some cuckoo coming into the nest, queering the pitch for her Penelope.'

'Penelope?'

'Aye, Penelope. Lindy's father took up with this other woman down south and once he wasn't tied to Mam, he married her and had another daughter. So our Lindy had a stepsister on both sides – me from Mam and Penelope from her dad.'

'Wasn't she jealous of Penelope?'

'Well, she pretended not to be, but of course I

155

always reckoned that she was terribly jealous of her. What that girl didn't have wasn't worth talking about. She'd had a governess, then went to a private school, had her own pony, all of that sort of thing. Lindy used to call her a stuck-up little cow behind her back, although she was always nice to her face. There wasn't much difference in their ages either – only a couple of years, and Lindy used to reckon that her father thought more of Penelope than he did of her. Well, it stands to reason, doesn't it? He'd watched Penelope growing up; she was his little darling. Then Lindy got it into her head that Mam and Dad preferred me to her as well. There were more and more arguments at home, and her father's influence just made matters worse. He wanted to send her to finishing school in France, but our mam wouldn't allow it. Putting ideas like that into a girl's mind! He bought her a car for her nineteenth birthday – a car, if you don't mind – and when she drove it into summat and smashed it up, he bought her another one. Guilty conscience, you see? Paid her no mind as a child, so he was spoiling her to make up for it. Eventually he set her up in her own little house. A young girl of that age! A little cottagey place on the edge of Bowness, it was, with a housekeeper and a cook. Mam and Dad tried to reason with him but they got nowhere, and I suppose it was a difficult time for him too. His wife had been took bad, you see, and they couldn't do nothing for her. It was obvious to everyone that she was dying.' Christina Harper paused for breath.

'And after his second wife died,' Fran prompted, 'did Linda go and live with him then?'

'No, she never did. Lucky for her, as things turned out . . . Anyway, she was coming up for twenty-one, and that's when she met Eddie Traynor.' Mrs Harper paused again to sip her tea, while Fran resisted the urge to beg her to go on.

'The funny thing is, Eddie Traynor seemed like a real good 'un at the time. He started seeing our Lindy regularly and there's no doubt that she changed for the better and calmed down a lot.'

Because she must have thought that she'd finally found someone who really loved her, Fran thought, and it turned her life around.

'They saw each other for the best part of six months, and our mam was expecting any day for Lindy to come bouncing in, showing off an engagement ring.'

'But she never did?'

'No, because Eddie Traynor threw her over for Penelope. We expected Lindy to be distraught, but I think she was so shocked that she just sort of . . . I don't know how to explain it. She closed down somehow . . . the fire went out of her and she went . . . cold. She never talked about it much, but I remember Lindy once saying that Penelope had always had what should have been hers, right down to the man she would have married.'

'So Eddie was going to marry Penelope?'

'He wanted to but her father wanted them to wait. Eddie had just qualified as an engineer. He wasn't out of the top drawer by any means and he hadn't a penny to his name, but he had a bright future, so folk said. The trouble was Penelope

157

stood to inherit an absolute pile and a rich daddy is always going to be on the lookout for chancers, isn't he? So he persuaded the pair of them to wait a while. Until Penelope was of age, at least. You can see his reasoning, right enough. I mean, young Eddie had already broken the heart of one daughter. Maybe, deep down, even Penelope thought it might be as well not to rush into anything. Anyway, it was all fixed up that Penelope would go off to Europe for the best part of a year to study paintings or something of that sort, and her father said that if they still felt the same when she came back, he wouldn't stand in their way – which in their world meant a nice cash settlement and probably a house thrown in.'

'So what happened? Did they get married in the end?'

Mrs Harper regarded Fran with the disbelief of a lecturer who has just been confronted with a particularly stupid question from a student at the back who hasn't been paying attention.

'No. Because the night before Penelope was supposed to leave for Europe, she and her father were murdered and the house set on fire.'

'Oh my God.' The words escaped from Fran's lips in a horrified whisper.

'You can imagine what it did to Lindy. She just went in on herself all the more. While they was waiting for the trial and everything, she came over all strange, reckoned the press were watching her every move. She even started to wear a wig because she said people were looking at her in the street and she didn't want to be recognized. She moved to a bigger house, up a long driveway, and employed a man to guard the gates – well, of course, she could afford to. She got everything, you see: sole survivor. Then she met David Dexter. Whirlwind romance wasn't in it. They were married within three months. I don't know what the attraction was for her, but if you ask me, he'd got his eye on her bank balance. He came from Carlisle way and that's where they bought a house. It was when she got married that she changed her name.'

'To Dexter.'

'To Linda. I don't think she ever did anything formal about it, but she let everyone know that from now on it would be Linda. It never made any difference to us because we'd always called her Lindy anyway.'

'What was her name before?'

'Belinda. My Mam liked fancy names. Belinda, Linda, not much difference, is there, but she said she'd never liked it. So Linda it was from then onwards, in public at least. So once she was married, she had different first and second names. I think she reckoned that would make it harder for people to find her.'

'And the marriage didn't last?'

'They parted after about a year. She made quite a bit of money over to him. I said to her there was no need. They hadn't been together for two minutes and he'd obviously married her for her money, but she just laughed and said it was cheap at the price. Glad to be rid of him, I suppose.'

'And wasn't there ever anyone else after him?'

'Not that I ever heard about. She just used to fool about collecting those children's books and going off to see where authors used to live and all that stuff. I could never see the point myself, though I daresay all those trips she took were very nice. She didn't stint herself, our Lindy – always had whatever she wanted. But if I'm honest, I think my George had the right idea about it. He always said she was soft in the head. Hiding herself away, spending her life on kiddies' books instead of having a proper life like other people. I think it was the shock that changed her. Eddie Traynor – that was the turning point.'

'And the murder of her father and sister – that must have been a massive shock to her.'

'Well, it was all wrapped up together, wasn't it? Didn't I say? That *was* Eddie Traynor. He was the one what murdered Penelope and her father. I'm surprised you didn't know nothing about it. It was all over the newspapers at the time – the Halfpenny Landing murders, they called it.'

Nineteen

As she rode home in the bus, Fran found that she was able to dredge up hazy memories of the Halfpenny Landing murders. That was what the papers had christened the case, after the name of the house in which the crime had taken place. An ironic sort of name, she thought, considering the value of the lakeside pleasure palace in question. She knew now where she had seen the house in the framed photograph that she had appropriated from Linda's sitting room. It wasn't associated with a famous author but with a notorious local murder: a case she had vaguely followed via the newspapers almost fifteen years ago, when she had still been at school.

Here at least lay the solution to the source of Linda Dexter's wealth and the reason why her sister's circumstances had been so different to her own . . . but while resolving one set of questions, it posed a variety of others. As soon as she got home, Fran sat down at her big old desk in the parlour and wrote down as much of her conversation with Mrs Harper as she could remember, then she read it through, making additions and corrections as she went. As she was doing so she heard the faint slam of a car door through the open window and, having raised her head enough to see out of the window, she uttered a word which her mother would have disapproved of. There was a blue Austin 7 parked at the gate and Stephen Latchford had just got out of it. She abandoned her notebook and pencil on the desk and fled into the kitchen. What luck that Ada had taken an extra half day to visit a sick relative, which meant that there was no one to answer the front door and no need for explanations either.

A moment later there was a brisk *rat-tat-tat* on the front door knocker. If she ignored it, he would have to go away. She waited in the kitchen and, sure enough, the sound came again. Her heart had begun to hammer in her chest. Stupid, she thought, because he will have to give up and go away in a minute. In the meantime, she would cut herself a sandwich for lunch. She had placed the loaf on the breadboard, positioned the bread knife carefully and began to saw through the crust. It didn't seem to matter how hard she tried to keep it straight, the knife always went off at an angle. What a good thing that Ada wasn't there to see her making such a hash of it. It was positively embarrassing that she could not manage the simplest of tasks that good servants took in their stride. She was just contemplating a slice which was twice as thick at the top than at the bottom when she was startled by the sound of the kitchen door opening behind her. She gave a shriek, dropping the knife with a clatter, as she turned to see Stephen Latchford stepping into the kitchen.

'Did I startle you?' He smiled as he closed the door behind him. 'I guessed that you hadn't heard the door, so I came round the back.'

The shock of finding him in the kitchen with her, coupled with the sheer cheek of it, rendered her temporarily speechless.

'I knocked twice,' he said. There was an element of reproof in his tone – as if it were she rather than he who was in the wrong.

'I must have been in the garden.' Why on earth was she lying? Why didn't she just tell him to get out? 'I've only just come back inside. You can't hear the door out there.'

'Just as well I thought to come round the back then. You need to get a nice loud bell installed.'

She tried to pull herself together. How did he manage to engineer situations in such a way that she would appear rude to complain of his unorthodox behaviour? 'You have caught me at rather a bad time again, I'm afraid. I'm just about to have my lunch. A friend is expecting me at two o'clock.' It sounded so transparent. She didn't think that he believed in her two o'clock appointment for a moment.

'Oh, do go ahead. Don't mind me. I haven't had anything myself, as it happens.'

She ignored the obvious hint. 'Did you want anything in particular?'

'I have brought something to show you. You remember, I called round with it before but you were having a bath.'

Something in the way he was looking at her made her feel deeply uncomfortable. She felt sick. Worse, she felt fearful, not properly in control of the situation. People did not simply walk into one another's houses upon the slightest of acquaintances. 'Yes, of course, I remember.

163

But this really isn't a very good time either. It would be much better if you would telephone and make arrangements in advance of calling in.'

'One doesn't usually telephone ahead – after all, most people are not connected to the telephone service. If it's inconvenient, I daresay I can come back another time.' The overly chummy tone had been replaced by irritation. He sounded like a haughty maiden aunt managing to retain her temper in the face of a considerable affront. If his presence had not been so upsetting, it might actually have been funny.

'No, of course,' said Fran quickly. 'I'm sure I can spare a few minutes if it's something that won't take too long.' If she looked at whatever this wretched thing was, then there would be no need for him to call again.

After a small show of token reluctance, he withdrew a single printed sheet from the cardboard wallet that he had been carrying under his arm. It was yet another magazine article pertaining to Robert Barnaby's alleged visit to some rather grand local house. It only took a moment to read it, but as she did so, Fran noted that the paper felt old between her fingers. The possibility loomed in her mind that he had a whole stock of these dreary cuttings which he could drip feed to her one after another to justify repeat visits.

'That's most interesting,' she said when she had finished reading. It wasn't all that interesting, but what could she say? 'Thank you for showing it to me.'

He ignored the note of dismissal in her voice

164

and continued to stand in the kitchen. It suddenly seemed like a very small space for two people.

Mrs Snegglington chose that moment to appear. She walked straight up to the visitor and began to rub herself flirtatiously against his trousers. Fran felt like strangling her. The one person she would have liked the cat to completely ignore.

'What a lovely cat. What's she called?'

Fran hesitated. She didn't want him to know that the cat was named after the housekeeper in the Magic Chair stories. Apart from anything else, it made her look childish. 'It's Tabby,' she said.

'Not very imaginative.' He tickled the cat behind the ears. 'Who's a lovely girl, then.'

Mrs Snegglington jumped on to the kitchen table, looking pleased with herself.

'Get down . . . Tabby. You know you're not allowed up there.'

Mrs Snegglington gave Fran an insolent who-the-hell-is-Tabby look, before strolling imperiously in the direction of the sink.

'Get *down*.' Fran got hold of the animal and plonked her unceremoniously on the floor. The cat headed straight back to her new friend, where she was rewarded with more petting and compliments.

'Don't let me stop you getting on with your lunch.' Stephen-with-a-ph had reverted to the role of an old friend, as if he was completely accustomed to hanging around in her kitchen.

Fran took a deep breath. 'Mr Latchford, the truth is that I don't really like people watching me eat. I – I've got a bit of a thing about it.'

'Oh dear, how awful for you.' The sarcasm was unmistakable. 'That must make things very difficult for you, when you eat at conferences and so on.'

'Yes,' said Fran. 'Very.'

'Well, in that case, I'll be off. I mustn't delay your lunch when your friend's expecting you at two.'

'And . . . and the other thing is that I'd prefer it if you didn't let yourself into the house like that again.' She ignored his hostile expression. 'I'm not at all comfortable with that. It's . . . it's not the way I was brought up.' Heavens, how pompous that sounded. Well, she did not care. 'If you plan to call on me again, it would really be better if you telephoned first, to make sure that it's a convenient time.'

Twenty

'So you think he knew that it was just an excuse to get rid of him?' asked Mo.

There was something steadying in hearing Mo's voice on the line. Fran could picture her in her chintzy drawing room, reaching for a cocktail glass. 'Oh, absolutely. It was totally obvious that I was lying. I've told him that the cat's name is Tabby, by the way. Oh, yes – and that I've got a thing about eating in public.'

'Fran, darling, have you been drinking?'

'I only wish I had.'

'So how many times has this chap been round?'

'Three, but he only got in twice, because the other time I wouldn't let him in.'

'Good plan. You shouldn't let him in at all.'

'I tried not to, but he let himself in. He came round to the back door and just walked straight into my kitchen.'

'Goodness, I don't like the sound of that,' said Mo. 'You're going to have to make a stand.'

'I tried. He didn't like it, but he must have got the message by now. Anyway, the thing I really wanted to talk to you about is . . . do you remember the Halfpenny Landing murders?'

'Vaguely. Isn't that the case up at Windermere before the war, where someone broke in at night, murdered the couple who lived there then tried to cover it up by setting fire to the place?'

167

'That's the one. It wasn't a couple, as such. It was a father and daughter.'

'Right-ho – so what about it?'

'Well,' said Fran, 'you're never going to believe this . . .'

After spending almost half an hour on the telephone with Mo, Fran was about to try Tom's number when she had second thoughts. Long-distance calls were terribly expensive, but that wasn't really the reason. Maybe it would be better to drop him a line in the post . . . not that there was any reason why she shouldn't speak to his wife, if she happened to answer. It was not as if there was anything improper going on. She wondered whether Tom had discussed the death of Linda Dexter with his wife and, if so, what she thought about it all. She decided that perhaps a note would be the best thing and sat at the big desk to compose it. There was a lot to put in a letter, and eventually she wrote: *Dear Tom, I had a very interesting conversation with LD's sister today. Much to tell you. Please telephone me when convenient.*

Fran

She pictured him ripping open the envelope the next day. She could see the lush dark hair and those clever brown eyes. He had a way of narrowing his eyes when he was reading something. He would be wearing his habitual flannels and that greenish brown necktie . . . The picture became hazy after that. Did he have a study, with a proper desk, or did he open his post at the breakfast table sitting opposite Mrs Dod? The vision faded. She had never visited his home and, in all probability, she never would.

Tom rang her the following evening at nine o'clock.

'It's quite a long story,' she said. 'Are you all right for time?'

'I've got the rest of the night, if you need it.' His voice always seemed a shade deeper on the phone, like someone speaking low, confiding something directly into her ear. He must hold the receiver very close to his mouth, she thought. Perhaps so that his wife couldn't hear him.

'Good. If you hear any paper rustling, it's because I'm looking at my notes. I wrote it all down when I got home so that I wouldn't forget anything.'

'Well done. I'm all ears. I've got *my* notebook and a pen on one side and a glass of port on the other.'

Fran laughed. 'And I've got a G and T.' She began by trying to tell him Linda's life story in chronological order, checking backwards and forwards in her notes to make sure she got everything right. He mostly listened in silence, only occasionally interrupting with a question or a minor exclamation of surprise.

'Well,' he said at last, 'that certainly opens up a whole new can of worms. Look, I've got an empty glass. Why don't I fill it up again and ring you back in say . . . four minutes. Is that long enough? How far do you have to walk to get a refill?'

'Only about six feet. I'm sitting right next to the kitchen door but I haven't finished my first glass yet.'

'Oh, come on, you've got to keep up. Anyway, I've got two flights of stairs to cover, so you've got extra time to empty your glass.'

'Two flights of stairs? Where on earth do you live – Buckingham Palace?'

'A very tall, thin townhouse, and my den's almost in the attic. Come on. Back on the line with refills in four minutes.'

His bossiness made her laugh. Some people were stilted on the phone, but talking with Tom was easy. Almost as good as having him there in the room . . . something else which was never going to happen.

'I've got something else to tell you,' she said when she was back in position on the sofa with her legs folded under her, feeling very slightly unsteady from gulping down her previous gin and tonic at speed.

'I've got something to tell you too – something I was going to tell you before, that Marcus Dryden told me when I was at Furnival Towers last week. Don't let me forget this time.'

'Very well then, but me first.' She told him about Stephen Latchford's three visits to the cottage and his behaviour on the way back from the conference, when he had appeared at the station and tried to persuade her not to take the train. 'And until recently,' she concluded, 'he lived very near to Linda Dexter.'

Tom didn't seem inclined to take it seriously. 'I think you've got to remember that he's new to your area. He's a lonely sort of chap, I'd say, a bit of a latcher-on and rather lacking in normal social skills. Hence this idea that you can come

170

into someone's house round the back way. As you well know, there are an awful lot of people who never use their front doors except for weddings and funerals, and I've always had a feeling that the chap's not exactly out of the top drawer. Combine that with the fact that he probably doesn't know many people round the neighbourhood yet, and add in that you're an attractive woman, apparently unattached, who shares his interest in Robert Barnaby. If you don't make him particularly welcome, he'll soon get the message. As for what happened on the way back from the conference, I might have done the same myself to save someone a roundabout railway journey if I realized that we were both going the same way. You would probably have forgotten all about it by now if he hadn't started dropping in.'

'He makes me feel uncomfortable.' Why didn't Tom understand? Mo did. Because Mo's a woman and Tom isn't, said a voice in her head.

'I expect you've done enough to put him off by now. He probably won't come round again,' Tom said.

'I hope not. Anyway, as far as I'm concerned, he's a suspect. He was at the hotel that night, in a room just across the corridor from Linda.'

'All right then.' Tom's tone had 'humour her' stamped all over it. 'I'll add him to my list. It's getting longer all the time. You remember when I said that Marcus Dryden let slip something interesting when I stayed at the Furnival Towers Hotel, the night before the committee meeting?'

'Yes?'

'Well, it seems that on the Friday evening of the

conference, Sarah Ingoldsby was in the hall when Linda Dexter first arrived. Marcus Dryden was in attendance, doing his mine host bit while people were checking in; and while he was welcoming someone else, he overheard Sarah Ingoldsby say to Linda, "I've got a bone to pick with you." Apparently the two of them started having some sort of bust-up, right there in the lobby.'

'What about?'

'Marcus didn't know.'

'What made him tell you about this?'

'I don't think he meant to. I got him talking in the bar and I said something about Linda not seeming to have an enemy in the world and always getting along with people, and he said yes, she'd always seemed on good terms with everyone, except for this one incident.'

'Did he seem to think it was important?'

'No. I don't think he attached any significance to it at all. Well, who would? Sarah Ingoldsby may be Little Miss Snappy but she's also a complete ninny. You can't honestly imagine her killing somebody and then setting fire to their car.'

'True. But she has to go on your list of suspects, just the same.'

'The way things are going, I'll have to start a second page. We've got Hugh Allonby, Sarah Ingoldsby . . .'

'The other thing is that although you called her Little Miss Snappy a minute ago, she's actually a Mrs. There's definitely a Mr Ingoldsby, because I remember her mentioning him once, ages ago.'

'And there's also a Mrs Allonby.'

'Precisely. And as we said before, it's most

unlikely that Mr Ingoldsby or Mrs Allonby would be too pleased to hear about the Sarah–Hugh connection. The society provides the perfect cover for their affair. He can say he has to be involved because of his books and she probably tells her husband she has to attend things on behalf of the museum, because of the Barnaby archive. Suppose Linda threatened to spill the beans?'

'Blackmail!' Tom said, as if he was relishing the thought of a particularly luscious slab of chocolate cake.

'It's a bit far-fetched, I know . . .'

'Maybe, maybe not. We can't necessarily assume that Mr Ingoldsby and Mrs Allonby are in complete ignorance. Some couples arrive at . . . unusual arrangements.'

Fran was trying to decide if he was laying particular emphasis on this phrase when he abruptly turned to another topic. 'You were the one who suggested that Linda present a paper to the conference. You've never told me how you came to know about her research in the first place.'

'There's nothing much to tell. We were having coffee together at that meeting in Durham – the one where we had that visiting Professor of Literature from Australia.'

'I couldn't make it to that meeting.'

'That's right, you weren't there. Linda and I happened to be the only ones left sitting at a table and we were just making conversation. She said that she'd been doing some really interesting research about Robert Barnaby and his sources. She didn't tell me anything specific, but because we're always on the lookout for new people to take part in the conference programme, I asked her if she thought there was enough material for a lecture, and when she said there was, I asked if she would mind me putting her name forward.'

'You're sure that she didn't give you any inkling of what it was about?'

'Definitely not.'

'And no one overheard you?'

'There wasn't anything to overhear. Why?'

'Because it has occurred to me that in order to want to stop Linda from giving her talk, you'd have to have a pretty good idea of what she was going to say. Anyway, let's get back to that list of suspects.'

She heard the rustle of a piece of paper at the other end of the line and smiled to herself. He really had got an actual list.

'Right then,' he said. 'Back to the suspects. There's the sister, Christina Harper.'

'Seriously?'

'Seriously. She gets the money. Money's always the number-one motive. In fact, there's a funny sort of pattern. One stepsister is getting most of the benefit of the money until she's murdered and someone sets fire to the evidence. Then her stepsister inherits – she gets killed and there's another fire, at which point stepsister number three gets her hands on the loot.'

'There was the better part of fifteen years in between. If Christina Harper did both murders, she's been prepared to play a jolly long waiting game. Anyway, she was only a child when the Halfpenny Landing murders took place.'

'Just thinking aloud,' said Tom. 'Then there's the ex-husband, David Dexter. We don't know anything much about him.'

'Except that he's dead.'

'We've only got Christina Harper's word for that at the moment. We ought to try and check.'

'There's an awful lot of things to check,' Fran said. 'Starting with Linda's research. Then there's the original murders, back before the war. There could be a connection to that which puts the Barnaby Society right out of it.'

'Where would be the best place to look for the lowdown on that?' asked Tom.

'The local papers would have been full of it. I think they've got back numbers of the *Westmorland & District Messenger* in Kendal Library.'

'I could come up and help you look at them,' Tom said. 'I can probably get up towards the end of next week.'

'That would be good.' For a moment, she thought of asking him if he needed a bed for the night but immediately decided against it. One did not offer unaccompanied male friends overnight accommodation and such an invitation could easily be misconstrued. She burned with embarrassment now whenever she thought of how she might have invited him up to her room at the Furnival Towers, and how dreadfully embarrassing it would have been if he had only made that remark about needing an invitation as a joke. I only like him as a friend, Fran told herself. He has a wife called Veronica and a son called William, named for the brother who was lost in the war. She had been the victim of an affair herself, and she knew that if

175

she went down that road everyone would get hurt in the end, and herself probably most of all.

'In the meantime, as I don't live far from the Vester House Museum, I could pop in and have a gander at their archives too.' Tom's voice cut in on her thoughts. 'It shouldn't take too long to confirm Linda's findings, as we have all the references and know what to look at. It isn't like starting from scratch.'

When Tom finally rang off the cottage felt suddenly empty, like a house when the last of the partygoers have departed and the host is left to clear everything away. Fran took her notebook back into the parlour and reached into the pigeonhole where she had put her Barnaby Society committee papers. In the course of the conversation, Tom had mentioned something about the next committee meeting and she wanted to double-check the date. The notes and doodles on the back of the last agenda caught her eye. *Why did Jennifer Rumsey resign?* She wasn't sure why the question bothered her, but it did. She glanced at the clock and saw that it was almost ten. Was it too late to ring Jean Robertson? Miss Robertson probably fell into that category of older woman to whom a telephone call after nine p.m. would only be made to flag up an ailing relative or some similar emergency. Better to ring tomorrow evening. She would put it on her list of things to do. If she wasn't careful, she would soon have to make a list of her lists.

Twenty-One

There was a note of surprise in Jean Robertson's voice when she discovered that it was Fran on the line. Their acquaintance had never stretched beyond the normal run of Barnaby Society activities, and this made it hard for Fran to think of a convincing excuse for telephoning. After giving the matter some thought, she had decided to tell Miss Robertson that she had been thinking about the reaction at the committee meeting, when she had suggested that they approach Jennifer Rumsey about resuming the membership secretary's job if John James stepped down. 'There was obviously some reason why we shouldn't,' Fran said. 'And I wondered if it was something I ought to know about as a member of the executive committee. After all, it's far better to be forewarned than to put one's foot in it.'

There was a brief silence, and when the older woman spoke again, her initially friendly tone had become cagey. 'I don't think there's anything you need to know, as such. It was recorded in the minutes that Miss Rumsey resigned because she had a lot on her hands, helping to care for a sick relative.'

'But that wasn't the real reason,' Fran prompted.

'Miss Rumsey had a difference of opinion with the other members of the committee. It was a sensitive matter and the committee voted not to discuss it beyond the four walls of the meeting room. It's never a good thing to start the rumour mill grinding or make the membership aware of tensions – washing dirty linen in public is always best avoided, don't you think? Miss Rumsey said she would not be coming to society meetings of any sort in the future, so the problems she had been experiencing with her mother's health seemed as good a reason to give as any.'

'Can I ask what this argument was about?'

'It was a confidential matter. It wasn't recorded in the minutes.'

'So, no good going back to Jennifer Rumsey for help if Mr James stands down,' Fran said as brightly as she could.

'No.' Miss Robertson was obviously not going to be drawn.

Fran tried Tom's home number next. If his wife answered, so what? It wasn't as if there was anything she shouldn't know about, but it was Tom himself who picked up the phone. She told him about her call to Jean Robertson, finishing with, 'I don't know why this Jennifer Rumsey thing is bothering me, but it is.'

'Why don't you ring Jennifer Rumsey and ask her direct?'

'I can't do that.'

'Why not? You've spoken to her in the past at meetings. Tell you what, why don't you say that you've heard that John James is about to step down as membership secretary and you were just wondering if her situation had improved, and if so, whether she might be willing to consider taking the job on again.'

'But that's lying!'

Tom ignored the protest. 'She isn't going to say yes because it's obvious that she's completely fallen out with the society over something. The thing is that she doesn't know you've already been warned off, so she will just think that you don't know the score. She might even come right out and tell you what happened.'

'Suppose someone on the committee finds out that I've rung her?'

'They won't. Why would she tell any of them? It doesn't exactly sound as though she's on friendly terms with them.'

'It's a funny old business,' said Fran. 'Jean Robertson sounded really uncomfortable. Of course, it's probably nothing to do with Linda Dexter . . .'

'Better to double-check, all the same. Her telephone number will still be in the membership list.'

'I'll think about it.'

Fran didn't have long to think. She scarcely had time to put the phone down before Mo rang wanting to know if she'd like to make up a four for tennis on Saturday afternoon.

'Who with?' asked Fran suspiciously.

'At the moment, there's only myself and Caro Lambert, who plays on the Ladies' B team. I was going to ask Mina Hendry to be the fourth.'

'Oh, go on then, count me in.'

'Jolly good. How's the sleuthing going on? What does Lord Peter make of all the latest clues?'

'Lord Peter? What are you talking about, Mo?'

'Lord Peter Wimsey, of course.'

'Ah, I assume you mean Tom – who doesn't have a Daimler, unfortunately. He thinks that I should ring Jennifer Rumsey.'

'Is that the sister?'

'No, sorry, that's the ex-membership secretary of the Robert Barnaby Society.'

'What on earth has the ex-membership secretary of the Robert Barnaby Society got to do with it?'

'I don't know.'

'You're not losing the plot, are you, Fran – telling people your cat is called Tiddles again and all that sort of thing?'

'I'm not sure that I ever found out what the plot was in the first place. That's the whole problem.' She decided not to confide in Mo that earlier in the day, while listening to the news on the wireless, she had indeed wondered whether being so fascinated with the obscure manoeuvrings within the Robert Barnaby Society while the rest of the country was still worrying about who would be prime minister might not indeed be indicative of someone who had completely lost their marbles.

She hadn't been off the telephone for more than two or three minutes when it rang again. Now what? She picked it up rather impatiently. 'Hello.'

'Hello, Mrs Black, it's Stephen Latchford. My goodness but you've been on the telephone a lot this evening. I've been trying to get through for about half an hour.'

'Yes,' she said. 'My telephone's been very busy this evening. What can I do for you?'

180

'It isn't bath night, then?'

For a moment, Fran didn't know how to answer. The question was intrusive, inappropriate. Why did he constantly overstep the boundaries of good manners and normal behaviour? 'No,' she said abruptly. 'Was there something specific that you wanted?'

'You remember how you said I should call first, to check whether you're at home?'

'Yes.'

'Well, that's what I'm doing. I'm calling to see if it's a convenient time – and if it is, I'm in the public telephone box out on the main road. In fact, I can see your chimney across the fields. I can be there in two minutes, in the car.'

She sank on to the sofa as if poleaxed. How long had he been hanging about out there? Had he actually been spying on her? There was still plenty of light left in the sky, so the curtains weren't drawn, and she couldn't remember when she had last looked out of the window.

'Well? May I?'

'What do you mean?'

'May I come in? I have something to show you.'

'No. No, you can't. Please go away.'

'I won't take up much of your time. And I did call ahead. It isn't as if it's bath night . . .'

'Go away!' she yelled. 'Just go away.'

She plunged down the bracket, which cut off the call, and dropped the receiver on the sofa before racing across to double-check that the front door was locked. Then she dragged the sitting-room curtains across the window, plunging

181

the room into premature darkness, before charging into the kitchen to check the back door and pull down the blinds. After that she took the stairs two at a time before entering the bathroom. She knew that the window was open at the top and the frosted glass would hide her. She kicked off her shoes, climbed into the bath in her stocking feet and adopted a half-crouching position in order to bring her eyes on a level with the opening. Was his car still sitting out there on the main road or not? The hedges were in the way and she couldn't tell.

The police. That was it, she would ring the police. She ran back down the stairs then paused in the doorway, conscious that she was shaking. How could she justify calling the police? What on earth could she say? That a man had parked out on the main road and called her on the telephone? That she had declined to invite him in and asked him to go away – which presumably he had done. There was no law against any of that.

Twenty-Two

Fran and Tom met by prior arrangement on the front steps of the Carnegie Library in Kendal on Thursday morning. The battery had gone flat in the wireless at the cottage, but she had learned by reading a morning paper over the shoulder of a fellow passenger on the bus that Ramsey McDonald was to form the new government, propped up by Lloyd George and the Liberals. She was still pondering what this might presage for the country when, from her slightly elevated position, she spotted Tom approaching from the direction of the town hall. He had a distinctive loping gait, and in any case stood out from the crowd, being head and shoulders taller than almost every other shopper.

As he greeted her and his brown eyes locked on to hers, a doubt crept into his smile. 'Are you all right?' he asked.

'Fine. I just didn't sleep very well.'

In fact, she had not slept very well for the past four nights. She kept waking from uneasy dreams, then having to restrain herself from slipping out of bed to peer through the window and check if there was a car parked outside in the lane. She had heard nothing more from Stephen Latchford, but that had not prevented him from becoming a constant presence in her thoughts.

183

One of the librarians conducted them to a quiet room on the upper floor of the library in order to examine the old newspapers. It appeared that demand for this kind of material was not high, so they had the place virtually to themselves and chose a table under the window, where it was possible to place two chairs side by side. Tom tossed the folder he had brought on to the table, removed his jacket and draped it over the back of the right-hand chair. He appeared almost childishly eager to get started.

'I went to the Vester House Museum yesterday.' He spoke in a loud stage whisper, which instantly earned a glare from a fat woman with greying hair dragged into a bun, who was hunched over a hefty ledger at a corner table. The only other occupant of the room, a middle-aged man who was poring over a reference book, also looked up and stared.

I'll tell you later, Tom mouthed – overdoing it so much that Fran had to stifle a giggle.

The newspapers for 1914 had been bound into four huge ledgers, and as they did not have a precise date for the murder they decided to split the year between them, with Fran taking the January to March volume, while Tom started on July to September. The fifteen-year-old papers already felt flimsy with age and needed to be turned with considerable care. After a couple of false starts, they both found that it was easier to work standing up, and Fran soon discovered too that the distractions of old, half-remembered news items slowed her down considerably. She was still in January when Tom's hand closed on

184

her upper arm, and she looked up to find him gesturing at the headline *Terrible Fire Claims Two Lives at Windermere*. The momentary presence of the hand was distracting, and in her imagination she continued to feel its lingering warmth long after it had been removed.

The initial story was brief and vague, the copy rushed in to meet a deadline, no doubt, but by the following day's edition the initial supposition of an accident had been replaced by speculation that there had been foul play and, by the third day, the headline was 'murder'. The inquest had been opened and adjourned after evidence of identity had been given, and by day five the paper had announced beneath yet more banner headlines that a local man, Edwin Edgar Traynor, had been arrested, charged with the double murder, appeared before local magistrates and been refused bail.

As they leaned over the table, reading the columns word by word, Fran tried not to be distracted by the way Tom's upper arm rested lightly against hers, his shirt sleeve brushing against her skin. For the first week or so after the fire, each edition of the *Westmorland & District Messenger* had been virtually devoted to the murders. The paper ran very few pictures, but one front page was dominated by a photograph of the burnt-out house. It was scarcely more than a shell, Fran thought sadly, like a cruel parody of the framed photograph which she had rescued from Linda Dexter's house. Windows gaped like sightless eyes in the face of a well-loved friend. The roof was gone and the interior looked like the end of a hideous game of Jack Straws, just a collapsed mass of blackened beams where there had once been an ordered structure of walls and ceilings. On an inside page, there were pictures of Andrew Chappell and his daughter, Penelope, both carefully posed studio shots, with him dressed in a morning suit, top hat in hand, while she had pearls at her neck and her hair piled up with what looked like real flowers woven into it – incongruous images when juxtaposed against the grim wreckage of their erstwhile home. The accompanying text had been provided by a local reporter, whose favourite adjectives appeared to have been *terrible, shocking* and *mysterious.*

In spite of the hyperbole, it was easy enough to piece the story together. Halfpenny Landing stood in extensive grounds on Windermere's eastern shore, at some distance from its nearest neighbours and protected from the road by mature laurel hedges which rendered the house invisible from the road. None of the servants lived in the main house, though the chauffeur had a room above what had originally been the stable block and was now the garages, while the cook and her husband inhabited the tiny lodge which sat just inside the front gates. On the night of the fire, none of these individuals had seen or heard anything amiss, and indeed all three remained soundly asleep until a passing motorist both saw and smelt the blaze at around half past two in the morning, and hammered on the front door of the lodge cottage to rouse the occupants. As a result, the fire had taken a good hold before the alarm was raised.

While the reporter on the *Westmorland &
District Messenger* may have been stylistically
suspect, he evidently had good local contacts,
writing within seventy-two hours of the tragedy
that according to a 'police source', the post-
mortems had revealed no signs of smoke inhalation,
which meant that both Andrew Chappell and his
daughter must have been dead by the time the fire
began, having presumably been murdered while
they slept. The paper had even managed to get
hold of the information that Mr Chappell had
been in the habit of taking pills to help him sleep.

It was the biggest thing to happen on the
Westmorland & District Messenger's patch in
years and they had milked the story for all it was
worth. The details of the incident itself were
almost lost among the columns devoted to local
reaction. Residents who had never even met the
Chappells queued up to say what a tragedy it was
– how mysterious and shocking. There was even
speculation about whether the double murder
would deter tourists from visiting the area (in
fact, it had the opposite effect, with ghouls
blocking the Bowness to Newby Bridge road in
their enthusiasm to get a closer look at the scene
of the crime).

'We'd better copy all this down,' said Tom. He
didn't need to raise his voice. They were standing
so close together that she felt his breath stirring
her hair. One millimetre to the right and her
shoulder would be resting against his.

'There's nothing at all here about Linda,' she
whispered.

'We need to keep following the story.'

187

Though it was time-consuming, they went back to the beginning and, by unspoken agreement, Fran began to neatly transcribe all the important details. Only when they had got further into the following week, by which time Edwin Traynor had been arrested and charged with the 'Halfpenny Landing Murders', as the paper was now calling the case, did the first reference to Linda appear.

'Here she is,' Fran whispered. '*Andrew Chappell leaves one surviving daughter, Miss Belinda Chappell, who is staying at an undisclosed location and is said to be too upset to talk to representatives of the press . . . It is understood that Miss Belinda Chappell had previously enjoyed a close friendship with the accused man, Edwin Traynor, a well-known local athlete who took two medals at last year's Grasmere Sports . . .*'

Though the *Westmorland & District Messenger* did its best to keep the story alive for as long as possible, as the days passed the murder became old news. Apart from reporting that a guard had been mounted over the wreckage of the '*burned-out mansion on the shores of Windermere*' in order to deter sightseers and souvenir hunters, they could find little to add except for some grumbling on the part of local businessmen about visitors going into the shops and hotels around Bowness, solely to ask for directions to the murder site.

'We need to find the trial,' Fran hissed. 'There will be a lot more about what actually happened when people start giving evidence.'

'Bound over to the December assizes, it said.'

Tom's deep voice emerged in a loud stage whisper and earned them an irritable, 'Shush.' After making a face at Fran, he turned to the volume which covered the final quarter of the year and began to turn over the pages in large chunks, pausing every so often to check the dates. When he reached the editions covering December they pored over page after page in vain. There were some references to the various cases heard that session at Appleby but nothing at all about the Halfpenny Landing murders.

Fran shook her head. 'We must have missed it.'

Tom obediently returned to the edition which covered the arrival of the judges and the opening of the assizes, this time reading carefully through the list of cases which were scheduled to be heard. 'Not here,' he murmured. 'It must have been moved to another district.'

'No!' Fran made a small excited noise, which she instantly stifled, while pointing to a tiny item at the bottom of the page. 'Now I know why I remembered the Halfpenny Landing case.'

Tom swiftly took in the words shadowed by her pointing finger. 'Crikey,' he said. The exclamation was greeted by the sound of a book being thumped down on a desk behind them, coupled with an irritated, 'Harrumph!'

'Let's have a break,' she whispered. 'I know somewhere nearby where we can get a cup of tea.'

They collected their things together in silence, trying not to incur any further overt disapproval from their fellow researchers. It was a relief to get outside and be able to talk in normal voices.

Fran led him to her favourite tea shop on the corner of Elephant Yard, where they found a corner table and ordered a pot of tea.

'I can't believe I had forgotten all this until now,' she said. 'The whole thing made such a huge stir at the time. We only lived about thirty miles away and of course everyone was beside themselves at the idea of there being a dangerous murderer on the run. Surely you remember it now?'

'I can't say that I do. Don't forget that I was still away at school in 1914. We didn't often get to read the newspapers, and when we did it was mostly for the cricket scores.'

'Not in December.'

'Of course not in December. The chap didn't escape in December, though, did he?'

'No, he didn't. It was while they were taking him to and fro from the prison for some reason or another, so far as I can recall. Probably to attend the police court, or the inquest, or something.'

'I say, though, it's pretty rare for anyone to escape, and specially someone who's up for murder.'

'You don't say. But the point is that after his "daring escape", as the papers put it, I don't think he was ever caught. And look here.' Her voice rose excitedly. 'I've just spotted the very person who would know.' She began tapping energetically on the window, then leapt up and hurried across to open the door, lest her quarry should escape.

Tom watched from their table and then

stood up politely as Fran, having brooked no refusal, ushered Christina Harper over to join them. 'No, no,' she was saying. 'I insist. We can easily get the waitress to bring us a fresh pot. I don't know if you remember Mr Dod, who came to your sister's funeral with me?'

After pleasantries had been exchanged, another cup and saucer procured and the tea pronounced perfectly fine following the addition of some hot water, Fran said, 'I know it sounds awfully morbid, but I'm afraid I was just telling Mr Dod about how Linda's father and sister were the people murdered at Halfpenny Landing. Is it true that the case against the man who was suspected never came to court?'

'That's right. Escaped the noose, he did, though they reckon that fate caught up with him eventually.'

'Really?' Fran smiled encouragingly. 'What do you mean?'

'Well, of course, after he did a runner, they hunted high and low for him, and then, round-about Christmas-time, there was a rumour that he'd been killed at the Front. The tale went that after war was declared, he joined the army under a false name.'

'But surely,' Tom said politely, 'he wouldn't have broadcast his whereabouts. And if he was serving under an assumed name . . .?'

'There's always some folk that are willing to shelter a friend, however bad the things he's done,' Mrs Harper said disapprovingly. 'It was said that he'd managed to get word back to his mother that he'd gone into the army, though

191

whether she knew under what name and so forth . . . well, I don't know about that. The police went round to his mother's time and again, but she wouldn't never tell them nothing. She believed that he was dead, right enough mind, because after that first Christmas of the war she started putting flowers in the churchyard, regular as anything.'

'But he wouldn't have been buried in the churchyard,' Fran demurred.

'No. She put them on her husband's grave, of course, but she was putting them there more often than before, and on Eddie's birthday and that type of thing. A lot of folk felt sorry for her, losing her only son like that, for all that he should have been hung.'

'Well,' said Fran, when Mrs Harper had finished her cup of tea and gone on her way. 'What do you make of that?'

'Rumours aren't the same as hard facts,' Tom mused. 'Then again, it would have made a lot of sense for a man on the run to enlist. If he chose another part of the country and a common enough name, he could easily have got away with it, especially in that first rush to join up, when everyone was saying that it would be all over by Christmas.'

'What about word getting back to his mother that he had died? How would that work?'

'Most chaps in the services have pals,' Tom said. 'He could have arranged some sort of code, whereby if anything happened to him, some other fellow could get word back – probably not directly to his mother – more likely to some innocent-sounding third party, who could have passed the information on to her.'

'So if Mrs Harper's right, justice was done in the end.'

'Mmm. I wouldn't be too sure about that. There are all kinds of stories about people going missing *presumed* dead and even swapping pay books with the fallen. The war was absolute carnage, of course, but it was also a godsend to anyone who wanted to enter the army under one name and come out at the end with another.'

'But surely,' Fran objected, 'he wouldn't have sent word to his own mother that he had died – she would have been devastated.'

'Someone who's ruthless enough to murder two people, then set fire to their house, may not be too worried about upsetting his mother. Think about it – it would have been a whole lot safer for him if she had believed him to be dead, and the best possible way of ensuring that the police lost interest in him. It was his mother's behaviour with the flowers that convinced Mrs Harper, don't forget, so it might have worked with the authorities too. No, here, let me get the bill.'

'So we're not going to be able to find out what happened from the witness statements at the trial after all.'

'Not from the trial, no,' Tom said. 'But there will have been preliminary hearings in the magistrates' court and at the coroner's inquest. We skipped past all that because we thought we'd find out everything from the trial, but as there was no trial, we'd better see what was said during the other proceedings.'

193

It was only as they left the little tea shop and re-crossed the road to return to the library that Tom told her about his experiences the day before at the Vester House Museum.

'They have a reading room there. You fill in a slip and shove it through this little arched window to a chap sitting in the next room, and then you sit and wait. I ordered the Barnaby diaries, and I'd scarcely been waiting five minutes when none other than Sarah Ingoldsby appeared from her lair, somewhere in the back of the building, and asked why I wanted to see them. I said I was doing some research and she asked what about. I felt like telling her to mind her own damned business, but I said "Robert Barnaby, obviously". She looked at me as if I was something she'd found on the bottom of her shoe and said that the diaries were an "irreplaceable resource"' – here Tom mimicked Mrs Ingoldsby's whiney voice – "and very rarely made available to anyone".'

'Oh, for goodness' sake!' Fran exclaimed. 'They're not even fifty years old! Anyone would think you were asking for the original copy of the Domesday Book.'

'Quite. Well, anyway, she went on in that vein for a bit – talk about the Keeper of the Sacred Texts. Eventually I said if that's the case, how did anyone ever get to do any research? How had Hugh Allonby managed it, for instance? She went very pink and said that Hugh Allonby was a recognized Barnaby scholar and naturally the museum made things available to him. So I said, very well then, how about Mrs Dexter? Hadn't she had access to them?'

194

'Oh, jolly smart move! What did she say?'

'It wasn't so much what she said as the way she looked. She went so red that I thought she was going to explode. I'm not joking. When I asked how Linda Dexter had got her hands on those diaries, it made her so mad that for a few seconds she could hardly speak. Then she said that Mrs Dexter had undermined her authority and deliberately arranged to visit while she – Sarah Ingoldsby – was away on holiday. After that, she told me that if I wanted to see the diaries I should put my request in writing and send it to her as the Barnaby archivist. I asked what was the point of asking her in writing, as she had apparently already turned me down, but she just stalked off, back to her hidey-hole.'

'Ah ha,' said Fran. 'Do you think that was why she went for Linda at the Furnival Towers when she said that she'd got a bone to pick with her?'

'I wouldn't be at all surprised.'

'Hold on, though . . . surely if it's museum policy that you have to apply in writing to Sarah Ingoldsby . . .'

'Yes.' Tom looked immensely pleased with himself. 'I thought of that too. If there were restrictions on people seeing the diaries, then arranging to go when Sarah Ingoldsby wasn't there wouldn't help you at all because you would still need to get her permission in advance. So, later on, after I got home, I telephoned the museum and asked to be put through to the top brass – the chap who's the head of collections or something. I spun him a line about being interested in the Barnaby archive and said that someone had tipped me off that to see certain parts of it you had to get permission from a woman called Mrs Ingoldsby, and I was just calling to find out if that was correct and what was the address to write to and so forth.'

'And what did he say?'

Tom grinned. 'He just laughed. He said that anyone was welcome to see any of Robert Barnaby's papers at any time and that Mrs Ingoldsby had no particular jurisdiction over them. Then he said something to the effect that some people like to give the impression they have more clout than is actually the case – not in so many words you understand, but that's what it amounted to.'

'So,' said Fran. 'Do you think she's just got an inflated opinion of her own importance, or is it something more sinister?'

'I don't know. She's always been a very self-important little person, hasn't she? Maybe she likes to see herself as the Barnaby person at the museum and is very possessive about the collection – we once had an office manager who was the same over the stationery cupboard. Made the devil of a song and dance about anyone having so much as a box of paper clips. Father longed to get rid of her, but the trouble was that she was frightfully efficient in other ways. Anyway . . . Linda Dexter had obviously got it worked out and resolved the problem by going to see the diaries behind Sarah Ingoldsby's back. That would have infuriated Mrs Ingoldsby and probably been quite enough to trigger the row at the hotel. I suppose that I will either have to go back and confront the wretched woman or else bide my time for a while before seeing the diaries. Either way, let's get back to the Halfpenny Landing murders. Must leave no stone unturned and all that.' There was such an obvious twinkle in his eye, so that she wondered for a moment if he was sending her up.

Back in the upper room of the library, there was no longer any need to whisper because the other occupants had both departed, leaving them with the room to themselves.

It did not take long to turn up the editions which covered the resumed inquest (which Edwin Traynor had been permitted to attend as an interested person), and the preliminary hearings at the magistrates' court, where the police had been required to produce evidence to justify his continued detention and committal for trial. Just as it had done previously, the *Westmorland & District Messenger* had reproduced that haunting image of the burnt-out shell in which the bodies of Andrew Chappell and his daughter Penelope had been discovered. This time it was accompanied by a picture of the two victims sitting together in a garden somewhere, informally dressed, smiling and laughing, and finally one of Andrew Chappell's surviving daughter, steadfastly ignoring reporters as she left the court, flanked by a couple of men in suits and bowler hats, who Fran thought were probably the family lawyers.

'Gosh, it doesn't look like Linda at all,' she said. 'Different hair style, I suppose, but I wouldn't have known her if it hadn't been for the caption.'

'Everyone changes,' Tom said. 'Don't forget, it's about fifteen years ago.'

They read steadily through the evidence, pausing every so often to draw one another's attention to something. The case against Edwin Traynor had essentially been circumstantial. No one had come forward to place him anywhere near the scene of the crime on the night of the murders, but the police had uncovered a strong motive, for it seemed that against her father's wishes, Penelope and Edwin had become secretly engaged and she had made a will, naming him the sole beneficiary in the event of her death. Although Penelope had little money in her own right, her father had been extremely wealthy, and the police had decided that Eddie Traynor must have assumed that in the event of the simultaneous deaths of father and daughter, the fortune would pass to Penelope and from Penelope to himself.

'And if he'd committed the murders last week, he'd have been right,' said Tom.

'What do you mean?'

'Because the law changed about three years ago. In English law, I believe it used to be dreadfully complicated if two people who were related died at the same time, but these days, if it's impossible to determine which of two people has died first, it's assumed for inheritance purposes that the older one predeceased the younger by a minute, so in a matter of those assumed sixty seconds of survival, Penelope would have come into a small fortune under the terms of her father's will, which would have fallen straight into the lap of her fiancé, Edwin Traynor, as she expired at his hands.'

Fran looked thoughtful. 'I didn't know any of that, but then, I suppose I've never needed to. The thing is,' she paused, then continued, 'Traynor's solicitor argued that he hadn't been within ten miles of his fiancée's home that night.'

'Quite so, but as it says here, the police came up with a theory which not only got Traynor to Halfpenny Landing but also overcame the problem of bypassing the heavy garden gates beside the little lodge at the top of the drive, which supposedly needed oiling and creaked like billy-o whenever they were opened. According to the police's hypothesis, Traynor took the last train of the evening from Kendal to Windermere, where he then melted into the countryside for the next few hours, eventually emerging to steal a dinghy from a boat landing in Bowness Bay and rowing himself down to Halfpenny Landing. By coming ashore off the lake, he would have placed himself on the right side of the gates and been in a position to let himself into the house with keys that he had either stolen in advance or else had been given to him on some previous occasion by Penelope. Once inside the house, he could slip upstairs and murder his victims before setting the fire, which he helped along with the tins of petrol that had been kept in the garden shed for use in the motor mower. Afterwards, he rowed back as far as the ferry, where he must have got onto the road and walked the eight or nine miles back to his home in Kendal. That wouldn't have been a problem for someone who was a champion fell runner. It says here that the dinghy was found next morning, drifting near the ferry.'

In her mind's eye, Fran could see the dark shape of a man heading silently through the garden towards the house, surefooted in spite of the darkness. She imagined the faint sound of a wavelet hitting the shore where the passage of the dinghy had disturbed the lake, and in the distance one tawny owl calling to another. He would have been deaf to all that, focused entirely on what he had come to do, one hand protectively enclosing the cigarette lighter and perhaps a ligature that he had earlier concealed in his pocket. She shuddered and pulled herself back into the present.

'Naturally Traynor denied ever having had any keys to the house,' Fran said, assimilating information as they both continued to read. 'You know, with no witnesses or anything particularly strong to back up the police's theory, the prosecution might have found it difficult to convince a jury of Traynor's guilt beyond reasonable doubt – except, of course, that he'd made such a mess of his alibi.'

'Traynor made a massive error there,' Tom agreed.

'It was idiotic. Whatever possessed him to tell the police on the day after the murder that he had bumped into his old flame, Miss Belinda Chappell, in Kendal and gone back to her house for supper on the night of the murder? Of all the people to pick – none other than Penelope Chappell's own half-sister, who, naturally enough, not only failed to corroborate the story but was able to provide the police with details of the party that she had attended the previous evening, where more than a dozen witnesses had seen her.'

'It says here that by the time of his second appearance in court, Traynor had changed his story completely, as of course he would have to, claiming that he had invented the encounter with Belinda Chappell because he'd panicked when the police first came to call on him. The snag is that this new version of events wasn't backed up by anyone either. All he could say was that he'd spent the entire evening alone at his mother's house and had already gone up to bed by the time she came home from visiting her sister.

'Making up that story about being with Linda was the worst possible thing he could have done,' said Tom. 'As you say, the police hadn't really got any evidence against him to speak of, but telling that stupid story showed him up to be a liar. The money wasn't that much of a motive, you know, because he wouldn't actually have inherited under the law as it stood then.'

'Just a minute.' Fran's mind had jumped ahead of the intricacies of inheritance law. 'I've just thought of something. Look at this – this elaborate story about how he got to and from the scene of the crime. I've just realized something really obvious that we've never thought of.'

'Well? Go on.'

'If someone abducted Linda from the Furnival Towers and then killed her on the railway line, that person must have either forced her to drive there from the hotel or else driven her car there himself. But the car was found close by the line, so assuming

201

that the abductor was someone at the conference, how did he or she get back to the hotel afterwards?'

'Another long hike?' asked Tom.

'I was thinking more in terms of another car, with a second person driving.'

'Meaning that more than one person was involved.'

'Hugh Allonby and Sarah Ingoldsby!' said Fran.

'Or Marcus Dryden and another member of his clan. There's that lemon-faced daughter of his who works on the reception desk occasionally.'

Fran looked doubtful again. 'In a way, it sounds like a brilliant theory,' she said, 'but then you look at it in another light and it just sounds barking. I wonder if the police found any evidence of a second car having been there. You know, tyre tracks and things.'

'Look out,' said Tom. 'Don't suck the end of your pencil like that. Now look – you've got black all over your lips.'

'I haven't, have I? Oh, bother. I'll have to go and wash it off.'

'I'll carry on copying all this lot out while you're gone,' Tom said.

By the time Fran returned from the ladies' cloakroom, Tom had reached the edition of the paper which covered the conclusion of the inquest. The verdict was 'murder by Edwin Edgar Traynor' and the report mentioned in passing that the surviving daughter of Andrew Chappell was applying to inherit the estate and would in all likelihood get everything. The paper speculated that rather than restore the house at

Halfpenny Landing, discussions were already underway to sell the site to a developer.

'Funny name for a house, isn't it? Halfpenny Landing,' Tom commented.

'Particularly considering what it must actually have been worth.'

'Anyway, I think we've got all that we're going to get from here. What do you feel about what we've found out?'

Fran considered the question. Her gut response was 'uneasy'. The picture of the burnt-out house had imbedded itself in her memory and she found it oddly upsetting. 'Honestly? I don't really feel as if we've managed to find out anything much at all.'

'Funnily enough, neither do I. It's hard to see how the first two murders have got any connection with the second one at all. If it was a murder, that is.'

Twenty-Three

Tom offered to drive her home again, and on this occasion he did not decline her invitation to come in for a cup of tea. Fran found her heart was skipping in a silly way as he followed her up the garden path and in at the front door. All those times that she had pictured him, ducking slightly to get through the sitting-room door, and now here he was, actually doing just that.

'Do sit down and I'll organize a pot of tea.'

Unlike Stephen Latchford, he did not attempt to follow her into the kitchen, where she found Ada pretending to bustle and clearly only too pleased to be instructed to provide tea for 'Mum and the gentleman' as it would afford the perfect opportunity to goggle at the visitor.

Tom had hardly had time to accept her invitation to sit down, and stretch his long legs out across the hearth rug, before the knocker sounded on the front door and they could hear Ada hastening through from the kitchen to answer it. Through the ill-fitting sitting-room door, Fran recognized Mo's voice. 'Hello, Ada, is Mrs Black at home?' And the next minute, Ada was announcing, 'It's Mrs Gallimore, Mum.'

Polite introductions were exchanged and Ada asked to provide an additional cup and saucer. After they had done the weather, Mo and Tom discovered a mutual liking for the lowlands of

Scotland and, in under half an hour, Tom had made his excuses and left.

'I'm so sorry, darling,' Mo said as soon as Tom had taken his leave. 'I would never have come butting in if I'd known. The fact is that I was calling in on spec, and when I saw the car I thought it might belong to that creepy fellow, what's-his-name, so I came barging in on the two of you.'

'Don't be silly, Mo. I'm glad you've met Tom.'

'But it's the first time you've had him here for a tête-á-tête: trust me to ruin everything, just when you were enjoying a romantic interlude together!'

'Don't be silly,' Fran repeated. 'We were just having a cup of tea, before he got back on the road. And there's nothing romantic in the air. As I keep on telling you . . .'

'Oh, come off it. You're obviously mad about him – the way you keep laughing at all his jokes, even the ones that aren't funny. And anyway, what's a family man doing, spending the day up here with you when he could be with his wife and son?'

'We're trying to find out what happened to Linda Dexter.'

Mo stared at her for a moment and then laughed. 'Oh my goodness! You really believe that, don't you? Well, you may think you're playing Watson to his Sherlock Holmes, but at the end of the day, he's a red-blooded chap. Don't fool yourself that there isn't an ulterior motive. Anyway,' she went on in an altogether different tone of voice, 'please bring me up to date on whatever it is that you've found out now.'

It was only after Mo had left that Fran noticed the day's post, which Ada had for once propped on the mantelpiece. The envelope at the front was addressed in a distinctive upright hand which she half-recognized, and when she had extracted and unfolded the single sheet of writing paper, she saw that it was from Hugh Allonby.

Dear Fellow Committee Member,

It has come to my attention that one of our number has taken steps to acquire the late Mrs Linda Dexter's research papers, having misled the family into handing them over, by representing herself as acting on behalf of the Robert Barnaby Society. I take this matter very seriously, as no doubt you all will. My own position is that the person concerned should hand over the papers and resign their position on the executive committee forthwith. Kindly let me have your views on this at your earliest convenience.

Hugh Allonby

Heat rose in her cheeks as she read the text. It was humiliating – like being a child called out in front of the whole school for some imagined offence.

She glanced at the clock and decided that she would need to give Tom at least another hour to get back home. She spent the next sixty minutes pacing about, making several false starts on responses to Hugh Allonby's letter and chewing at her nails. When she eventually picked up the phone and asked the exchange to connect her, she was relieved when Tom answered the telephone himself.

'This is probably because I went to the Vester

House Museum,' Tom said. 'I bet that wretched Sarah Ingoldsby has put two and two together. You remember that I asked her how Linda Dexter had managed to see parts of the Barnaby archive? Well, she must have worked out how I knew and reported back to Allonby.'

'"Herself", the letter says. How did they know that it was me?'

'I'm sure I never mentioned you. Allonby must have contacted Christina Harper and she must have told him that you'd got the papers. Funny that she never mentioned it today.'

'I suppose she didn't think of it. And we were too busy getting her to talk about the Halfpenny Landing murders.'

'Anyway, you never told her that you were acting on behalf of the society.'

'Umm . . . I rather think that I did. Not outright, perhaps, but I gave her that impression.'

'Well, there's no real damage done. You can tell the committee that you did represent the society because you always intended to hand them over – which you can, because we've read them now.'

'Which is presumably what Hugh Allonby's got a problem with.'

'Quite. But they can hardly chuck you off the committee if you say that you thought you were doing the right thing: saving the papers before they got thrown on the fire. Just tell them that it didn't occur to you to run it past the committee first.'

'I don't much care if they do chuck me off the committee,' Fran said. 'It's Hugh Allonby's reaction that interests me. He's obviously really keen to get his hands on those papers, and so is Sarah Ingoldsby. They're in it together. I know they are.'

'Don't forget how proprietorial they both are about all things Barnaby. I still can't help thinking about the Dryden family. They're the ones with the really strong financial motive. Do you think—'

'There's also Stephen Latchford,' she interrupted.

'I know you've got a bit of a thing about old Stephen-with-a-ph,' Tom said gently, 'but I can't really see where you're going with that. I know you don't like the guy and he's a bit of a creep, but apart from that, what have we got on him? Anyway, we need to get our story straight about how you come to have these papers. It'll be obvious that I know about them, because it was me who went sniffing round the museum and put Little Miss Sulky Face in a huff.'

'You know, Tom, I really don't care. Let Hugh Allonby throw me out. The committee's pointless anyway. They all just do whatever he says.'

'But if we're going to get to the bottom of this, we can do it more easily from the inside. And think of me still stuck on the committee without you – you're the only person who makes the meetings bearable.'

Fran sucked in a gulp of air. 'I suppose so,' she conceded.

'I suggest we say that it became obvious at the funeral that Linda's family weren't interested in the Barnaby stuff and, because you'd struck up a rapport with the sister, you thought an informal approach would be most likely to succeed and I agreed. Once you got hold of the papers, you fully intended to hand them on to Sarah Ingoldsby, as society archivist, at the next committee meeting. You didn't bother mentioning it before because it's hardly an urgent matter.'

'Good idea – sort of . . . Where's the fire?'

'Exactly. That might calm him down, and even if it doesn't, he won't want to make too much fuss just in case anyone else starts to suspect that there could be something important in those papers. Anyway, Allonby has asked for our views, so I'm going to write to him now, but I suggest that you leave it until tomorrow. That way the letters won't arrive together and it might look less like a collaboration.'

After Tom rang off, she read the letter again. Although her gut instinct was to tell Hugh Allonby that he was a pompous fool and could go to hell, it was still humiliating to think of the rest of the committee reading an accusation of impropriety. Good grief, she thought. Did none of them have any sense of perspective? It wasn't as if she'd run off with the subscriptions or something. To all intents and purposes, the fuss amounted to the contents of a few old note-books about a long-dead children's author. It wasn't something serious, like finding a dead body on a railway line.

She let her mind run back to the weekend of the conference. When Linda had first been missed, someone had suggested checking to see if she was still in her room and Hugh Allonby had gone off to look for her, but he hadn't known which room to look in – he'd had to ask John James. Mr James had handled the bookings in cooperation with the hotel, so he had a list of who was staying in which room. Could Hugh Allonby's asking for the room number have been a double bluff? Delegates would not normally know which room anyone else was in, but whoever had abducted Linda must have known where to find her. However, if Hugh Allonby was responsible, he wouldn't have wanted to let on that he knew which room she was in.

'Excuse me, Mum.' Ada had appeared in the doorway with her outdoor coat and hat on. 'Should I feed the cat, Mum, before I go, only she's been asking these past twenty minutes.'

'It's all right, Ada. You had better go or you'll miss your bus. I'll take care of the cat.'

After she had dealt with Mrs Snegglington's requirements, Fran gave in to temptation and poured herself a large gin. She carried it into the parlour and set it down on the desk while she consulted her membership list for John James's telephone number.

The operator connected the call swiftly and after a brief exchange of pleasantries, during which he sounded unmistakably surprised to hear from her, she said, 'Mr James, I hope you don't mind my calling you like this, but I was just curious about something. When the conference was being organized this year, I wondered how the room allocation worked. Am I right in thinking that the society looks after all that?'

'That's right. The bookings officer – that was me

this year – does it all. Apparently it's always been done like that, so that friends who want to share a room or be adjacent to one another can be put together. It saves the hotel having to bother with it.'

'So people sometimes know which rooms their friends are in?'

'Sometimes.' His tone had become cagey.

'Does the hotel know who's in which room?'

'Of course. I gave them a complete list. For billing purposes. Why do you ask?'

'Oh, no particular reason.'

'You don't ask questions like this without a reason.' John James's voice had turned cold. 'I don't think I want to discuss this with you any further. There's already some trouble over you getting hold of Mrs Dexter's papers, isn't there?'

'What makes you think that the letter's about me?'

'Well, it isn't going to be Miss Robertson or Miss Winterton who's involved, is it? And I can't imagine our chairman sending out a letter like that if everyone's favourite archivist was involved.'

'Did Mr Allonby know which delegate was in which room?' Fran asked.

'What is this, Mrs Black? No, wait – I get the picture. You fancy yourself with a pipe and deer-stalker, don't you?' His obvious derision cut her like a knife. 'Well, if you want to know anything else regarding the arrangements, I suggest you raise it in the committee. I know Robert Barnaby wrote for children but that doesn't mean we all have to behave like one. May I suggest you just grow up, stop playing detectives and leave the police to get on with their job?'

211

The line went dead. Fran realized that her cheeks were burning as hard as they had been when she'd first read Hugh Allonby's letter. She steadied herself with a couple of gulps of gin.

She had gone too far in ringing John James, a man she had met only twice before, first at the conference and then at the subsequent committee meeting. And his words, while wounding her, had also been a wake-up call. She and Tom were trying to solve a mystery which was already under investigation by a professional police force, who probably had heaps of evidence about which she and Tom knew absolutely nothing. It really was childish to imagine that they could team up and solve the case, like Mickey and Ronald in the Two Boy Detectives series. She thought about Mo's comment earlier that afternoon: '. . . You may think you're playing Watson to his Sherlock Holmes, but at the end of the day, he's a red-blooded chap. Don't fool yourself that there isn't an ulterior motive.'

Did Tom have an ulterior motive? What was a married man doing, leaving his wife and son at home while he went chasing around after clues with another woman? If he was interested in having an affair, he hadn't so far done anything to initiate one. Then another conversation came back to her, when Tom himself had mentioned that he'd had a room in that same downstairs corridor from which Linda had gone missing. She went into the kitchen and topped up her glass again, finding that it had unaccountably emptied itself. It would really be much more convenient to have a cocktail cabinet in the sitting room as she and Michael had once done, she thought. Civilized people did not keep their gin in the pantry.

Back in the sitting room, she reverted to her previous line of thought. Suppose you had abducted and murdered someone and you thought that some other person was getting too interested in finding out what had happened . . . wouldn't it make sense to pretend to help, so that you could keep an eye on what they were finding out?

It wasn't as if she had particularly good judgement when it came to men. Right from school, she had been attracted to the wrong sort. Her first love had been an unrequited passion for a boy down the road, who had gone on to be a charming, feckless bounder who'd found brief notoriety after embezzling the local Liberal Club funds. There had been that short-lived romance with a local solicitor, who'd had wandering hands and a drink problem, to say nothing of the cheater she had eventually married. Good God, she must have some sort of beacon which attracted them, like a silent dog whistle.

Twenty-Four

Tom had evidently managed to get his letter into the last collection of the evening, for she received a copy of it the following morning.

Dear Fellow Committee Members,

It is generally accepted that one of the central themes of Robert Barnaby's work is fair play, so I assume that none of us would wish to be party to a situation in which pressure was placed upon a committee member to resign without there having first been a proper investigation into whatever offence that person was supposed to have committed.

As it happens, I am aware of what has occurred in this instance, and I hope Mr Allonby will not be offended when I say that I believe he has completely misunderstood the situation in regard to the late Mrs Dexter's papers.

As you are all aware, Mrs Black and I repre-sented the society at Mrs Dexter's funeral, where we met her sister, Mrs Christina Harper. Mrs Harper told us that the vast majority of the late Mrs Dexter's possessions were shortly going to be turned over to a house clearance firm, and that as she had no interest in her sister's research on Robert Barnaby, if we wished to acquire it on behalf of the society, we were welcome to do so. While we did not suppose that the items involved would be of any particular value, given a choice between acquiring them for the society or standing

214

by while they were disposed of, it seemed sensible to accept them on the society's behalf, and I assume that any other committee member faced with this situation would have done the same thing.

Mrs Black and I agreed that as she happens to live within a few miles of Mrs Harper, it was more practical that she should be the one to undertake the collection of the notebooks, etc., and bring them to the next committee meeting. It did not occur to either of us that there was any urgency about this, or that one member's unwanted notebooks were capable of causing such a storm in a teacup. Under the circumstances, talk of misleading anyone or offering resignations seems completely inappropriate.

Tom Dod

By the next day, Fran had received a copy of a note circulated by Jean Robertson.

Dear Fellow Committee Members,

In the light of Mr Dod's explanation, I think we can all see that he and Mrs Black believed that they were acting for the best, and that talk of resignations is not appropriate in this case.

J. E. Robertson

Tom rang that evening to tell her that Ruth Winterton and the journal editor Richard Finney had both contacted him in support. Even John James, from whom Fran had half expected a degree of hostility after their recent conversation, had telephoned Tom, saying that he did not consider there was any need for talk of people standing down.

Fran felt like cheering. Hugh Allonby had attempted to get the committee to gang up on her and it hadn't worked. Well done, Tom. The only note of dissent came from Sarah Ingoldsby, who had circulated a rather rambling letter suggesting that it was always best if members made sure that the 'proper people' were kept informed, and that when it came to the acquisition of papers, as society archivist she was self-evidently that person. 'Pompous little prig,' Fran said aloud on reading it.

'Do you think those two were just infuriated because they like to be in control of everything?' Fran asked. 'Or do you think Hugh Allonby really does want to suppress Linda's research?'

'Well, he certainly won't like what's in those notebooks. The general upshot is that his own research was pretty shoddy. That doesn't make him a murderer, though.'

'He didn't exactly seem sorry when Linda didn't turn up to give her paper.'

'You're right there.' The line went quiet for a moment. Tom was obviously thinking.

Fran breached the pause, saying, 'You know, we should both watch our backs. Hugh Allonby doesn't like to be gainsaid and you can bet that he's smarting over this defeat. It must be the first time in years that his executive committee hasn't backed him up.'

'What could he possibly do?'

'Nothing, I suppose,' Fran said. But she could not help recalling that the last person who had attempted to cross him over something to do with Robert Barnaby had ended up dead on a railway line.

Twenty-Five

It was three days before she heard from Tom again, and in the meantime Fran had received her telephone bill. It seemed a staggering amount – all those trunk calls to Tom, probably – and she blanched as she wrote the cheque. The trouble was, she thought, that this whole business over Linda Dexter and the Barnaby Society had become the most interesting thing going on in her life – something to focus on over and above the humdrum day-to-day activities like shopping and gardening and changing her library books. It was only like having a very expensive hobby, she thought as she folded the cheque into an envelope, then glanced across at her shiny black telephone, of which she was rather proud as it was one of the new designs with a handset which combined both mouthpiece and earpiece, making it much easier to use than the old candlestick models.

It was different for Tom Dod, of course. He must be very busy, with his job and his wife and son, all of them living in the tall mews house, where several flights of stairs separated his study from the ground floor, and where she supposed that Veronica gave instructions to their cook, planned little family outings and received callers. She wondered if Tom's wife minded about all the time he spent on the Barnaby Society and the Linda Dexter mystery. Did they talk about it together? He never really mentioned his wife. But then, why should he?

Mo called in on her way home from a trip to see her dressmaker in Grange, and once the obligatory tea had been provided (it was too early for cocktails), she curled her legs beneath her on Fran's sofa and leaned back luxuriantly. 'Come on, then. Let's have the latest on the crime of the century . . . No, no, get down, Mrs Snegs. I'm too full of cake to have a cat on my lap.'

'Well, my list of suspects isn't getting any shorter. In fact, if anything, it's getting longer.'

'Go on.'

'Stephen Latchford. He telephoned me again yesterday evening, asking if it was convenient to come round and discuss a Barnaby Society matter. I can't believe that he called again after I had slammed the receiver down on him and told him to leave me alone, but he behaved as if that had never happened. How much plainer can one be? Anyway, I said it wasn't convenient and couldn't he put whatever it is in a letter or just tell me about whatever it was there and then, on the telephone, but he wouldn't. He said he would call me again in a day or so. It's hard to explain, but somehow he sort of made it sound like a threat. He's got this really peculiar way of . . . oh, I don't know . . . manipulating the conversation somehow so that the sort of polite disinterest which would discourage other people makes me sound as if I'm being rude or unreasonable. And he just won't take no for an answer.' She found it difficult to explain, even to Mo, how unnerving she had found the call.

'Very well then. The chap has obviously taken a fancy to you, but what's his connection to the victim?'

'None, really. Except that until recently he lived quite near to Linda Dexter. Oh, yes, and he mentioned that the police had asked him if he heard anything suspicious that night because his room in the hotel was opposite to Linda's. Of course, if he intended to abduct Linda, I don't know how he could have found out in advance which room she was in.'

'I should think that would be quite easy,' Mo said. 'If I wanted to know what room someone else was staying in, I would just ask at the front desk.'

'That's a bit chancey if you are up to no good. Suppose someone remembered afterwards that you'd asked about her room? It's drawing attention to yourself.'

'Well, so is starting to make a nuisance of yourself to someone else immediately after you've just done away with your first victim.'

'Yes and no. Linda's death might be passed off as suicide. And, of course, there's no evidence that he was bothering her.'

'Would she have told anyone?'

'I suppose not. I mean, who does one tell? It's not as though we have a member responsible for policing the behaviour of other members. No one in the society knows that he's been bothering me. Well, only Tom, and I don't think even he takes it all that seriously.'

'Mmm,' said Mo. 'What about your other suspects?'

'Well, Tom's a bit of a suspect too.'

'What? Mr Death in several Scandinavian languages? I thought you had cast Tom as Bulldog Drummond, the detective hero?'

'His room was on that downstairs corridor too.'

'But that isn't very much to go on, is it? I mean, just being on the same corridor. As you've already said, that doesn't mean you would know where the intended victim's room was. And anyway, your Tom's a thoroughly good guy – well, except for flirting with you when he is married.'

'He hasn't – *ever* – flirted with me. But I agree that his being married and somehow never mentioning it, is . . . well . . . maybe part of what makes me wonder.'

'Who else is on the list?'

'I've added John James, the membership secretary, for the same reason as Tom.'

Mo laughed. 'Don't tell me he's got a wife hidden away at home too?'

'No. He had a room on the downstairs corridor. Oh, yes – and he's one of the few people who would definitely have known which room Linda Dexter was in, because he organized room allocations with the hotel.'

'I'm not sure that's particularly significant. What's his motive?'

'He hasn't got one. In fact, I don't think he'd ever met Linda prior to that weekend, because the conference was the very first society event that he had ever attended.'

'Did you notice anything about him on the Friday evening? Was he paying her a lot of attention?'

Fran thought hard. 'If he was, I don't remember. No, hang on a minute, he wasn't even there. A couple of delegates didn't turn up until Saturday morning, and I think he was one of them. I remember Miss Robertson introducing him to me when I was on my way out of the dining room, after breakfast. She knew him from executive committee meetings, you see.'

'That must put him out of it. Who else is there?'

'Marcus Dryden. He keeps the hotel, would have known the room allocations and probably wouldn't have wanted Linda's revelations about the magic chair to come out. The hotel is his livelihood. It doesn't exactly sit in on the normal touring route, so they rely quite a bit on the Barnaby connection. It's mentioned in all their advertising.'

'He sounds like a definite possibility.'

'The snag is that Marcus Dryden would have to have known in advance what was in Linda's paper.'

'Perhaps he did.'

'I don't think so. I don't think anyone else really knew what she'd turned up until Tom and I read through all her notebooks.'

'But if they didn't know what she was going to say in advance, why would they have murdered her? It doesn't make sense, Fran.'

A knock at the front door interrupted them. Ada's workman-like shoes could be heard on the stone flags of the hall and then, as she opened the door, a familiar deep voice reached them through the sitting-room door. Fran rose to her feet at once. 'It's all right, Ada,' she called. 'Show Mr Dod straight in. Hello, Tom, what on earth are you doing here?'

221

'I've been visiting some damson growers up the Lyth Valley and realized that I was virtually passing the end of the road, so I thought I would come and report back from my latest visit to Furnival Towers. I'm sorry to come barging in like this, Mrs Gallimore.'

'Nonsense,' Mo said. 'We already know each other, and please drop this Mrs Gallimore business and call me Mo – everyone does. Well, everyone who's halfway worthwhile, anyway.'

'Mo's as intrigued to hear anything new as I am,' Fran said. 'Ada.' She turned to the young woman who had followed the visitor into the room and was about to bear his hat off to the hall stand. 'Please can you bring in a fresh pot of tea and a cup for Mr Dod – and if there is any of that delicious fruitcake left, please bring that in too. Now then.' She turned her attention back to Tom again. 'Do sit down and tell all.'

Tom took a vacant armchair and began. 'Well, I had to go up to see a grower on the Fylde, so I made a bit of a diversion and called in for lunch at Furnival Towers en route. The place was really quiet, so I managed to engage old Dryden in a long chat in the bar, before I ate. I was pretty straight with him, actually. I said that I'd read Linda's research, gave him the gist of it, then asked him if he thought there was anything in it, and if so, whether it could make a difference to him and the business if it got around?'

'Gosh! That was jolly direct. What did he say?'

'I nearly fell out of my seat, because he just laughed and said that he had suspected for years that the magic chair was a fake. "My father was

222

a canny old fellow," he said. "There must have been some story about a possible Robert Barnaby connection, and the old boy evidently read some of the books and installed an appropriate piece of furniture – it wouldn't surprise me if he hadn't had it made specially – and, of course, the rest is history. When Hugh Allonby came round, asking about the Barnaby connection, Father was still in charge and it was a marriage made in heaven, really – each used the other. Hugh's books were always on sale in the hotel; the hotel was name-checked as *the* epicentre of all things Barnaby. A mutually lucrative exercise."'

'But surely,' Fran said, 'all that was going to be ruined once Linda's research is made public?'

'Dryden doesn't think so. He said, "It takes more than a few facts to destroy a legend."'

'I can see that,' Mo said thoughtfully. 'The link between Robert Barnaby and Furnival Towers must appear in thousands of newspaper articles and magazines by now. You could never correct every one of them.'

'That's perfectly true,' Tom said, 'but not exactly the whole story. Dryden said something else which struck a chord with me. "People want to believe it's the real magic chair," he said. And I think he's right. A few people might say, "Oh, it's not the real place," or "it's not the real chair," but the majority want to see the chair and want to believe that Barnaby himself once sat in it. They don't want truth, they want fairy dust. They won't go digging around in the archives to check whether Linda is right or not. They will choose to assume that she's got it all wrong.'

Fran nodded, recalling that she had entertained similar thoughts herself. 'So you think the Drydens really aren't at all bothered about Linda's research? Are you sure he wasn't just bluffing?'

'No, I genuinely don't think he's worried by the results of Linda's research or its publication. What he's not a bit happy about is the hotel being associated with a suicide or a murder. "Wrong sort of publicity attracting the wrong sort of interest," was the way he put it.'

'So Marcus Dryden is hardly likely to be our murderer,' said Mo. Fran noted the 'our'. For all the mockery, she knew that Mo was becoming increasingly intrigued.

Aloud, Fran said, 'So Mr Dryden turns out to be not much use after all.'

'Not as a suspect, no, but something else came out of the conversation which was very interesting.'

'Go on.'

'It was perfectly obvious that nothing I said about Linda's research was news to Marcus. He already knew what was going to be revealed in that talk – Marcus is a member and he would have got the programme like everyone else, but the programme only carried the title of the lecture – *The Magic Chair: Fact or Fiction*. In the context of Barnaby's work, that's open to a whole variety of interpretations. You wouldn't be able to guess from the title that the contents would completely debunk the provenance of a piece of furniture.'

'But how could he possibly have known what Linda was going to say?'

'After we'd been chatting for a while, I said

that he didn't seem surprised by what I'd told him, and he said that he wasn't because he'd been tipped off in advance. Apparently none other than the Robert Barnaby Society's Ninny-in-Chief, Mrs Sarah Ingoldsby, had contacted him about a week before the conference. "Wittering on" were his exact words. Mr Dryden might flatter dear Mrs Ingoldsby to her face, but it was pretty obvious from the way he spoke about her that he finds her as irritating as just about everyone else does, and he was therefore perfectly willing to be bitchy behind her back. First of all, Dryden reckons that Mrs Ingoldsby isn't actually involved with the Barnaby archive and hasn't been for quite a while, which of course fits perfectly with the attitude of the museum director when he spoke with me last week. I reckon our Mrs Ingoldsby has tried to keep this under wraps, because she's always gained a lot of kudos within the society thanks to her supposed connection with the archive. She gets an honorary member-ship and an automatic place on the executive committee off the back of it, and that must help to convince the unseen Mr Ingoldsby that she is an essential fixture at every meeting, which of course provides the perfect cover for her involve-ment with Hugh Allonby.'

'But how does she get away with it?' Mo asked. 'Surely people must find out if they get in touch with this museum place?'

'Most of the membership would be none the wiser, because the woman still works at the museum in some capacity. It's easy enough to keep up the pretence that she is still involved with the Barnaby archive because the majority of enthusiasts are perfectly happy to leave any actual research to other people. But, of course, people will occasionally find her out, as Linda Dexter obviously did.'

'She wouldn't like it to get around that she isn't the queen bee at Vester House.' Fran's tone was thoughtful. 'Sarah Ingoldsby has rubbed an awful lot of people up the wrong way, ever since the society got started. She can be quite nasty when she gets her claws out. I reckon there would be more than a few members happy to see that free membership and automatic committee place stopped if they realized that she was getting it under false pretences.'

'Is there much money involved?' Mo asked.

'Virtually none.' This from Tom. 'A single membership costs twenty-five shillings a year. Committee members only get travelling expenses and there are no other perks. But with Sarah Ingoldsby, I'd say that there's a whole package of other things. The complimentary membership is nothing – the loss of status would hurt her more. She's a sad little woman who's worked all her life behind the scenes in a museum, but then, with the formation of the Robert Barnaby Society, she suddenly became a big fish in a little pond. More importantly, if she lost her place on the committee, she would lose the cover story that she uses in order to conduct her affair with Hugh Allonby.'

'If this woman is having an affair with the chairman, then presumably she was spending the night with him,' Mo ventured. 'Which means that if she was the murderer, he's got to be in on it too.'

'Two people would actually make sense,' Tom said, 'because of the car. Linda's car was found at the scene, so either the murderer had to make a long walk back or there was a car driven by a second person which would bring both parties back to the hotel after Linda's car had been torched.'

'That's good thinking. But how did Sarah Ingoldsby find out what was in Linda's paper?'

'I've been thinking about that,' Tom said. 'When you want to look at something from the Vester House archives, you have to fill in a request slip. I suppose those slips are filed somewhere, which means that when Sarah Ingoldsby got back from her holiday she probably found out that Linda had been visiting the museum behind her back. Then she would have received the conference programme and seen the title of Linda's lecture. At that point, she could have gone back to those request slips, and she or Hugh Allonby could have had a look at the same material as Linda had and worked out what Linda was going to say.'

'Which would have provoked big-time wittering,' said Fran. 'So the Dryden clan are looking less and less likely, but Ingoldsby and Allonby as a double act would work.'

'We were talking about Fran's list of suspects when you arrived,' Mo said, giving her friend a mischievous look which Fran attempted to ignore.

'Jolly good show,' Tom said. 'Do let me in on the picture.'

'Well, there's Stephen Latchford.' Fran began to outline her argument while trying to ignore Mo's face-pulling.

'And of course there's you,' Mo put in cheerfully when Fran had finished. 'But only on the basis that you had a room in the downstairs corridor.'

'Fair enough.' Tom seemed completely unfazed by his inclusion on the list. 'Though it has occurred to me that while proximity would be useful, it isn't essential. The important thing would be to know where the room was, and you could easily find that out.'

'By asking at Reception,' put in Mo.

'Too obvious. Why not just wait until Linda was going to her room, then discreetly follow her and watch where she went? If anyone queried what you were doing, you could pretend that you'd lost your way. You could say that you didn't know the layout of the place or had forgotten that your room was upstairs, instead of downstairs where it was last year, or basically make any old excuse at all. It's the Barnaby Society. Fifty per cent of the membership are as mad as hatters, so no one's going to query the idea of someone forgetting where their room is located. Oh, and if being on the same corridor gets you on to the list, I suggest you add dear old Miss Leonard and Miss Coward, because they had the room right next to mine.'

Twenty-Six

'He didn't do it,' Mo said as soon as Fran returned to the sitting room after seeing her latest visitor out. 'He's just too nice.'

'I bet Ethel Le Neve thought Crippen was nice too. 'Specially when he gave her his dead wife's fur coat.'

'How creepy is that? To find out that the chap you've moved in with has murdered his wife?'

'Well, if you ask me, there's more than a chance that she was in on it all along.'

'Who?'

'Ethel le Neve. Do try to keep up.'

'It's the alcohol intake rotting my brain cells. Or maybe I just need another top-up.'

'Don't worry. Ada's gone for her bus but I can take a hint,' Fran said over her shoulder as she headed into the kitchen to fetch the bottles and glasses.

As she entered the kitchen, she thought she saw a movement in the garden, but when she turned to face the window properly there was nothing there. Must have been a bird, she thought, flying low and glimpsed momentarily from the corner of her eye. Back in the sitting room, as she set down her cargo and began to pour, she said, 'In a way, that's what happened to Linda Dexter. Her ex-boyfriend turned out to be a murderer. I suppose a thing like that would

229

affect you for ever – change your whole outlook. It's no wonder her marriage failed and she became . . . well . . . almost a recluse, in a funny sort of way.'

'It was an odd kind of life,' Mo mused. 'Just pursuing your passion for children's books. I mean . . . it wouldn't have done for most people. Though I suppose if you've got the money you can do whatever you want. Didn't you say that she travelled quite a bit?'

'Exactly. I suppose we wouldn't think it was so odd if, say, she had been a massively wealthy tennis fan who followed the stars around the world, showing up at every major tournament.'

'You're right. Different people have different passions.'

'Or obsessions.'

'Quite. And although it wouldn't seem important to anyone else, being perceived as the source of all knowledge about Robert Barnaby and at the top of the pecking order within the Robert Barnaby Society could be massively important to a person like this nasty Allonby man and his sneaky little accomplice.'

Both women paused to sip their drinks, then Mo asked, 'Do you honestly still think that it was an inside job?'

Fran hesitated. 'It sounds farfetched, but so far as we can see there's nothing else in Linda's life to provide a motive. She scarcely had a private life. She had pots of money but there's no jealous husband or lover who might benefit.'

'What about the ex-husband?'

'Oh, Tom's already looked into that and he's

definitely dead – a motoring accident, several years back. The sister gets the money but, as we all agreed, it's hard to see how the sister could have pulled off an abduction and murder from the Furnival Towers Hotel. The Harpers don't even own a motorcar. We just don't have any realistic suspects beyond the society itself, and the suspects that we do have, have jolly puny motives.'

'It's a massive coincidence,' Mo mused. 'Being involved in a sensational murder case and then getting murdered yourself.'

'Except that in real life coincidences happen all the time. When I was a child, two separate families in the village each lost a child in drowning accidents, a few years apart, at almost exactly the same spot in the river. What are the odds of that?'

'Really? I suppose it depends how dangerous the river was at that point.'

'That's just it. The river wasn't dangerous there. We all went to bathe there in summer, when I was a child, but it seems to have been a freak accident in both cases. Lightning striking twice and all that.'

'Goodness, how awful.'

'I'm just nipping up to the bathroom,' Fran said. In fact, her trip upstairs had a secondary purpose, as she did not want Mo to drive home after several gins and decided that it would be a good idea to check that the spare room bed was ready for an overnight visitor, just in case it was needed. Sometimes she left the spare-room door open by mistake and Mrs Snegglington took advantage of the situation for an impromptu grooming session, leaving a carpet of cat hair all over the quilt, but on this occasion Fran found that all was well. As she crossed the room, she paused to look out into the lane. Mo's car was parked on the little grassed area to the side of the cottage, where she always left it so as not to obstruct the occasional passing traffic, but to Fran's surprise there was now a second car parked in the lane. It was not directly outside the cottage, where it would be obviously noticeable to the occupants, but a little way down the hill, where it was partially screened by the start of the hedgerow. She might not have noticed it at all but for the angle of the evening sun reflecting off the bonnet.

Someone out for a walk, perhaps? Trippers did leave their cars in the most inconvenient of places, but now that she had focused on it properly she could clearly make out the bulk of a person occupying the driver's seat. Someone was sitting out there, watching the house.

She hesitated for a moment, then stepped back into the room, just in case her outline was visible at the window. Better not to give away that she had noticed anything. Once she had cautiously withdrawn a couple of feet, she raced downstairs, not daring to shout, almost falling into the sitting room, where an astonished Mo said, 'What on earth's up?'

'There's someone outside. I think I caught a glimpse of them prowling round the garden earlier on. I saw something when I went into the kitchen, but I thought I was imagining it. Then

I just looked out from upstairs and there's a car, half hidden, out in the lane.'

'Good heavens! Is it burglars, do you think?'

'I've got nothing to steal. I know you'll think I'm being silly, but I think it's Stephen Latchford.'

'Right.' Mo didn't even hesitate. 'It's definitely time to call the police.'

'I think so too. Wait, though. You go up and have a squint through the bathroom window. Just to make sure I'm not imagining it.' Even in the horror of the moment, Fran was abruptly seized with disbelief. Virtual strangers did not sit outside your house or creep around the kitchen garden, peering in through your windows. That sort of thing couldn't really be happening.

'Why the bathroom?'

'Frosted glass. Not so easy to see us as it would be through the spare-room window.'

Mo made her way up into the bathroom as cautiously as if she was expecting to meet the mysterious watcher on the way. Fran followed her, displaying only a marginally lesser degree of trepidation. It took Mo only a moment to confirm what Fran had observed. There was definitely a car parked out there in the lane.

'I think it's his car,' Fran said.

'That's it,' said Mo. 'We telephone the police at once.'

Though there was no possible way that anyone outside the building could see them, they both crept back down the stairs. They had almost reached the bottom when Mo, who was in the lead, said, 'What's that on the doormat?'

It was an ordinary white envelope, which had

233

evidently been hand-delivered. Fran picked it up as if it were a hand grenade with the pin removed. There was nothing written on the outside, but she opened it to find two typewritten pages headed 'Robert Barnaby Society – Proposed Publicity Initiative'. She flipped on to the second page, which concluded with a handwritten note. *For your comment and consideration, Stephen.*

'That proves he's been here.'

'How long has it been lying there, do you think?' Mo asked.

'I don't know. I'm sure it can't have been here when I saw Tom out, but it could have arrived just about any time after that. I wouldn't necessarily have noticed it, going up or down the stairs. Of course, you can generally hear the letterbox from the sitting room, but maybe we wouldn't have done if we were talking.'

Mo considered the aperture in question. 'You could easily close it quietly if you wanted to. You might also be able to hold it open and listen through it.'

They had been standing in the hall, staring down at the missive and its point of entry, but now Fran stirred into action again. 'I'm ringing the police,' she said.

It seemed to take an age to get through and then to communicate the details of their situation to a policeman at the other end of the line, but once Fran had done so, the man reassured her that another officer was not far away and would be with them in a matter of ten to fifteen minutes.

'Let's go upstairs and see what happens,' Fran suggested.

The bathroom was too small for more than one person at a time to look out of the window.

'What's happening?' whispered Mo.

'Nothing. His car's still there. Shush – I can hear another car coming along the lane, travelling quite fast. Gosh, it must be the only police car in the entire county. Imagine it happening to be this near. Ah ha, look at that! Our unwanted visitor has fired the ignition and he's starting – yes, he's pulling away and – and – ouch, let go' – in the excitement of the moment, Mo had grabbed her arm – 'the police car is going after him.'

With both cars out of sight, the two women stared wide-eyed at each other. The sounds of the two engines faded into the distance, then out of their hearing altogether.

'Gosh. Will they catch him, do you think?'

'Maybe. Let's go back downstairs. They're sure to come and tell us what's going on.'

It was a full twenty minutes before one of the cars returned and disgorged two police officers, one in plainclothes and the other in uniform. Fran had the front door open before they had the chance to use the knocker. The policemen were unsmiling as they each removed their headgear and dutifully wiped their boots on the mat before following her into the sitting room and accepting her invitation to sit down. Fran saw them taking in the empty cut-glass tumblers and felt instinctively that a judgement was being made.

While the man in uniform took out a notebook and pencil, the other rather gravely asked Fran if she would like to explain, in her own words – hard to see how you'd be using anybody else's words, as Mo said later – why she had telephoned the police. Fran explained that she thought she had seen a figure outside the kitchen window and, having gone upstairs soon afterwards, she had seen that there was a car parked outside in the lane. 'I thought it might belong to a Mr Latchford, who had been bothering me lately. He has been to the house before.'

'Did you recognize Mr Latchford's car?'

'Not at first. I couldn't see the car properly.'

'Has Mr Latchford dropped anything off here this evening, madam?'

'Yes,' Fran said eagerly. She reached over to the table and proffered the white envelope.

'And can I ask you what's in the envelope?'

'Yes – it's some information about the Robert Barnaby Society. You know, Robert Barnaby, the author, but that's just an excuse—'

The policeman politely interrupted. 'So there's nothing . . . for example . . . threatening in what's written?'

'No, but . . .'

'We've just stopped Mr Latchford, up there on the main road, and he told us that he only came here to post something through your letterbox. He says that you are an acquaintance of his and both belong to some sort of club. Would that be correct, madam?'

'Yes. It is . . . sort of . . .'

'According to Mr Latchford, he rang you a day or so ago and asked whether it would be convenient for him to call in tonight. You told him that it was not and asked him to put this information into a letter. Is that correct?'

236

'Yes, it is.'

'Apparently Mr Latchford was passing so he dropped it through your letterbox.'

'Well, yes . . . but he was lurking about outside.'

'You say that you saw him "lurking about", madam? Can you explain what he was doing, exactly?'

Fran hesitated. 'I didn't exactly see him. First I thought I saw someone outside the kitchen window. Then I saw his car parked outside the house.'

'How long would you say it was between thinking that you were seeing someone outside the kitchen window and actually seeing his car parked outside?'

'I don't know. A few minutes.'

'And you thought you saw someone – you're not quite sure?'

Fran shook her head.

'When did you find the note through your door?'

'Mrs Gallimore – my friend – saw it when we came downstairs, after I'd seen the car.'

'That man was not just posting a note through the door,' Mo broke in. 'He'd had plenty of time to do that and drive away. He didn't drive off until he heard you coming and realized that it was the police.'

'Mr Latchford admits that he didn't drive off immediately after posting the note through the door. He says he got his map out to check his route first, as he was on the way to visit a friend in another part of the district. He also says that it did not occur to him that he was causing any alarm, because of course he had no idea that anyone might be watching him through the window.'

'We weren't watching him,' Mo protested. 'He was watching us. He's been bothering Mrs Black for a couple of weeks now.'

The officer turned back to Fran, his face still impassive. 'Can you give us some specific examples of that? Has this man made any threats, any, er . . . improper suggestions, anything of that nature?'

'Nothing like that, no,' Fran said wearily. 'He's been round here a couple of times and it's made me feel uncomfortable, that's all.'

'That wretched man has made us look like a pair of hysterical idiots,' Fran said the moment the police had gone. 'He'd got his story all ready and they just accepted it. I thought any minute that older guy was going to pat me on the head and tell me not to be a silly little girl.'

'Looking at the other side of the coin,' Mo said, 'it must have put the wind up this Latchford fellow when the police pulled him over. He'll surely think twice before he hangs around here again.'

Twenty-Seven

The northern branch of the Robert Barnaby Society were due to meet on the following Saturday afternoon in Middleham, a visit to the castle having been arranged by way of a nod in the direction of *By Sword and By Book*, the Barnaby title which involved an excursion into medieval England.

'You should come as my guest,' Fran told Mo, 'and see some of the suspects for yourself.'

'No, thanks,' said Mo. 'I'd prefer not to spend my afternoon squatting on a toadstool, or whatever it is that you all get up to.'

'There's no squatting involved, I assure you. If asked to squat, the vast majority of our members would never make it back on to their feet unaided.'

Fran had therefore travelled to the event alone, taking the bus service which trundled through Sedbergh, Hawes and Leyburn. She had always liked that part of the Dales and her spirits were lifted still further when the motor coach finally came to a standstill in the market square of Middleham and she recognized Tom's car parked among a group of other vehicles on the cobbled paving.

The meeting proved to be well attended for a regional event, with thirty or so people present, all of whom already knew one another to a greater or lesser degree. Ruth Winterton was there and

Richard Finney, though Gareth Lowe had sent his apologies, which meant that everyone was spared his inevitably eccentric costume. Hugh Allonby and Sarah Ingoldsby were also prominent absentees, though Stephen Latchford was much in evidence, chattering excitedly to everyone except Fran, whom he pointedly ignored. Even Marcus Dryden had taken an afternoon off from hotel-keeping to come along. Marcus rarely attended meetings as the weekend was one of his busiest times, but he explained that he was also a member of the Richard III Society and could not resist a visit which coupled his interest in Robert Barnaby with the castle where the king had spent so much of his life, and he was therefore giving himself what he described as a 'well-earned treat'.

'Good heavens! I didn't know there was such a thing as the Richard III Society,' Tom said.

'Yes, indeed. It's been going for several years now and membership is growing all the time.' Marcus Dryden might have elaborated further but they were interrupted by Richard Finney, who had just spotted what he took to be a buzzard soaring high above them and wanted to know if anyone had brought a pair of field glasses.

Blessed with a sunny day, the group was able to thoroughly explore the castle ruins and visit the nearby church before assembling in the large tearooms which were a feature of the main square. Afternoon tea had been pre-booked for the entire party and Fran found herself sitting at a table with Tom, Marcus Dryden, Ruth Winterton and Richard Finney.

240

It was the first regional meeting since the conference and therefore inevitable that the conversation would turn to Linda Dexter.

'A terribly sad situation,' Mr Finney said. 'I wonder what drove her to do it?'

'It isn't certain that it was suicide,' Fran said. 'The inquest hasn't brought in a verdict yet. They won't resume proceedings until the police are ready.'

'Oh, but surely it can't have been anything but suicide?' This from Ruth Winterton.

'As Mrs Black says, the police are still investigating,' said Marcus, picking up and handing around a plate of cheese sandwiches as he spoke. 'Though I think they will ultimately come down on the side of suicide. It can hardly be anything else, the way Mrs Dexter's bag was packed and her room was left completely tidy, just as if she'd checked out.'

'Had her bed been slept in?' Tom asked in a chatty tone, as if he was merely making polite conversation.

'They asked our chambermaid about that and she said "no".'

'I suppose it might just be possible for someone to get into her room and be waiting there for her when she came down from the bar that night. I mean, there must be other keys to the rooms?' Tom prompted, still adopting that casual, only-making-conversation type of voice.

'We've got pass keys, of course.' Fran noted that Marcus Dryden was not in the least fazed by the direction of the conversation. 'I was asked about all that at the time, but, you know, the layout of

241

the room is against anyone lying in wait. You can see the entire room from the doorway. If a woman were to walk in and see a stranger waiting for her, I would imagine that her normal reaction would be to scream the place down, but no one heard anything, apparently.'

'Who was in the room next door?' Tom asked, but Marcus said he couldn't remember, and the conversation got diverted by Mr Finney asking Miss Winterton if she wanted more tea.

It was only when the waitresses were beginning to clear away that the conversation returned unexpectedly to Furnival Towers.

'I see that Mr Allonby and Mrs Ingoldsby aren't with us,' Marcus Dryden said. His tone was slightly mischievous. 'I assumed that they would be, as they are both staying with us at the Towers this weekend.'

'Another unofficial committee meeting for two?' enquired Tom.

'So it would seem. Of course, our policy at Furnival Towers is discretion at all times.' The hotelier winked and adopted a mischievous expression, while Miss Winterton pursed her lips in disapproval.

'Do you get a lot of visitors through the Robert Barnaby connection?' asked Richard Finney.

'Goodness, yes. It's probably our biggest single selling point. Some people are terribly funny. I had a chap the other week who wanted to lie full length on the floor to take photographs of the magic chair. I mean, honestly! I had to stand guard while he was doing it, in case any of my other guests tripped over him.'

242

'Quite a lot of the guests must be members of the society, I suppose?'

'Not so many as you'd think. Barnaby Society members have mostly already stayed with us during the annual conference, so it's non-members as often as not, though we did have quite a spate of members just before the conference. Gareth Lowe and some of his pals came about a month beforehand on a Barnaby walking weekend. I don't know how much walking got done but they certainly downed a lot of beer.

'Then Mr James, the new membership secretary, came for a night – getting the feel of the place, he said, on account of being tasked with organizing the conference bookings. I thought myself that it was more to do with getting a first look at the chair and everything. A lot of people – even society members – don't like to admit that they're desperate to see it. They don't want to be thought childish, I suppose. Mr James had never been to a conference before, of course. I believe he was living abroad until recently.'

'I am sure that Mr James was also checking the layout to help with the room allocations,' Miss Winterton said. 'He seems to be extremely conscientious in everything he does. If he has to stand down, it will be a real loss.'

'Thoroughly good sort of chap,' Marcus Dryden agreed. 'I got on splendidly with him myself. Of course, the Barnaby connection has been an absolute godsend, because back before the war we were almost entirely reliant on people who came for the shooting, and a small band of loyal regulars. Funnily enough, Mr Latchford's mother . . .'

Marcus Dryden paused momentarily to jerk his head in the direction of the table in the corner, which included Stephen Latchford, '. . . was one of our regulars, and he came for a weekend himself, during the war.' He lowered his voice conspiratorially and added: 'He didn't serve, you know. I'm not sure if he wasn't a conshie.'

There was a moment's awkward silence, then Miss Winterton pointedly changed the subject, turning to ask Mr Finney if it wasn't true that Middleham was a well-known centre for training race horses?

'That was a bit naughty of old Marcus, mentioning the Allonby-Ingoldsby tryst,' Tom said a little while later. 'And it evidently irritated Miss Winterton no end.' He and Fran were standing on the edge of the large group who were exchanging farewells outside the tea shop. The late afternoon bus was due and one or two people were already climbing into motorcars.

'She didn't much like it when he suggested that Stephen Latchford might have been a conscientious objector either,' Fran said, keeping her voice too low to be overheard by anyone but Tom.

'It's not the sort of thing anyone should be spreading around,' said Tom. 'A rumour of that sort could end up getting the chap ostracized. Look here, are you in a hurry to get off? Because if you like we could drive partway out of the Dales, then stop for a drink and catch an early supper at a pub somewhere on the road. I could easily drop you home afterwards.'

She knew perfectly well that it was miles out of his way, but even so she heard herself saying,

244

'After that huge afternoon tea, I'm not sure that I've got room for anything else to eat, but I'd love a drink.'

'Good show – what say we drive back to Hawes and stop at one of the pubs there?'

Over two halves of beer, Fran told Tom about the episode with the police and Stephen Latchford. The trouble was that she found herself feeling nearly as foolish as when she had tried to get the problem across to the police, because with every retelling, the story sounded increasingly flimsy and pathetic.

'No wonder old Stephen-with-a-ph was giving you the cold shoulder today,' was all Tom said.

After that they went over the Linda Dexter question again, but nothing new emerged.

Neither of them seemed to be in any hurry to leave. When Tom's knee accidentally rested against her thigh under the scrubbed wooden table, she let it stay there. She wasn't hungry for food, she thought, not just because of the scones and dainty sandwiches which they had already consumed, but because she felt full up with desire. Tom had never seemed wittier, his brown eyes never more entrancing. She found herself noticing his hands, unusually graceful for a man's, as they closed around his glass. The thought came to her that if she couldn't have Tom, then just sitting here as long as possible, being with him, being his friend, laughing at his jokes and making him laugh in turn, was – well, basically as good as it was ever going to get. Then she noticed that the pressure of his knee was gently increasing.

'I don't feel much like eating either,' he was

saying. 'Tell you what, why don't we take a stroll up to the edge of the village? It's a lovely evening out there.'

As she stood up and wriggled out from between the table and the bench seat, his hand rested momentarily on her shoulder, as if he was assisting her progress in some way.

She must not give way. He had a wife called Veronica. Veronica was at home with her little boy, William, at that very minute, and even if she had never heard of Frances Black and never would, Veronica was relying on her to do the right thing by that great sisterhood of married women to which they both belonged.

They had left the pub now and were walking along the deserted street in silence. When they reached the turn which led to the railway station, Fran said, 'I suppose it's time to head back.'

'Do you have to get home? I wondered whether we might make a night of it.' He was looking right into her eyes. There was no mistaking the message. 'I know a really nice little hotel just down the road.' When she said nothing, he put an arm around her shoulder, ready to draw her into a kiss. For a split second, the prospect of melting into his arms danced enticingly before her, but it was interrupted by a vision of a faceless woman holding a little boy by the hand.

Fran pulled away abruptly. 'Please don't do that, Tom. It's not . . . appropriate.'

He drew back, as if she had struck him, but recovered quickly. 'Oh.' He hesitated. 'Right. I see. I'm so sorry.'

'I have to get back. Home. I've got a cat. She'll

be getting hungry.' The words tumbled out, ridiculous, incongruous. 'I'll see you . . .' She faltered to a halt, not knowing when she would see him again, or in fact how she was now supposed to get home. The situation had become hopelessly awkward, embarrassing.

'It's quite all right,' he said quickly, almost as if he had read her mind. 'I will run you straight home, of course.'

'Thank you.' She turned back towards the pub where they had left the car, retracing her steps so briskly that she arrived alongside the Hudson slightly out of breath, and climbed in without waiting for him to hold the door for her. He gunned the motor into life and began to drive at his habitual speed, but all the usual pleasure of travelling alongside him was crushed beneath the stifling silence which enveloped them. She longed to say something which would reinstate good relations, even if their easy camaraderie could never be restored, but it was as if her mind had been completely emptied of words and she was ridiculously afraid that if she attempted to talk she might begin to cry. His own silence seemed to be born of awkwardness rather than hostility. On two occasions he cleared his throat, as if in readiness to speak, but nothing emerged. Eventually, after they had put Hawes some miles behind them, he began to say what sounded like, 'I am most terribly sorry—'

She cut across him at once. 'Please don't say anything. I would far rather not talk about it.' Stupid, stupid, words coming out all wrong. Of course they must talk, but somehow she could not take it back, and so they drove on and on in silence.

It was getting dark when they drew up at her gate. For the last fifteen minutes or so she had been wondering whether she should invite him inside, so that they could try to put things right, but as she had rejected his attempt at an apology and had no idea what else to say, what possible use would it be to prolong matters? So instead, she said, 'Thank you very much for bringing me home.'

'I'll telephone – if I find out anything else about Linda Dexter,' he said, turning half towards her, his expression masked by the encroaching dusk.

She knew it was a question. 'Yes,' she said. 'Of course. I expect we'll speak during the week.' She was still fighting back tears and her voice sounded clipped and abrupt, like someone dismissing a tradesman. She had not meant it to come out that way at all.

She did not wave goodbye or watch as he drove away, but instead stood at the gate, focusing all her attention on her handbag while she fumbled for the door key. I am not going to cry. I am not going to cry. She opened the gate and walked up the path, trying to forget the expression on Tom's face when she had pulled away from his attempted embrace. He had seemed so surprised and hurt. It was her own fault, she thought. She had led him on. Her eyes must have betrayed her a thousand times, and now she had rejected him in an abrupt, humiliating way, when in reality . . . 'Stop it,' she said aloud. 'You are not going to be that person.'

It was only when she had reached the doorstep that she actually looked up properly at the cottage and saw the damage. With trembling fingers, she unlocked the door and reached for the matches to light the lamp in the hall. Mrs Snegglington trotted forward to greet her.

'Hello,' Fran called nervously, but the only reaction she received was a curious look from the cat. Carrying the oil lamp before her into the sitting room, she went straight to the telephone and asked for Mo's number.

'Hello,' the blessedly familiar voice sounded in her ear. 'What's up?'

'I've just got home and discovered that someone has put my front windows through.'

'Say that again?'

'I've just got home after a Barnaby Society meeting and found that someone has smashed my downstairs windows. I don't know what to do, Mo.'

Twenty-Eight

Mrs Snegglington was not at all happy about the transfer to Mo's house, where she was being confined to the drawing room. She intermittently prowled around, looking for an exit, before settling disconsolately in an armchair and refusing all suggestion of fuss or laps, having adopted a strict policy of non-fraternization.

'If only she could tell us who did it,' Mo said, nodding in the cat's direction. 'She must have seen them come or go.'

'She might have been asleep – let's face it, she usually is. She probably knew nothing about it until she heard the rocks come through the windows.'

Mo hesitated. 'I know you told the police about that Latchford man, but did you mention Tom Dod?'

In the day and a half since the Barnaby Society meeting at Middleham, Fran had brought her friend fully up to date with the Tom situation.

'I didn't mention Tom, because he couldn't possibly have done it. He was with me, remember.'

'Unless for some reason he did it on his way to the meeting. He could have come a different way and still have got there in a shorter time than it took you to get there by bus.'

'That doesn't make any sense, Mo. And anyway, why would it be Tom?'

'The more scared you are, the more likely to fall into his arms?'

Fran said nothing. There was a time when she would have ridiculed such an idea, but then hadn't she also ridiculed Mo's constant assertions that Tom was romantically interested in her? Perhaps this latest suggestion was no more bizarre than the fact that her windows had been put through. The situation felt unreal, as if her whole life was sliding into chaos. The policeman who had attended the cottage in answer to her call on Saturday evening had not been one of those who had previously answered her call for help a few nights earlier, when Stephen Latchford's car had been parked out in the lane. This latest policeman had arrived while she and Mo were sweeping up the broken glass and waiting for the local handyman to arrive and do some temporary boarding up. After a lifetime of never having had anything to do with the police, Fran reflected, it now seemed as if various members of the constabulary were beating a regular path to her door. The latest model was tall and thin, with a ponderous, north country accent. When she told him that she suspected a Mr Stephen-with-a-ph-Latchford might be responsible for the damage, he said that the police would call on this Mr Latchford, of course, but that they could not jump to any conclusions when there was no real evidence about who was responsible. 'It might just be a random act of vandalism, Mum, or a case of mistaken identity.'

In the meantime, Mo had insisted that Fran and the cat stay with her, at the very least until the new glass could be cut and the windows were mended. 'As long as you like,' Mo had said, but Fran knew that it wasn't fair on the cat, who liked to be in her own territory, where she could make believe that she was a great feline hunter, though in fact she was far too lazy to catch even a catnip mouse on the end of a string.

'You know, I can't help feeling that this is all mixed up with Linda Dexter,' Fran said.

'Don't,' Mo said. 'Next thing you'll be thinking that you're going to be the next victim, or something.'

'You have to admit that all this business with Stephen Latchford only started the weekend that Linda Dexter died.'

'That's true – but mightn't that just be coincidence, because that was when he realized that he lived so near to you? Didn't you tell me that he has only just moved into the district?'

'From the area where Linda Dexter used to live,' Fran reminded her.

'Fair point.' Mo brushed back a strand of hair which was escaping across her forehead. 'Try to think back. Were there ever any signs that there was some kind of problem between Latchford and Linda Dexter?'

'Not that I noticed.'

'Let's try going through things systematically again. Could Stephen Latchford perhaps have some connection with Linda's family, either the sister who stood to inherit, or else the murder back in 1914?'

'The sister gets everything,' Fran said. 'She's married, and I saw her husband at the funeral. It isn't Stephen Latchford.'

252

'Well, of course not.' Mo laughed. 'The connection couldn't be that obvious, not least because Linda Dexter would have recognized anyone who was close to her sister, and probably ditto her ex-husband . . . And probably the chap who murdered her father and stepsister too – weren't they quite close?'

'The killer was her ex-sweetheart, so I suppose she would still know him if she saw him again, even after all this time. I know people change and a man could dye his hair, or grow a beard, or something like that, but people don't generally change that much. I saw people at the unveiling of the village war memorial who I haven't seen in years, but I still recognized them and knew who they were.'

'Assuming that this person didn't have a key to Linda Dexter's hotel room, one supposes that she must have let them into the room herself,' Mo mused. 'Of course, she may not have bothered to lock the door behind her. Lots of people don't. What kind of locks are they?'

'Oh, the old-fashioned kind. You have to turn the key on the inside to lock them.'

'And you say she wasn't a particularly strong, athletic type?'

'Just the opposite.'

'So there are really quite a lot of possibilities. To begin with, if she didn't bother to lock her door before she went to bed, the killer could have simply walked in and taken her by surprise. Or he could have knocked on the door then grabbed her when she opened it, without giving her time to cry out. If he was watching, waiting for her to come to bed, he could have barged straight in after her, again taking her by surprise and not giving her time to cry out.'

'There's nowhere to hide in that corridor, but Stephen Latchford's room was right opposite and he could have been watching through the keyhole. You're absolutely right that if the attack came out of the blue, she may not have had time to shout for help.'

'I believe it's not that difficult to strangle someone, using a gent's tie or something similar,' Mo said. 'Particularly if you have come prepared. Once Linda was dead, you could pack up her things and move them down to her car, then you choose your moment and carry the body out the same way, dumping it on the railway line and trusting to luck that the train would make such a mess of the poor woman that the doctors wouldn't be able to say exactly what had happened to her.'

'Tom said he thought it would have been quite easy to carry her.'

'Let's hope he wasn't speaking from personal experience.'

'Oh, really, Mo!'

Mo did not immediately reply. She knew that Fran had not spoken with Tom since parting from him at the garden gate on Saturday night. After a lengthy pause, she said, 'Cheer up, old thing. We're off to Wimbledon next week, don't forget. Remember when we saw Lili Alvarez in 'twenty-six? Gosh, but she was pretty. Do you think she will make the final again this year?'

Twenty-Nine

Mo drove Fran back to Bee Hive Cottage the following morning, where they found that the windows had been replaced and the handwritten bill for the work was propped in front of the other post, which Ada had picked up and placed on the mantelshelf. The rest of the place looked spick and span and just as usual. It took more than a bit of broken glass to divert the stolid Ada from her normal routine.

Fran shuffled through the envelopes, immediately recognizing the distinctive handwriting on one of them. 'Hello,' she said as she tore it open and swiftly scanned the contents. 'There's one here from Hugh Allonby, asking me to telephone him, on what he describes as "a matter of urgency". I wonder what on earth he can want.'

'Only one way to find out.'

'Somehow I don't think it's going to be good news. Mr Allonby has been furious with me, ever since Tom and I sort of defeated him over getting hold of Linda's papers before he managed to procure them himself and bury the contents forever.'

'Perhaps the Grand Master of the Barnaby Society just wants to talk to you about the handover of those precious notebooks.'

Hugh Allonby did not want to talk about the notebooks. When he found that it was Fran on

255

the phone, he did not bother to beat about the bush. 'I was trying your telephone number for most of yesterday,' he said. His tone was accusing, as if she had been avoiding him on purpose.

'I'm not at home at the moment. I'm staying with a friend. I came back to pick up my post and only found your letter a few moments ago.'

'Really?' Hugh's tone was acerbic. Fran was uncertain which aspect of the statement he doubted – the reality of her absence or the possibility of her having a friend. 'As you know, I have entertained reservations about your being on the executive committee ever since your conduct over those papers belonging to Mrs Dexter, but yesterday I became aware of another matter, which is surely the final straw.' He paused, but as Fran said nothing, he was forced to continue. 'Mr Stephen Latchford, one of our most valued and respected members, telephoned me in great distress. He informs me that you have now told the police not once, but twice, that he has been harassing you in some way. Mr Latchford is a very fair-minded man, and he said that, on the first occasion, this could have been the result of no more than an innocent misunderstanding. Apparently there was some suggestion of a prowler at your property and he had coincidentally been there that evening to deliver something – something which he tells me that you had actually *asked* him to drop off.'

'That's not entirely correct,' Fran began, but Hugh Allonby ploughed on regardless. 'It now seems that because someone has committed some act of vandalism at your property, you have

256

suggested to the police that Mr Latchford may have been responsible, and they called on him again and questioned him at some length. As he said to me, it is very difficult for a single person, living alone, to rebut these kinds of allegations, however misplaced. He is talking about slander and involving solicitors, and he has pointed out that your being a member of the executive committee gave you access to a membership directory, which in turn enabled you to send the police straight to his door. Naturally, I have assured him that I will take appropriate action at once. I'm afraid I will have to ask you to stand down from the committee immediately. It is possible that you mean well, but you're a loose cannon, Mrs Black, and we cannot afford loose cannons. If you don't resign voluntarily, I will have no alternative but to convene a special executive meeting and have you removed. I simply will not tolerate members bringing the society into disrepute.'

'But that's ridiculous.' Fran attempted to take breath in readiness for a fully thought-out protest, but again Hugh Allonby gave her no opportunity.

'As chairman, I have to put aside any personal feelings and consider the interests of the society. My duty, first and last, is to protect the reputation of Robert Barnaby and the society convened in his name. We already have this unpleasant business of a member's suicide hanging over our heads, and I cannot afford suggestions that one member is accusing another of harassing them. By all means, take a couple of days to think about it, but I shall expect to receive your letter of resignation and a copy of your formal apology

257

to Mr Latchford by the end of this week. It goes without saying that this must be kept between ourselves. It will naturally be put about that you have had to resign for personal reasons.'

'Apology!' Fran exploded, but it was unlikely that Hugh Allonby heard her as he was already in the process of hanging up the telephone.

'What will you do?' Mo asked, after Fran had repeated Hugh Allonby's side of the conversation.

'I don't know. I don't much care about being on the wretched committee, it's just that I don't want to let him win. Which, of course, he will do, either way. Tom managed to sway everyone last time, but I think the committee would support Hugh Allonby over this.' She did not add that Tom probably would not care about her having to resign from the committee anyway, now that she had finally rebuffed his attentions.

'He's a crafty one, this Stephen Latchford,' Mo said, thoughtfully. 'He's completely turned the situation around, making himself into the victim, instead of you. Properly, they ought to be looking at it the other way, or at least in a neutral way, because if he *is* pestering you, then it's him who should be penalized, not you.'

'Hold on a minute.' Fran stood up from the chair in which she had sat to make her telephone call and, somewhat to Mo's surprise, marched into the parlour. 'I'm just fetching something.' She returned a moment later with what was clearly an amateurishly produced booklet – essentially a lot of typewritten sheets of paper, stapled together.

'Now what are you up to?'

'I'm about to misuse my membership list again.

Do you remember my telling you something about the membership secretary?'

'Some new chap who helped to organize the conference?'

'No, not him. There was a previous membership secretary and she stood down for what were officially described as "personal reasons" too.'

Mo shook her head. 'Darling, I haven't got an inkling as to what you're talking about.'

'Jennifer Rumsey. I'm going to telephone Jennifer Rumsey. Oh, damn!' she exclaimed a moment later. 'She's not on the telephone. Well I'll have to drop her a note and arrange to see her somehow. This isn't the sort of thing you can put in a letter.'

Thirty

The inquest into Linda Dexter's death was resumed the following day. Fran had been watching for the date to be announced in the newspaper and had briefly considered the possibility of attending in person, but it seemed rather like the sort of morbid behaviour – which her mother had often remarked upon – among those lower-class women who could hardly wait to go and see the laid-out body of a deceased neighbour, so Fran had held her curiosity in check until the evening paper arrived, and she was able to read an account of the proceedings instead.

To her irritation, the jury had brought in a verdict of suicide while temporarily of unsound mind. As she read the evidence, Fran found her indignation bubbling up to boiling point. When Christina Harper had been asked about her step-sister's life, the coroner had adopted a line of questioning which served to emphasize the relative loneliness of Linda's situation, and then Hugh Allonby had been questioned about Linda's role in the conference and had managed to imply that the theories which she had intended to share with her fellow members were questionable to the point of eccentricity. The coroner (who sounded like a pompous old fool of her mother's vintage, Fran decided) had made some remarks to the effect that it was distinctly abnormal for a woman to lead a life 'so lacking in purpose, without the normal constraints of husband, family and home which would inevitably lead to a more balanced outlook'.

'Bloody man,' Fran said aloud. 'Doesn't he realize that living with some husbands would be *exactly* the kind of life which could lead a woman to throw herself under a train?'

The sergeant who had appeared as a witness on behalf of the local police informed the court that their investigations had failed to throw up anything which suggested foul play.

After she had tossed the paper aside in an untidy manner of which her mother would have thoroughly disapproved, she felt enveloped by a sense of hopelessness. She and Tom had assumed that it was taking so long to bring the legal formalities to a close because the police were undertaking a thorough investigation and had been pursuing some interesting clues, whereas what the newspaper report actually revealed was that the resumption of proceedings had been delayed due to some 'indisposition' on the part of the coroner, which had led to a backlog in the business of the court. Ever since Linda Dexter's death, she had become more and more convinced that it was a case of murder, but now she was confronted with the plain fact that the police – who were surely the experts – had found nothing to underpin that idea. Under the circumstances, could she realistically attempt to continue with some kind of investigation on her own?

The telephone rang right on cue.

'Fran?' It was Tom, sounding less than certain of what his reception might be.

'Yes, yes, it's me.' Who else would it be? After all, she was one of those unbalanced women who lived alone.

'The inquest took place this morning.'

'Yes, I know.' She tried not to sound too eager. 'I've just been reading about it in the evening paper.'

'The police have given up.'

'I know.'

'But . . . we're not going to give up, are we?'

'No.' She gulped. 'We won't give up.'

'I'm not sure that there's much to be gained from my going back to the Vester House Museum.'

'Probably not. It's pretty obvious that Linda was right about the magic chair. The question is whether that actually matters to anyone. In the meantime, I've had another letter from Hugh Allonby.'

'*Another* letter?'

'Yes.' She told him about the broken windows, her call to the police and its aftermath, but Tom's reaction was somewhat different to that which she had expected.

'I can see why old Allonby finds himself between the Devil and the deep blue sea on this one.'

'What on earth do you mean?'

'Whatever we may think about Allonby, he does have to put the society's interests first, and if Latchford is cutting up rough and threatening to sue, he will naturally want to mollify him.'

'But what about me? Surely it's hardly fair to cave in the minute that wretched man threatens him. Why . . . it's positively cowardly.'

262

'Some might say that he's merely taking a diplomatic line.'

'Just suppose,' Fran tried to keep the annoyance out of her voice, 'that Stephen Latchford had done this before and knew that he could get away with things by pretending that he had been falsely accused.'

'But there's nothing to link him to Linda Dexter.'

'I'm not talking about Linda Dexter. Jennifer Rumsey lives up in Cumberland – just as both Linda Dexter and Mr Latchford did until recently. Don't you remember that Jennifer Rumsey was supposed to have stood down for "personal reasons" too? I'm convinced that there was something fishy about her resignation. No one is willing to talk about it.'

'I'm inclined to agree with you, but it may be absolutely nothing to do with Latchford, and anyway, I'm not sure how you're going to get to the bottom of it. Didn't Miss Robertson say that it was a confidential matter and it hadn't been minuted?'

'She did. But I'm not going via the committee members or the minutes. I'm going straight to the horse's mouth. I've written to Miss Rumsey, saying that I have to go up to Carlisle on some errand and asking if I can meet her while I'm there.'

'Talking of meeting,' Tom said, 'I think it would be a good idea if we could meet too, face-to-face, because there's something I would like to discuss with you which can't easily be said on the telephone.'

Thirty-One

Fran had initially written to suggest that Jennifer Rumsey nominate a tea shop where they could meet on the day when she 'happened to be up in Carlisle', but Miss Rumsey's response had been to invite her to call at her home instead, so Fran made her way to an address not far from the cathedral at the appointed time. A smartly dressed parlour maid answered the front door and conducted her into a positively Victorian drawing room, complete with a stuffed fox on a plinth in one alcove and side tables draped with cloths which almost reached the carpet and were so laden with ornaments that they looked for all the world like chronically over-decorated iced cakes.

'I'm afraid my mother's tastes are rather old fashioned.' Miss Rumsey had evidently caught Fran's expression.

'How is your mother? I heard that she was unwell.'

'My mother's as fit as a flea. She is currently chairing a meeting at the Women's Institute, which gives us a chance to enjoy our tea without your being asked a million and one questions. I'm afraid my mother mistakes interrogation for polite conversation. Tell me, what made you imagine that she had not been well?'

Fran decided that there was no point in beating about the bush. 'I expect you know that I've

264

recently been elected on to the Barnaby Society committee . . .' She received a nod of confirmation and continued, 'There is a possibility that the new membership secretary may have to stand down, and I asked whether you might be prevailed upon to resume the task, but I was given the impression that your mother, or perhaps some other relative, was in greater need of your assistance.'

'Oh, heavens!' Jennifer Rumsey burst out laughing. 'So that's the way Mr Allonby and his cronies tried to dress it all up, is it? I can assure you, Mrs Black, that at the slightest sign of my mother or anyone else requiring any kind of ministrations, I engage the services of a private nurse at the first possible opportunity.'

A tap on the door heralded the arrival of the maid, bearing an impossibly large tea tray. When she had gone and Miss Rumsey had dealt with the little ritual of pouring their tea and offering thinly sliced cucumber sandwiches, she fixed Fran with a rather determined look and said, 'Would I be right in guessing that this is not purely a social call? You have come to find out the truth behind my resignation, isn't that so?'

Fran smiled. 'I'm afraid you have found me out.'

'I am perfectly happy to explain, but first I have one condition. Will you tell me why you want to know?'

'Certainly. On Tuesday this week, I myself was privately invited to stand down, and it was suggested that a story be put out that my resignation had been tendered for personal reasons.'

'Well, well.' Jennifer Rumsey laughed again. 'And may I ask what offence you are supposed to have committed which has rendered Mr Allonby so eager to be rid of you?'

Fran swallowed. 'I complained to the police about the behaviour of a fellow member.'

'Did you now? Chap's name wouldn't be Stephen Latchford, would it?'

'You have it in one. Can I take it that he had been bothering you too?'

'Not bothering me, no. I live here with Mother, you see. Mr Latchford's activities are, so far as I know, usually directed only at women who live alone.'

'But . . .'

'I promised to explain and now I will. You see, as membership secretary, I get to hear about all resignations from the society. Almost two years ago, a woman member from Darlington resigned. There was a bit of a fuss because she had complained to the committee about Mr Latchford calling on her and making a general nuisance of himself. At that time he was living over in North Yorkshire. She wanted the committee to do something about his having a copy of the membership list. As you may know, although he isn't on the executive committee, he acquired one some time ago, supposedly for the purposes of a project he had suggested which involved plotting how many members lived in different parts of the country, or something of the kind. It was supposed to help determine the organization of regional events, though I'm not at all sure that anything ever came of it. Anyway, the woman's complaint was pretty much dismissed out of hand. Mr Allonby said that the committee could not get involved in personal spats between members and, at the time, I have to admit that I agreed with him.

'However, about a year later we got another complaint. A woman informed Miss Winterton, of all people, that Stephen Latchford had been making a nuisance of himself. She brought it to the committee and Hugh Allonby was all for dismissing it again. He didn't want "some sort of bandwagon", as he put it, developing against Mr Latchford. Miss Robertson and I protested at once. Neither of us could see how a bandwagon could have been developing because, so far as we knew, there wasn't a connection between the two women who had complained, but of course the rest of the committee fell into line behind Allonby as usual and nothing further was done.

'The whole business left me feeling very uncomfortable, and when I got home from that meeting I had a look through all the resignations from the previous year and noticed that there were two from women who happened to live in this same area of the country, and I decided to contact them, to check why they had resigned. It's a perfectly reasonable step for a membership secretary to take.'

'Of course.' Fran nodded, mentally noting that she and Tom were by no means the only amateur detectives in the society.

'One of the women was extremely cagey. I felt that something had gone on which had clearly upset her but she was not willing to talk about it. The second was more forthcoming. She went so far as to say that Latchford had called repeatedly and eventually tried to . . . well . . . take advantage of her. She did not wish to involve the police – what woman wants to give evidence about such matters in a court of law?'

'Quite so.'

'Needless to say, I took my findings to the next committee meeting. I pointed out that we now had the word of at least three of our members that Latchford had made improper approaches, and strong suspicions that he had done so in the case of a fourth. Essentially the man had gained access to our membership list and was using it in order to intrude himself into the lives of various women. Naturally their confidences had to be respected, so we could not take the matter to the police, but I felt that Mr Latchford ought to be made to return his membership list and, at the very least, be warned in some way about his conduct. To my absolute astonishment, Hugh Allonby became furious – not with Stephen Latchford, but with me. He said that we could not give credence to unsubstantiated allegations of this nature, accused me of snooping and virtually claimed that I had encouraged these women to invent these stories.

'I had at one point suggested confronting Latchford and requesting his resignation, but according to Allonby that was tantamount to slander and liable to bring the society into disrepute. As you can imagine, I was furious. I said there and then that it was my intention to stand down. I could not countenance being part of an organization which ultimately placed its reputation ahead of the welfare of the very members who financed it. I initially decided to have nothing further to do with the society, but later I thought better of it. After all, why should that nasty little man rob me of the enjoyment I get from reading the society journals?'

'But you no longer come to any of our meetings,' Fran said.

'I thought it over and decided that it was better not to. I don't want to have to lie to members, if anyone asks me, as for example you did today, about the circumstances of my resignation. You see, the problem is that, in one sense, Hugh Allonby does have a point. Until one of the recipients of Mr Latchford's unwelcome attentions makes a complaint to the police and has it upheld in court, he can continue to bluster about suing anyone who says anything at all about what is going on.'

'It's an impossible situation,' Fran said. 'It is very . . . intimidating . . . when he keeps hanging around, but if you complain to the police, he justifies it in such a way as to make you look like an idiot.'

'Precisely. And if – as I believe must have occurred on at least one occasion already – things go too far, no respectable woman will want to damage her reputation by making a complaint.'

'What use would it be to complain anyway?' Fran said bitterly. 'No court in the land will take a woman seriously if she appears to have befriended the man and invited him into her home before such an act took place.'

'I trust,' Miss Rumsey said, carefully focusing her eyes on the teapot as she lifted the lid and added hot water from a jug, 'that nothing too dreadful has occurred in your own dealings with Mr Latchford?'

'He has done nothing worse than make repeated attempts to visit me. I became alarmed and reported him to the police, at which point he returned and smashed my windows. Or at least I suspect that it was him – I could never prove it.'

'Past behaviour suggests that although nothing can be proved, the involvement of the police at this stage will ensure the cessation of his visits. No doubt he will now transfer his attentions elsewhere.'

'Tell me,' Fran said, 'was Mrs Dexter one of the women who complained?'

'I am not prepared to name names, I'm afraid, because people spoke to me in confidence. However, I don't see any harm in telling you that she was not.'

'Though that doesn't guarantee that he wasn't bothering her.'

'And you think that may have been what led her to take her own life?' Jennifer Rumsey looked thoughtful. 'I suppose there might be something in that, but I can only repeat that she was not one of the women who had actually complained.'

'I have found myself wondering whether she did take her own life,' Fran said carefully.

'I can't see how there would be any doubt about it,' Miss Rumsey said. 'After all, it can't possibly have been an accident and it struck me from what little I read about in the newspaper that it would be a frightfully complicated way of choosing to murder anyone. To begin with, the person concerned would need to know that

Mrs Dexter was going to be at the conference at all. Then they would need to know where and when the trains ran – oh, yes, and which room she was staying in at Furnival Towers . . . that place is a fearful rabbit warren. If you wanted to murder her, why not just break into her house one night, taking care not to rouse the servants, stab her, or strangle her, and then creep away into the night? It surely wouldn't have been any more difficult to break into her house than it would have been to break into a hotel?'

'I don't know,' Fran said. 'Well . . . I expect you're right.'

'There was probably some deep-seated unhappiness there which drove her to do it. That's the thing about organizations like the Barnaby Society, of course. We none of us know anything much about one another's lives. Occasionally one comes across the most astonishing things. Did you know, for example, that our journal secretary, Richard Finney, won a VC in the last war? Such a pleasant, unassuming man. I only found out by accident because I have a cousin who was in the same regiment.'

'Gosh,' Fran said. 'I had no idea.'

'There we are. Bertram Winterbottom, who preceded Miss Robertson in the role of Minutes Secretary, sings solo tenor in his church choir and my replacement, Mr James, coaches junior athletics teams. None of us knows a thing about one another.' There was a faint note of triumph in Miss Rumsey's voice, as if she had established an important point.

271

Thirty-Two

'She sounds like a far better detective than you or Tom,' Mo said when Fran had finished relating the conversation to her that evening. 'How on earth does she know so much about all these people anyway?'

'She stumbled across the information about the VC by accident and it was the same with John James really. Apparently they arranged to meet, so that she could hand over all her membership files, and he was tying the trip in with attending an athletics meeting somewhere. I've no idea how she knew about Mr Winterbottom and the singing – just from casual chit-chat, I suppose.'

'But all that business with that horrible Latchford man and those other women. I think it's absolutely scandalous that this Miss Rumsey went out of her way to look into the whole business, but then, when she finally got to the bottom of it, the wretched committee refused to do anything about it.'

'Basically that's because he blackmailed them into keeping quiet.'

'Tommyrot!' exclaimed Mo. 'They ought to have stood up to him. If that Allonby fellow had told him to sue and be damned, he would have soon backed down. You can't win a slander case if what people are saying about you is true. If you ask me, I think your society behaved in a pretty cowardly, shabby kind of way. Anyway, after what Miss Rumsey has told you, I assume that Stephen Latchford goes right to the top of the list of suspects?'

'You suppose right, except that I can't quite see what he stood to gain by killing her.'

'What do you mean?'

'Well, murdering someone is pretty drastic.'

'I should say so.'

'To murder someone in this particular way required a lot of advance planning and must have carried a certain amount of risk.'

'I'm with you so far.'

'One woman had complained to the committee about Latchford bothering her and her complaint had got her precisely nowhere. Jennifer Rumsey had uncovered other victims of his attentions and still nothing was done, and Linda Dexter had never shown any signs of complaining about him at all, so where's the motive?'

'We can't be absolutely sure that she hadn't said anything about him bothering her.'

'If she had complained to the committee recently then I'm sure that Tom and I would have heard about it, and if she had gone direct to the police that would have made him a suspect after she died – particularly as they knew that he was in the room opposite to hers – so the fact that he wasn't treated as a suspect and that the police believe there were no suspicious circumstances rather suggests that there was no complaint.'

Mo considered this with her head on one side. 'Right,' she said. 'In which case, as you say, what is Latchford's motive for getting rid of her?'

'Oh dear . . . Well, there's possible gain, but for that we would need to tie him to the Harpers somehow, because Mrs Harper is the only one who inherits. There's the need to silence Linda over her research . . .'

'Which brings in the hotel people and your society chairman, but not Mr Latchford.'

'And Mr Chairman has a secondary motive inasmuch that he probably doesn't want news of his affair getting back to Mrs Allonby. Although I have to admit that there's nothing to suggest Linda Dexter even knew that something was going on between him and Mrs Ingoldsby – I didn't, until Tom pointed it out to me.'

Mo shook her head and clicked her tongue in mock disapproval. 'And you call yourself a detective?'

'Finally, there's the Halfpenny Landing murders.'

'I'm sorry,' Mo said. 'But I just don't see how that comes into it at all.'

'Nor do I, really. It just sort of hangs about, like a bit of jigsaw puzzle that won't fit.'

'How old is Stephen Latchford?'

'I'm not entirely sure. In his forties, I would guess.'

'So he's the right age to have fought in the war?'

'Easily.'

'Well then, couldn't he be your escaped murderer? This chap who was rumoured to have joined up and then been killed, but who could just as easily have managed to circulate a rumour of his death, survived the war and gone on to make a new life for himself elsewhere? How old was that chap when the Halfpenny Landing murders took place?'

'About twenty-one, twenty-two, something like that. I've got it written in my notes. But Stephen Latchford can't have been the Halfpenny Landing killer, because Marcus Dryden knew him and his family before the war.'

Mo was still reluctant to let go of the idea and used her fingers for some swift arithmetic before saying, 'If he was twenty-one in 1914, then he would be thirty-six now. That does fit – or nearly fit – with Latchford.'

'And half the other men in the society. We've got a lot of ex-servicemen.'

'How old is Tom Dod?'

'I don't know.' To her annoyance, Fran felt her cheeks colour. 'He doesn't seem as old as thirty-six.'

'How old is his son?'

'He had his tenth birthday last month. Tom mentioned it.'

'Most men don't marry until their mid-twenties.'

There was a moment's silence before Mo said, 'But anyway, why would the Halfpenny Landing man want to murder Linda Dexter now, after all this time?'

'I don't know. Clearly there was something very peculiar about the whole business at Halfpenny Landing. You have this young man, Edwin Traynor, who first of all sets his cap at the sister who doesn't have any money and then jilts her in favour of the younger stepsister who is an heiress. He becomes secretly engaged to this girl and gets her to make a will in his favour, and then he murders her and her surviving parent, hoping to inherit the family fortune. What's the first thing that strikes you about that situation?'

'That he's a nasty, greedy little beast?'

'Apart from that?'

Mo favoured her friend with a blank look. 'Go on, Sexton Blake, I know you're dying to tell me.'

'He would be the obvious suspect.'

'Well, yes, clearly.'

'Think about it. You have gone to all that trouble to get the girl to fall in love with you, make her will and so forth. You commit an elaborate murder which involves, from memory, stealing a boat and hiking miles across the countryside, and then when the police come knocking at your door, as you know that they inevitably will, you don't have an alibi ready and waiting.'

'It would be pretty difficult to have an alibi if you had been out murdering your fiancée and her father. On the other hand, I suppose that if you said you had spent the entire night at home, alone, although that's pretty lame, it's then up to the police to prove that it wasn't the case.'

'But don't you see?' There was a growing note of excitement in Fran's voice. 'Edwin Traynor did something far worse than provide your "lame" alibi. He told the police a story which they were able to disprove straight away.'

'Remind me?'

'He told them that he had spent the evening with Linda, the stepsister and his old flame. It was a lie and, worse still for him, she could easily

276

prove that it was a lie, because she had spent the evening with some other friends at a party.'

'Why on earth . . .'

'Would he say that?' Fran finished the sentence for her. 'One can't help thinking that if he really was innocent, bumping into the stepsister would have provided a perfect alibi because no one would expect someone who had previously been thrown over by young Mr Traynor to volunteer him a false alibi, whereas people might suspect that someone like his mother would lie to save him from the gallows.'

'Well, yes, I can see why it would have been a godsend for him, *if it had really happened that way*, but what would be the point of saying it when it wasn't true? Quite obviously the jilted girlfriend would tell the truth and say that he had not been with her that night.'

'Bear with me. We agree that if he was guilty and had to choose someone who he hoped would lie for him, then his mother, or a good friend, or basically almost anyone, would be a far better proposition than the girl he'd thrown over for her richer stepsister . . . unless, that is, you'd been planning the whole thing with her from the very beginning.'

'But surely . . . No, hold on a minute . . .'

'It's far-fetched, I admit, but you can see, can't you, that it is possible?'

'So,' Mo mused. 'How would it work? He would do the evil deed and inherit the money, and she would be the person who provided him with his perfect alibi, thanks to this apparently accidental meeting.'

'And later on,' Fran took up the theory, 'they would be drawn together again in their supposed mutual grief and, after a respectable interval, they would get married and the money would be theirs.'

'Except, of course, that it didn't pan out like that at all.'

'No,' Fran said, 'because if I'm right about this, the plan was even more complicated than that. Suppose you were the jealous, impoverished step-sister who had secretly always hated the father who had deserted you, and his other daughter, the spoiled little rich girl who had always had so much more than you. Then let's suppose that you met a young man who was not only besotted with you, but was as black-hearted as you were. Let's imagine that you dangled the prospect of that fortune under his nose and, between the pair of you, you came up with a plan for the perfect murder. The actual murder was to be committed by the boyfriend, for whom you, the jilted sister, would unexpectedly provide an alibi. Or, rather, you promised him that you would provide the alibi, but in fact you had a quite different plan.'

'Oh my goodness.' Mo clapped a hand to her mouth. 'Now I see it! The police turn up to question him and he tells them the story that he and Linda have planned together, but then she doesn't back him up. He would be in a cleft stick, because he couldn't possibly tell the police about her part in the scheme without also admitting that he did the murder and putting a rope around his neck.'

'Precisely. Telling the truth about her would not

278

have got him off – even if the jury believed him. His best hope was to come up with an alternative alibi and hope to get off completely.'

Mo gasped. 'She meant to get him hanged, at which point she would have inherited everything.'

'According to Tom, she would probably have inherited anyway. The police assumed at the time that he didn't understand the way the inheritance laws worked, but the real explanation was that under the plan as he understood it, it didn't matter who was going to inherit, because the two of them would live happily ever after, sharing the loot.'

'She persuaded him to commit her murder.'

'Precisely. Remember what her stepsister said about Linda's secret jealousy? I thought she had kept that photograph of her father's house for sentimental reasons, but it wasn't that at all. If she had really cared about her father, she would have kept a picture of him. She kept that photograph of the house as a kind of trophy. It was proof that she had had the last laugh.'

'You have to admit,' Mo said, 'that it would be a jolly clever plan. Far better to frame someone for the killing, because that would put you completely in the clear, instead of leaving everyone forever speculating about an unsolved mystery.'

'And the plan almost came off, except for one loose end – he escaped.'

'Would he have come looking for her?'

'Not straight away,' Fran said. 'His first thought would have been to make good his escape and, if the rumours are right, he did that by joining the army.'

279

'And then by managing to have it put about that he'd been killed, when really he had taken on some other identity. The thing is . . . I know that revenge is a dish best served cold and all that, but isn't ten years rather a long time to wait?'

'That's what I thought – initially – but then I realized that he had a problem.'

'Darling, I should imagine he had a whole hatful of problems.'

'I'm focusing on one in particular. In order to pay Linda Dexter back, he first had to find her. Just think about it for a moment . . . When he last saw her in 1914, she was Belinda Chappell – wasn't that her maiden name? By the time the war was over, she had become Linda Dexter and was living miles away. Christina Harper actually said something to the effect that she thought one of Linda's reasons for rushing into a marriage was as a means of changing her name and leaving the district. When the old boyfriend came back from the war, pretending to be someone else, he could hardly just drop in on her remaining family and ask them where she'd gone.'

'Oh, jolly good point. He would have had to track her down. Good heavens, where on earth would you start?'

'In the case of an heiress, you'd probably start with the gossip columns, but he'd get no joy there, because Linda Dexter didn't lead that kind of life.'

'From what you've said, quite the opposite. She was a virtual recluse. And this is probably the reason why.'

'It does seem to fit. It mightn't have been too

difficult to find out her married name, because the wedding would surely have been mentioned in the papers, but getting to know where she went to live afterwards would be much more problematic, so eventually you would have to try to second guess what she might be doing. Mrs Harper told me that Linda had always been fascinated by Robert Barnaby's books, so if you found out that there was a Robert Barnaby Society, it might well be worth joining it, on the off-chance that it led you to Linda.'

'That's a brilliant piece of sleuthing,' said Mo.

'But is it the correct solution?'

'How long has Stephen Latchford been a member?'

'Oh, absolutely ages.'

'And did he always live near Mrs Dexter?'

'As it happens, I don't think he did. Jennifer Rumsey said something about him living near Darlington, before he moved across the Pennines and lived somewhere in the vicinity of Carlisle.'

'Ah ha. So he joined the society, invented a pretext to get hold of a membership list, found out where Linda Dexter lived and went to live nearby, but then he realized that instead of breaking into her house one night, it would be easier to murder her at the conference. You could see why he'd want it to look like an accident or suicide, because so long as everyone went along with that, no one would start poking about and making any other connections.'

'My problem with all this is that Linda Dexter would surely have recognized him – and if she did, all she needed to do was report him to the police and have him arrested.'

'Oh.' Mo sounded deflated. 'So basically it's a brilliant theory, but it doesn't actually work.'

'Unless he somehow persuaded her not to give him away. If I'm right, then they had been in league together once before, remember. If she had him arrested, there was always the possibility that he would be able to convince people that she'd been in on the original murder plot all along, and that would mean her standing trial alongside him, whereas if he persuaded her that he'd forgiven her the double-cross, she might agree with him that it was better for them both to keep quiet.'

'I'm not sure that I would trust someone who had murdered my father and my stepsister.'

'But you're not someone who would have plotted that murder in the first place. Linda had played a very high stakes game and won, but at a price. She must have wondered all the time whether Edwin Traynor was still alive, and if so, whether he might one day seek retribution. If he turned up in the Barnaby Society and appeared to be perfectly harmless after all, mightn't it be a relief?'

'I suppose so. The question is how do you prove that Stephen Latchford is Eddie Traynor?'

'I'm not at all sure that Stephen Latchford *is* Eddie Traynor. In fact, I don't see how he can be, not if what Mr Dryden said is true.'

'Then it must be one of the other men in the right age group.'

Fran sighed. 'One of the problems is that I can't even remember exactly who was there. I tried to make a list at one point, but I only managed to remember about sixty names and I think the attendance was much closer to a hundred.'

'Oh, Lord. That will throw up dozens of possible suspects.'

'It isn't just a question of being in the right age group,' Fran said. 'Jennifer Rumsey made an interesting point when she said that we hardly know anything about one another, and of course that's true of a lot of members, but there are some that we've gleaned odd bits and pieces about which would completely rule them out. For example, Marcus Dryden has lived at the Furnival Towers for years, helping to run the family business. There's continuity there which goes back before the war, and therefore he cannot possibly be Edwin Traynor. By the same token, Hugh Allonby has been a literature buff for ages – he's too old to be Edwin Traynor anyway, but even if he was the right age, he has a known past.'

'I see what you mean. Whoever Edwin Traynor is now, he can't have been that person before the war.'

'Exactly. So that means no family, no old school chums, nothing in his life that goes back more than ten years, whereas Marcus Dryden definitely mentioned that Stephen Latchford's mother used to stay at the Furnival Towers before the war, and that he stayed there himself on a couple of occasions.'

'What about Tom Dod? Does he have any family, apart from a wife and child acquired after 1918?'

Fran did not reply.

Thirty-Three

'Hello, is that Mr James? It is? Oh, jolly good. It's Frances Black here.'

'And what can I do for you, Mrs Black?'

Fran was relieved to note that the membership secretary's tone was cordial, particularly as their last telephone conversation had ended on a rather hostile note.

'Well, I expect this will sound like a strange request, but at the conference I was talking to a gentleman about poetry and he lent me a little volume of poems by Robert Frost, which I obviously intended to return. I know it's dreadful of me, but I have forgotten his name and there is nothing in the book to indicate ownership. Of course, I know an awful lot of the members, but this was someone I haven't come across before. I've been pondering how I can return the book and it occurred to me that if you could give me a list of the people who attended I might be able to work it out by process of elimination, or at least narrow down the numbers of people I need to contact. I had hoped that I might have recognized the man at the Middleham meeting last Saturday,' Fran ploughed on. 'But of course that wasn't so extensively attended as the annual conference, and he may live in another part of the country entirely.'

'I'm sure I have a spare copy of the delegate list,' he said. 'I will look it out and let you have it.'

'Oh, thank you, that is so kind. One doesn't want to purloin another member's book.' She could hardly believe how easy it had been. He was obviously unaware of Hugh Allonby's latest demand that she resign or he would never have agreed – evidently the chairman was trying to keep the latest resignation request a close secret. 'Oh, and Mr James, I hope you won't mind me asking before I go, but I was at the unveiling of the war memorial in our village a week or so ago – the village where my brothers and I grew up – and I somehow mentioned the society, your name cropped up and my mother reminded me that my brother, Cecil, served with a John James. You did not happen to know a Cecil Ford, did you? He was in the Durham Light Infantry.' Goodness, Fran thought, how easy it was to invent when the moment required – or as her mother would have said, to tell lies.

'Not my lot, I'm afraid. Must have been a chap with the same name.'

'Yes, of course.' She hesitated, wondering if there was some way of drawing him out further, but her powers of improvisation had reached their limit. 'Well, thank you very much; I look forward to receiving the list.'

'Don't worry,' he said, 'I won't forget.'

After she ended the call, she paused for a reality check. Did she really imagine that she would be able to establish the background of every man in the right age group who had attended the conference? And suppose she was barking up the wrong tree entirely? She ran her eye down the list that she had already compiled from memory. Richard

285

Finney, the journal editor, who according to Jennifer Rumsey was a holder of the Victoria Cross. Well, that proved that he was resourceful and daring. Gareth Lowe – he was a bit old to be Edwin Traynor and such a buffoon too, always dressing up and thereby drawing attention to himself. Surely you wouldn't do that if you were on the run?

She smiled at the remembrance of Hugh Allonby's expression at the conference, when he had first caught sight of Mr Lowe's latest effort. Of course, Gareth Lowe would probably argue that in adopting various guises he was not merely showing off but enhancing the fun for the other members. Hadn't someone once said something of the kind? Yes, it had been dear old Miss Leonard on the morning after Linda Dexter had disappeared. A memory rose unbidden of a hitherto forgotten remark, made on the final morning at Furnival Towers, when she said that she had observed the Black Shadow climbing in through a bedroom window. 'Oh my goodness!' Fran exclaimed aloud. Surely not? Had sweet, dotty Miss Leonard mistaken the murderer's return for a prank by a member in fancy dress?

On consulting the membership list yet again, she was relieved to find that Miss Leonard was among those listed who were on the telephone, and a moment later she was through to the exchange and asking for the number. It seemed to take an age for the connection to be made, the telephone answered and the man servant on the other end of the line agreeing to fetch Miss Leonard to the telephone.

Fran had been prepared to observe polite preliminaries, but Dora Leonard was obviously unsettled by the unexpected call and asked at once, 'Is there anything wrong, Mrs Black?'

'No, no, nothing at all.'

'Oh, goodness me, I am so glad to hear it. When Hodgkiss told me who was calling, I said to myself at once that it could only be some terrible news from the committee – an accident to dear Mr Allonby, perhaps, with you calling members personally to soften the blow. So terrible to read something like that in the newspapers without prior warning. And, of course, dear Amy has a bad heart, you know, and cannot cope with sudden shocks of any kind. But it is nothing like that, you say?'

'No. Nothing like that.' Fran hesitated. 'Though it is connected with something rather tragic which happened at the conference.'

There was a pause, then Miss Leonard said, 'You must mean poor Mrs Dexter.'

'Well, yes . . . perhaps. Miss Leonard, it may be nothing at all, but do you remember, the morning after Mrs Dexter had disappeared, a group of us were talking and you mentioned that you had seen someone dressed as the Black Shadow climbing in at a window?'

'I may have said something of the kind. I'm afraid that I can't really recall.'

'But you did see someone dressed up like that?'

'Oh, yes, dear, I did. I assumed that it was Gareth Lowe. Mr Lowe is always the first to don a costume at the least excuse, isn't he?'

'But you don't know that it was him?'

287

'Oh, no. I didn't see who it was. He would have been wearing a mask, of course, being dressed as the Black Shadow – and in any case, it was pitch-black dark.'

'When was this, exactly?'

'My dear, you sound like a policeman asking all these questions. I really couldn't say when it was. I am a very poor sleeper, you see. And when I wake up, I don't put on the light for fear of waking dear Amy, but sometimes I creep out of bed and look out of the window. There was moonlight that night, and I drew back the curtains a crack and peeped out at the stars. I was just thinking that those would have been the same hills and the same stars that Robert Barnaby looked out at when he stayed at Furnival Towers all those years before, when I saw the Black Shadow coming towards the building. As you can imagine, I thought for a moment that I was dreaming, but then I realized that it would just be one of the members having some high jinks – and naturally I thought of Mr Lowe, as it's just the sort of thing that he would do.'

'Yes, of course,' Fran prompted. 'And then you saw the Black Shadow climb in through a window?'

'That's right. It was the window right next door to ours. It wasn't difficult, of course, because our room was on the ground floor.'

'And what happened next?'

'Well, nothing. I stood looking out little longer and then I went back to bed.'

'You didn't happen to mention this to anyone else, did you?'

'Well, I told Amy the next morning, of course – while we were drinking our morning tea in bed. I'm afraid it wasn't very hot. I remember saying to Amy that the girl who brought it must have dawdled. Why do you ask? Is it something important?'

'Well,' Fran said carefully, 'it might be. Did the police ask you any questions after Mrs Dexter disappeared?'

'Of course not – why ever would they? I hardly knew her.' Miss Leonard was starting to sound flustered again.

'No, of course not. It's just that, you know, someone climbing in at a window, the very same night that Mrs Dexter disappeared from the hotel . . .'

'I'm afraid I fail to see the connection.' Miss Leonard's voice had developed an edge.

'There's probably no connection,' Fran said.

'Indeed there is not. A harmless prank and a sinful act like that. What possible connection could there be?'

'Please don't upset yourself,' Fran said quickly. 'It was just an idea I had.'

'Well, I would appreciate it if you did not mention this idea to anyone else. It was most inconsiderate of Mrs Dexter to behave in the manner that she did, mixing the society up in something so horrid. The least said about it in the future, the better it will be for everyone.'

'Yes, of course, I quite agree,' Fran said, despising herself for taking the line of least resistance. The Barnaby Society was so universally keen to brush unpleasantness under the carpet,

she thought, that it might eventually become difficult for the organization to negotiate its way over
the various lumps and bumps it had created.

The conversation with Dora Leonard left her
feeling embarrassed, uncomfortable and worried,
all at the same time. What exactly did she think
that she was doing, telephoning harmless old ladies
and quizzing them about what they had or had not
seen at the conference? She recalled an earlier
bruising telephone encounter with Mr James, when
she had asked him about the disposition of the
members' accommodation at the conference.
Who was she to imagine that she could work her
way to the truth when the authorities had looked
into the matter thoroughly and already reached
a firm conclusion? Why was she doing it all
anyway? Was it really because she believed that
Linda Dexter had been murdered, or was it – as
a treacherous voice in her head intervened to
suggest – because it continued to provide a
splendid excuse to speak regularly with Tom Dod
on the telephone and to justify meeting up with
him more frequently than the normal run of
Barnaby Society activities allowed?

Mo had suggested in the first place that Tom
himself was only using it as an excuse, and it
was noticeable that since she had rebuffed his
attentions, his interest in their supposed detective
work seemed to have dwindled. There had been
only one telephone call this week, when he had
said that he needed to talk to her face-to-face.
They had agreed to meet on Friday, which was
tomorrow. She wondered what it was that he
wanted to say to her which could not be discussed

on the telephone. Presumably it did not concern the Linda Dexter mystery.

Her thoughts slipped back to some of their previous conversations and she abruptly heard Tom's words again about the suspect list. *I suggest you add dear old Miss Leonard and Miss Coward, because they had the room right next to mine.*

An invisible ice cube traced a sharp trajectory down her spine. What possible reason could Tom have had for dressing up as the Black Shadow and climbing in through his hotel-room window? Then again, had this person Miss Leonard had seen really been dressed as the Black Shadow at all? Pitch-black dark was the way Miss Leonard had described it. Would she have had her spectacles on, having just got out of bed? What it probably amounted to was that she had seen a figure in dark clothes, which she had assumed to be the Black Shadow. Even so, there was no legitimate reason for anyone to be entering the hotel via a bedroom window.

Think, think . . . what had Tom said about rooms on that bottom corridor? Linda Dexter had occupied the room next door to the fire escape and Tom had established that this fire door, which could only be opened from the inside, could easily have been propped open and used to transport Linda, or her body, out of the building. Why, then, would anyone involved in her murder have needed to climb in or out of an open window at all?

Got it, she thought a moment later. It was all very well to slip out for a few minutes for a pretend cigarette, but the killer must have been away for at least a couple of hours, taking the body to the railway line in Linda's car then walking all the way back, and anything might happen in that time. Someone might come along and close the door, which would leave you stuck outside, when surely part of your plan was to return to Furnival Towers and get up for breakfast on Saturday morning, just as if you had never been away. Moreover, you could choose your time to slip out, checking that the coast was clear by peeking out of the bedroom door first, whereas re-entering the building via the fire door might mean bumping into someone on their way for a nocturnal trip to the bathroom. Climbing back into your empty bedroom, on the other hand, you did not risk bumping into anyone at all.

By way of an insurance policy, she thought, it would actually have been a clever idea to dress up as the Black Shadow because the mask provided an effective disguise if anyone saw you returning to the hotel. It would be jolly bad luck for anyone to have been looking out anyway, and particularly bad luck for it to have been a person close enough to identify which of the many windows you had entered by. The odds against the person in the next-door room being the one to see you must have been extremely high, and yet seemingly that long shot had come in.

But Tom . . . Surely it could not really have been Tom?

Thirty-Four

She met Tom outside the same tea shop in Elephant Yard where, just over two weeks before, they had excitedly discussed the Halfpenny Landing murders and their discoveries in the library. Fran remembered clearly the wave of pleasure she had experienced on first catching sight of Tom loping towards her as she had waited on the library steps. It was different today. A barrier had come down between them and they greeted each other with the politeness of relative strangers.

After this initial exchange, Tom said, 'Let's not go in for tea just yet. Will you come and sit in my motor, so that we can talk in complete privacy?'

For a split second, she hesitated. After all, since her conversation with Miss Leonard the day before, Tom had climbed well up her list of suspects, but on the other hand it seemed both melodramatic and ridiculous to refuse. He had had her at his complete mercy in the car on several other occasions without her coming to the least bit of harm, so she said, 'Yes, of course,' and they walked the necessary few hundred yards down the road to where he had parked. It was turning into a warm afternoon and she slipped out of her jacket, which he took from her and laid on the back seat, the upturn in the weather providing a brief but welcome distraction on which to comment until

293

they were both settled, he in the driver's seat and she in the passenger's.

'I owe you an apology first and foremost,' he said. 'No, no, don't try to say that I don't. I am afraid that I made some assumptions and it was wrong of me to do so. Firstly, having realized that you lived alone, I took you to be a widow, which of course you are not, but even after you had explained your circumstances, I still assumed that you were . . .' He faltered awkwardly to a halt.

'Attracted to you and available for an affair,' Fran prompted gently.

He hesitated, then said, 'Both of those. Yes.'

'And that I would be a party to you deceiving your wife.' She tried to be censorious, but only managed to sound sad.

'That is something else that I ought to have explained. My marriage is . . . somewhat unusual. No, please . . .' He had seen Fran pursing her lips. 'You must allow me to explain. I will not ask for your word, because I have no right to do so, but I hope that when you have heard me out, you will understand and respect my desire that what I am about to tell you should go no further.'

He paused and looked at her in a way which made her heart melt. A whole series of thoughts, every one seemingly more foolish than the last, chased through her mind, including both the ideas that she should open the car and run far, far away, but simultaneously that she should simply lean in and kiss him.

'I think I once mentioned to you that I was one of two brothers,' he said.

'You did.'

'My brother Will was five years older than me and I rather idolized him. He was a splendid chap in every way. Bright, funny, elected captain of his house and played for the first fifteen at school. He was also, of course, nineteen years old when war was declared and exactly the sort of fellow to volunteer straight off. I respected him enormously for that, as you can imagine.'

Fran nodded, though she could not really see where this was going at all.

'I was still at school through most of the war. I came to dread those morning assemblies, when one name after another would be added to the list of the fallen. The toll among the old boys was quite terrible, and sometimes it felt inevitable that one day Will would be among them, but then, at other moments, I had complete confidence in his survival. Do you see?'

Fran nodded again. She did see, because she envisaged his brother Will as being another Tom – large, solid, invincible.

'Will and Veronica had known each other all their lives. Her parents were great friends of my parents and for years there had been a sort of understanding that one day Will and Veronica might marry. Will finally proposed to her on his last leave at home, and they became engaged. Veronica and Will wanted to be married straight away and talked of getting a special licence, but in the end the parents persuaded them to wait. That was in the late summer of 1918, and we all hoped that the rotten war would be over very soon.'

'But Will did not make it to the end,' Fran finished for him.

'He was shot by a sniper, just three weeks before the armistice. It was almost the cruellest thing of all. We were still fresh in our grief when everyone else was putting out flags and hailing a great victory at last.'

Fran nodded. 'My mother said it was impossible to rejoice when you had lost everything you had held dear. Of course, she still had a daughter.' She gave a little hollow laugh. 'But one daughter doesn't equal two sons.' She was looking straight up the road, watching the shoppers in their summer clothes, not meeting his eye.

'I told you that the parents had persuaded Will and Veronica to wait, but in one respect, well, they had not waited . . . and before long Veronica was forced to confess to her mother that she was carrying Will's child. There was consternation in the family, as you can imagine. If it had got out, Veronica would have been ruined and my brother's child raised under the worst of stigmas. So I offered Veronica marriage.' He paused. 'It seemed the only honourable thing to do.'

'You were . . . not in love with her?'

'No. She knew that. There was no deception on either side.'

'But you were giving up your whole life.'

'Will had already given up his.'

Fran said nothing. She understood the guilt which went with being the surviving sibling.

'I had sat out the war at school,' Tom continued quietly. 'Only volunteering right at the end, when it was too late to see active service. I was only nineteen when we married, of course, but my parents naturally gave their consent. Veronica was not quite of age either. Luckily the baby came late, though it was given out that it had come early. Either way, my nephew is being raised as my son and will inherit the family business, just as everyone always intended that he should. When he's old enough, I intend to tell him the truth, because I believe he has a right to know. No one apart from our immediate families knows anything about this. You are the first person outside that circle that I have ever told.'

'Why are you telling me?' she asked quietly.

'Because you have a right to know. Or perhaps that's too strong. I'm telling you because I made that suggestion to you, in Hawes, and although that is completely behind us now, I suppose I wanted you to know that I would not have made such a suggestion if I had been a party in a normal marriage. I am very fond of Veronica and she is of me, but we have essentially lived as brother and sister. The one thing we have in common – perhaps the only thing really – is that we both loved my brother, Will. Veronica told me a long time ago that if I should ever wish to stray, she would have no objection, providing that I was discreet.'

'And how many times have you strayed?'

'Never. Until now.'

'The pressures of one's family are a terrible thing,' Fran said. 'My husband, Michael, has asked me to release him, but the scandal of a divorce would kill my mother, so I have little choice but to cling to some vestiges of respectability by refusing to cooperate with him. In the event that he got the slightest whiff of my having an affair, he would of course be able to divorce me, for my infidelity.'

'I understand. Perhaps it's better to keep the gate bolted on both sides?' He took her hand and squeezed it. She wanted the moment to last, but he released the hand again immediately. She felt tears of regret rising in her eyes. She had always known, deep down, that nothing could ever come of it.

'I hope,' he said, 'that we can still remain good friends?'

'Of course,' she said. 'Very good friends.' She must not cry. She really must not cry, but there, he was reaching a big, sensible white hand-kerchief out of his pocket and pushing it across at her while mumbling something about slipping out for a breath of fresh air.

When he returned a few minutes later, she had managed to repair her face and comb her hair, and she saw that he was the normal, friendly Tom of old.

'Let's go and have our tea now,' he said, holding the car door open in readiness for her to climb out. 'I've got some very exciting news to tell you, hot off the press, as it were. Though of course this is actually the sort of news that will never find its way into the press at all.'

'Well, come on, don't leave me in suspense.'

'Hurry up, then,' he said. 'Leave your jacket where it is for now. Come on, I'm dying of thirst.'

'All right, I'm coming. So what's this exciting news?'

'Last night I got a telephone call from none other than Hugh Allonby. The old boy was in a regular tizzy, I can tell you. It looks as if Stephen-with-a-ph-Latchford has finally overstepped the mark.'

'Has he been bothering someone else? Do you mean the committee is going to do something about him at last?'

'Not the committee, no. Matters have already been taken out of their hands.'

'By the police?'

'My dear Mrs Black, if you would only stop interrupting with questions, I might be able to get to the gist of the tale.'

'Of course. Sorry. And there is really no need to call me Mrs Black.'

'Well,' said Tom as they set off up the road, 'it transpires that Latchford had been annoying yet another member of the Barnaby Society, Miss Julia Spencely. Miss Spencely asked him to desist and he took no notice, so she mentioned the matter to a friend – a close friend. It seems that Miss Spencely has become romantically involved with our magazine editor, Mr Finney.'

'Gosh! I always thought him a confirmed bachelor.'

'Still waters run deep, as they say. Anyway, it seems that Miss Spencely had originally complained to old Allonby about Latchford's activities, but as you might expect, she got nowhere, so Mr Finney decided to take matters into his own hands, waited at Miss Spencely's flat for Latchford to turn up and gave the fellow a damned good thrashing. When Latchford bleated to Allonby and started waffling on about solicitors, good old Finney stuck to his guns: better yet, he said, that unless Allonby demanded Latchford's resignation, he would see to it that the whole scandal was published in the next society mag.'

'Good heavens! He couldn't do that, surely?'

'I don't honestly know, but anyway, Allonby caved. Latchford has been given his marching orders and he's accepted defeat.'

'What about his solicitors?'

'It was all a bluff, just as we always supposed that it would be. And as for Finney and Miss Spencely, rumour has it that there will be an announcement shortly.'

'A happy ending.' Fran tried to keep the wistful note out of her voice.

'Who would have thought that the Barnaby Society was such a hotbed of romance?'

'In the meantime,' she intervened briskly, 'I have been giving a lot more thought to the Linda Dexter mystery and I've also got some exciting new information.'

'I'm pleased to hear it, because I have been so tied up with a delegation of peach growers from Italy that I've scarcely had a minute to think about it at all.' He held the tea-shop door open for her, then followed her inside, pausing on the threshold to remove his hat.

Over a pot of tea and some rather indifferent tea cakes, she brought him completely up to date on the theory that she had developed with Mo, saving the revelation about Miss Leonard's sighting of the Black Shadow until the end. When

300

she reached the part about the figure climbing in through the window, Tom pursed his lips and whistled: an activity from which he immediately desisted on catching sight of the horrified glares from their fellow customers.

'He must have been climbing back into his own room,' Fran said casually. 'Because that's the only room where he could guarantee that no one would have come and closed the window while he was away.'

'That narrows the field considerably,' Tom said. 'Because I was in the room on one side of them. All we have to do is find out who was next door on the other side. Thinking about it, that room would have been right next door to Linda Dexter's. You could have watched through the keyhole for her to pass, or even just listened for the sound of her bedroom door.'

A wave of relief rushed through her. Of course, she thought. There would have been a room to either side of Miss Leonard and Miss Coward. How stupid of her not to think of that.

'We've nearly done it, haven't we?' she said in disbelief. 'We're just one step away from finding out who it was. Do you think we're ready to talk to the police?'

'Suppose it turns out that there was a woman occupying the room next door to Linda's?'

'What on earth do you mean? Are you suggesting that the murderer could have been a woman after all?'

'No. I'm just suggesting that we might still be bowled a googly. Before we go to the police, we have to find out who was staying in that room.

Once we've got a name, we can see whether it's possible to tie that person to the Halfpenny Landing murders.'

'Because you think that we still might have got it all wrong?'

'Not necessarily. But let's take it one step at a time. If I get my skates on I can be at Furnival Towers in just over an hour, providing you don't mind taking the bus back home.'

'What will you do at Furnival Towers?'

'I'm going to see if I can find out from Marcus Dryden who was staying in that room.'

'Suppose he won't tell you?'

'Then I'll steal the blasted register if I have to. Of course, I really ought to offer you a lift home . . .'

'No, no,' she said eagerly. 'You get off to Furnival Towers. Taking me home will only delay you.'

Thirty-Five

It was not until she was climbing into the bus that Fran remembered her discarded summer jacket still lying on the back seat of Tom's car. It was warm enough not to need it, but a nuisance all the same, as there was no saying when she might get it back from him and it went with everything in her wardrobe, whereas her green one was more problematical to match and the black one only came out for funerals. She found herself wondering what the unseen Veronica would make of discovering a garment belonging to another woman in the back seat of Tom's car and whether she would be so understanding, as he expected, if he ever breached his marriage vows. Well, it did not matter because whatever Mrs Dod surmised, there was nothing going on, and there never would be. They would content themselves with being good friends.

Now that summer had finally arrived, the unaccustomed heat had turned the walk down the lane from the bus stop into rather a trudge, despite her sensible shoes, and she was grateful to kick them off as soon as she got into the sitting room.

It was well after Ada's going home time, but at least Mrs Snegglington was there to greet her, fussing around her ankles and emitting squeaky demands for food. As she dealt with the cat, she noted that Ada had left a dish of macaroni cheese, ready to be heated up for her own supper. The only decision now was whether to put the kettle on or reach for the gin bottle and mix a celebratory cocktail – for after all, she and Tom had nearly cracked the case. Or had they? A part of her still hankered after the idea that Stephen Latchford was responsible, for while he had not occupied the bedroom next door to Linda Dexter's and could not possibly be Eddie Traynor, his behaviour towards various women in the society argued in favour of his guilt. Could it be mere coincidence that he had a habit of harassing female members of the society? She supposed that it must be. After all, wasn't it her who had said that coincidences happened all the time? Tom was right: the answer lay in the hotel register. They only had to identify who had stayed in that room next door to Linda and everything would fall into place. Then she remembered that once the mystery of Linda Dexter's death had finally been resolved, there would be far less excuse to meet up with Tom, good friends or not – and a mantle of loneliness suddenly descended. She thought of ringing Mo, but remembered just in time that Mo had driven south that morning to spend the weekend with a cousin in Shrewsbury. Never mind, at least she had their Wimbledon trip to look forward to next week.

At that moment the familiar bangitty-bang of the front-door knocker made her jump. For a horrible moment, she froze, picturing Stephen Latchford on the doorstep, but then she remembered that it would almost certainly be Tom, who, having discovered her jacket, must have belatedly turned back to reunite her with it. She rushed into the hall, where the stone floor felt cold under her stocking feet, and threw open the door. It was not Tom. John James was standing on the step, smiling shyly.

'I was going to put the list you asked for in the post,' he said. 'But then I realized that I had business up in this direction today, so I decided to drop it in by hand. I'm afraid I hadn't realized quite how far off the beaten track you lived.'

'Oh.' Fran had been completely taken aback, but she recovered swiftly. 'Well, it's very kind of you to go to the trouble. You must come in for a drink, of course.' She hesitated, glancing up and down the road in vain for a parked car. 'You haven't come by bus, have you?'

'Oh, no. I made a mistake over the house – missed the name on the gate, so I parked the jalopy further up the lane and walked back to check.'

'Oh, I see. Well, do come in. Would you care for a cup of tea?' One should not encourage drivers to drink cocktails. It had said so in the newspaper only the other day.

'Thank you, that would be very nice.'

He followed her into the sitting room, where he stood on the hearth rug, declining her invitation to take a seat. 'I've been sitting in the car for hours,' he said. 'I'm glad of the chance to stretch my legs. You're a long way out here, aren't you? Do you live here on your own? But I suppose you have help.'

'The help goes home to her mother's for the night,' Fran said. 'But I can make tea.'

305

'I say, before you go off making tea,' he said, arresting her progress in the doorway, 'is there any chance of my getting a look at that volume of Frost's poetry that you mentioned? I'm pretty keen on the Dymock poets myself.'

Fran felt the colour rising in her face. What had seemed to be a clever invention on the spur of the moment now dangled like a trap before her eyes. 'I'll go and fetch it,' she said.

How? How could she fetch a book which didn't exist? she thought as she hastened across the hall and into the parlour, then made a noisy show of moving various books and papers about. 'Now where on earth has it gone?' she said, overacting for all she was worth. 'Do you know, I had it in my hand only yesterday.' She returned to stand in the doorway of the sitting room, shaking her head. 'I'll go and make the tea and perhaps it will come back to me.'

'Tell me,' he said. 'How is your detective work coming along?'

'I'm sorry, but I don't know what you mean.'

'Oh, come now, Mrs Black. You didn't really want that list because of some book you had borrowed. You were wondering which of the men whose names were on it would turn out to have a connection to the Halfpenny Landing murders, weren't you?'

Fran said nothing, but she knew that her face had given her away. She wanted to move, but her feet seemed to have become rooted to the spot.

'I take my hat off to you, I really do. I think you have been most frightfully clever.'

306

No, Fran thought. I have actually been utterly, utterly stupid. The man who had made all the conference arrangements, had handled the room allocations, the new member who had unexpectedly volunteered to become membership secretary, and thereby custodian of all their names and addresses. This longstanding member of the society that Linda Dexter had never seen, because he had arrived too late on Friday night to join them at dinner and had never been to any meetings before. The man who, along with Tom, had had a room on the ground-floor corridor . . .

'I suppose it was my slip of the tongue that did it.'

'What?' Fran was genuinely bewildered. 'I'm afraid I have no idea what you are talking about.'

'Calling her Belinda that first evening, when you and Miss Robertson were fussing around, wondering where your precious speaker had got to.'

'I didn't notice – or if I did, I don't remember.'

'Really?' He raised his eyebrows. 'Ah, well. Not so clever, as I thought.'

'Look here; I really don't know what you're getting at.'

'Don't be silly, Mrs Black.'

Fran said nothing. She had never before understood the paralysing effect of fear. Her feet refused to move and, in any case, her thought processes were no longer functioning fast enough for her to decide what to do next. If she tried to make a run for it in just her stocking feet, he would easily outpace her, and in any case, he had once been a champion fell runner and still coached junior

307

athletics – another clue, if only she had managed to spot it.

Out of the corner of her eye, she saw Mrs Snegglington sliding around the edge of the room, heading for the hall and the sanctuary of the spare-room bed, well aware that there was something not right in the air. If only she could send Mrs Snegglington for help. Good God, had she actually entertained such a mad thought? It was then that she heard the faint sound of a car engine. It was growing nearer and must be coming to Bee Hive Cottage . . . surely it must be? The engine slowed, idled for a moment and was then cut off.

John James moved with astonishing speed, grabbing her around the head and waist and dragging her further into the sitting room, where he wrestled her on to the floor and pinned her down, with one of his hands clamped firmly over her nose and mouth. Not only was she prevented from crying out for help, but she was barely able to breathe. Any lingering doubts about his ability to prevent a victim from screaming were instantly dispelled.

He's going to kill me, she thought. Then he will arrange it somehow to look like another suicide. That's why he has parked his car a good distance from the house, so that no one who passes by will connect the vehicle with me. Anyone who sees it will just assume that it belongs to someone who's gone for a walk.

The door knocker sounded, exactly as it had just a few minutes before. It was far too early to have switched on any lights and too warm to have put a match to the fire, so from outside the cottage, there was nothing at all to say that there was anyone at home. After waiting a moment or two, the door knocker sounded again. It must be someone persistent – someone who expected her to be in there.

She heard the flap of the letterbox raised, a sound familiar from the postman's twice daily visits. 'Fran? Are you there? I've brought your jacket.' It was Tom.

In a single, stupendous effort, she flung herself sideways. She knew that she would only have one chance, but she also had the advantage of knowing the positions of her own furniture to the inch. The little table on which Mo invariably placed her drinks was supported by a single twisting stem, which was perfectly balanced on three equidistant feet, but it was a lightweight piece, not designed for a determined onslaught which combined the weight of a pair of human beings locked together, and it toppled to the floor with a gratifying crash, scattering its normal contents, which included a green glass ashtray, the fragments of which skittered in all directions well beyond the rug and across the stone floor.

'Fran!' The shout which came through the letterbox this time was laced with anxiety. 'Fran, is that you? What's going on in there?'

She tried to respond, but the hand was still clamped firm. One of her own was free, however, and she used it to grab a cast-off shoe which had come within reach and flung it towards the window. She had not generated enough force to break the glass, but the impact evidently suggested a new idea to her latest visitor, whose face she now saw, momentarily pressed against the glass. Was he able to see the writhing figures on the floor? Impossible to tell, but a moment later she heard a sound which could only be indicative of Tom, hurling himself hopelessly at the solid oak front door. As she continued to struggle with her assailant, one of whose hands was suffocating her while the other attempted to close around her neck, she heard another couple of bone-crunching impacts, which preceded a short pause. She could feel herself becoming light-headed; she was losing her grip on everything in a hot, red haze of pain. Next second there was a sound like an explosion, the pressure on her face and neck simultaneously ceased and warm air rushed into her lungs. Thrusting her violently aside, John James had picked himself up from the floor and raced into the kitchen, where she could hear him dragging back the bolt on the kitchen door while she simultaneously turned the other way to see that, lying in the centre of the sofa, surrounded by broken glass, there was now a stone garden urn, spilling out most of its earth and a selection of spring pansies which were well past their best. And there was Tom, heedless of the dangers posed by the jagged remnants of glass, reaching his arm inside to operate the window latch.

'The front door,' she managed to gasp. 'It isn't locked.'

Thirty-Six

'I still say that everyone is making far too much fuss.'

'Fran, darling, people have sent flowers, and hot house grapes, and boxes of chocolates,' Mo said, helping herself from one of the latter items. 'You really must learn not to discourage that sort of attention.'

'I wasn't meaning that. I meant things like Doctor Jenks being called in and prescribing me a sedative.'

'Well, goodness me, most women would have needed a sedative after being attacked by a homicidal maniac. Thank goodness they caught him this time round.'

'Tom said it was more luck than judgement,' Fran said. 'I suppose you know that after John James escaped through the kitchen door, he made off across the fields at the back? Tom didn't see which direction he went in, but it seems that he didn't try to get back to his car, because I suppose he thought the police would soon get hold of the registration number and spot him on the road. Anyway, he set off across country, where old Ned Braithwaite managed to wound him in the leg after taking a pot shot at him in mistake for a deer. Ned is really getting far too doddery to make a successful poacher.'

'I can't help thinking that it's rather a comical end to it all.'

'It wasn't very comical when he attacked me, I can assure you, and I don't imagine that it will be particularly comical when he comes up for trial,' Fran said. 'I wonder which case they will bring against him? The original Halfpenny Landing murders, or the murder of Linda Dexter?'

'No, what I mean is that it's sort of comical, the way Tom tried to bash down your front door when it wasn't actually locked in the first place.'

'Well, believe me, it didn't seem very funny at the time.'

'Do you think the two of you will be wanted as witnesses at the trial?'

'Oh, I do hope not. My mother would see it as a dreadful scandal – a member of the family being mixed up in any kind of court case.'

'But if you're not involved in the case anymore, and you're determined not to have anything further to do with the Robert Barnaby Society, you won't ever see anything of Tom.'

'So?'

Mo, who had been speculatively contemplating the open box of chocolates again, switched her full attention back to her friend. 'You say that as if you don't care. No, wait a minute . . . don't give me that innocent face, Fran Black. We go back far too long. What's going on? Come on, I demand that you tell all.'

'It's nothing really, but I had a call from Tom today, about his aunt.'

'His aunt! What about his aunt?'

'Well, it's his great-aunt, actually.'

'Yes? Well? What about his great-aunt?'

'He says that there's some rather strange goings-on at her church. Some mystery involving the death of a parishioner. He was wondering if we might try to look into it.'

'And?' demanded Mo.

'We've arranged to meet and discuss it, the week after next, once the Championships are over. You know, I must say that I am really looking forward to the tennis on Thursday. A girl needs a bit of excitement in her life, every now and then.'